Dirty Trouble

by

J.M. Griffin

Dedication

For Judi, who's always there waiting
with a hot cup of tea to listen to me whine.

Acknowledgements

Rhode Island State Police Major, David Neill, has been a valuable source of information and inspiration on police matters, along with retired State Police Major, John Leyden. They have shared facts, stories, and contacts, while answering many of my questions with much humor and indulgence. Thanks so much.

I also want to thank the Providence Police Department in Providence, RI for their patience in explaining various weapons, dealing with bad guys, the arrest process and more. Rhonda Kessler has been an invaluable contact, and friend, at the department. I couldn't have done this series without all of you.

Reviews:

4 Cups from *Coffee Time Romance*
"If you enjoy humor along with romance and suspense, then you simply must read *Dirty Trouble*."

5 Hearts from *The Romance Studio*
"*Dirty Trouble* is an action packed read filled with humor, sexy men, and some of the best characters you'd ever want to see in a story."

Also available in the Esposito Series from this author:

FOR LOVE OF LIVVY

SOON TO BE RELEASED RE-EDITED & REVISED:

DEAD WRONG
COLD MOON DEAD
SEASON FOR MURDER
DEATH GONE AWRY
DEADER THAN DEAD

UPCOMING RELEASE:
VINNIE ESPOSITO
NOVEL #8
DOWN DIRTY DEAD

OTHER NOVELS AVAILABLE FROM THIS AUTHOR:

A CRUSTY MURDER
A CROUTON MURDER
THE FOCACCIA FATALITY
FAERIE CAKE DEAD
FAERIE DUST DEAD
TANGLED TO DEATH
MURDER ON SPYGLASS LANE
THE CADENCE CAPER
THE MAN, THE DOG & MURDER

Dirty Trouble

Chapter 1

Tractor-trailers jockeyed for position among speeding cars and buses. Everyone drove at breakneck speed past Narragansett Bay as they rounded the curved highway approaching the bridge. It was six in the morning when I made it onto Rhode Island's Interstate 95 headed toward the George Washington Bridge. In the low-speed lane, my car worked hard to keep pace with the others. Speeds increased, akin to those at the Daytona Speedway.

Cars and trucks thundered across the highway of never-ending construction. Orange cones lined the high-speed lane and curtailed traffic. In a flash, everyone squeezed into my lane. Vehicles jostled, maneuvering for a new spot.

Intent on my own strip of road and the line of drivers ahead, I never saw the vehicle to my rear left side. My fender was slammed hard. I swerved to the right, losing control of the car. There were no barriers to stop me as the car careened right. It left the road, and we took flight over the temporary curb. The car bounced out of control, pointed nose first down a knoll toward an embankment. I clenched the steering wheel and twisted, but the car seemed to have a mind of its own.

Things happened fast, yet it seemed like slow motion. Hardly aware of our sideways skid over the terrain, we continued the downhill journey. I tried to straighten the wheel again, but the airborne vehicle hurtled toward a pile of stone and sand. With a loud crunch and a thud, we landed. Perched precariously on top of a concrete bridge abutment just before Narragansett Bay, the car and I teetered on the brink of disaster.

The State of Rhode Island was in the process of constructing yet another ramp – it's an ongoing construction thing. A T-shaped abutment stood out over the road far below. I balanced on the top edge of the concrete while the groan of bending metal resounded in my ears.

When my body jerked forward the airbag had inflated and smashed into my face. I thanked God for seatbelts. So much had happened in so few seconds.

I fought the airbag while it deflated. With the view before me, I suddenly wished it was still inflated. The hood of the car pointed downward and seemed to hang in mid air. The windshield, crinkled and cracked, offered a terrifying bird's eye view of my surroundings. No way could I get out of the car.

Scared, and perched high above the ground like a bird on a creaking branch, I took stock of my body while rational thought crept in. Reaching up to pull the visor down, I stared into the attached mirror. My reflection assured me there were no facial injuries – just pasty white skin and huge brown eyes surrounded by my erratic, dark swarm of curls. My hands and arms still worked, as did my legs and toes.

How the hell was I gonna get out of this car? The dashboard was shoved upward from the impact to the car, when it bent in the middle, and left little room to maneuver.

Within my jacket pocket, the cell phone jingled a lofty tune. I struggled to retrieve it. I'm not sure how I managed it, but the phone suddenly sat in my hand and I answered the call. *Why didn't I use it to scream for help?* Well, I don't know – just call me stupid.

The voice on the other end of the phone wanted to know if I might be interested in an increased limit on my credit card. I held the phone away and gawked at it. I struggled to breathe while the seatbelt squeezed the shit out of me.

"No, I don't want a freakin' raise in the limit. I'd like to be rescued though," I yelled into the phone and hit the end button. Sales people do call at such inconvenient times.

Within seconds I dialed 911. I took a breath and glanced around to get my bearings. Some person answered and asked a bunch of foolish questions about my condition and location.

"I'm stuck over a bridge abutment somewhere near the George Washington Bridge, eastbound in Providence," I said. I started to shake and realized shock was had set in. Another inconvenience.

"Okay ma'am, I'll notify emergency services for you. Are you injured?"

The disembodied voice was calm as a cucumber. *Why not?* He wasn't hanging forward, God knows how many feet in the air, with his boobs divided by a seatbelt instead of a cross-your-heart bra. My hips would never be the same, and I was sure there'd be a permanent strap mark on my skin. My shoulder strap was another matter. A burning sensation ran along my clavicle and down my left arm.

"No, I don't think so. Everything is movable, just uncomfortable. The car is slanted downward and I think I'm quite far off the ground. The view is poor at the moment."

"Is there a street sign nearby?"

What the hell? Did he really think I was that fortunate?

"No. Just get me the hell out of here," I bellowed and disconnected.

Sirens wailed in the distance overhead, and I could hear them zoom past. Damn. As the sounds receded a fresh batch approached. My cell phone jingled again, and I answered the summons.

"Hello," I said, and then glanced around. *Can't anyone find me?* Providence is, after all, a relatively small city.

"Vinnie, it's Marcus. Are you all right?" His voice echoed over the phone.

My frustration level climbed, and as relieved as I was to hear his voice, I just wanted to get out of the car. Unfortunately, I was afraid to unclasp the seat belt. Courage isn't my strong suit. I just pretend a lot.

"I'm great, having the time of my life. Why don't you join me for a Margarita?"

He mumbled to someone in the background. If I heard it right, he said I was my usual smart-assed self. Fuming inside, and about to lose control over my temper, I took a deep breath. It seemed they were taking forever to find me. *What if I were bleeding to death or something equally disgusting?*

"There are more than six patrol cars and a couple fire trucks in the area where you went off the road. Someone should be with you momentarily. By the way, save me a Margarita, will you?"

Breathing heavily now, I tamped my rising sense of panic, while my nerves stretched to the limit. *Would someone please get me the hell out of this damned car?* I was suffocating in this vehicle and couldn't put the window down.

"Vinnie, are you there?"

With a grunt, I eased the seat lever back and felt the strap across my body loosen a bit. The car teetered, and I gasped.

"Yeah, this damned seat belt is choking me to death. Get me out of here, Marcus. Hurry." Anxiety filled my voice and tensed my fraught nerves. A tear slid down my cheek.

Sounds of cars screeching to a halt were accompanied by flashing colored lights that reflected off the concrete abutment across from me. Ropes and safety lines appeared over the car as a fire truck aerial ladder rose into view. The next thing I knew, two fire fighters leaned toward the car.

One of them yelled to me and asked if I was all right. *Geesh, I thought I established that fact.* When I nodded, he gave me the thumbs up sign and turned to the other man with him. They conversed for a few seconds – an eternity to me – and then focused on the car.

"We'll secure the vehicle. Can you get the door open, ma'am?"

Heavy ropes sloped over the car and tightened. Only the two men were in view.

I really dislike that 'ma'am' thing but didn't say so at that moment. Instead, I nodded affirmatively and tried the door handle. The lock clicked as I forced the door open a crack. Brisk fresh air swept into the car.

With the nose of the car bent, the contorted interior refused to allow the door to open wide. I leaned into it and the seatbelt tightened against my skin. My glance went back to the rescue personnel and I shook my head.

Within minutes they pried the door open with heavy equipment while I waited. I recognized the scissor-like Jaws of Life. I'd seen them used on a television program, but never the real thing. *Some folks have all the luck.*

Drenched in sweat, my body shook as the adrenaline rush receded. If I didn't get out soon, I'd throw up or wet my pants, I just knew it. Another embarrassing moment in a life filled with them.

Would it be too much to ask for a mundane life? What is a mundane life, anyway? Do people really have such a thing? These questions tumbled one after another through my mind as I waited for the professionals to do what they did best – save my sorry ass – that's what.

The door peeled back like a sardine can lid and I sucked in fresh air, gulping great draughts of it. The closest rescuer checked me over. When he finished, he smiled at me, his blue eyes sparkling.

"What's your name?"

"Vinnie," I said.

"Well Vinnie, I want you to put your arms around my neck, if you can." His calm voice soothed my frayed nerves. "The seat belt is snagged. I'll cut it and remove you from the car on a count of three. Okay?"

"On the count of three, right?"

"Yep." He smiled again.

His confidence bolstered mine, and if I trusted him, I had nothing to lose. With a white-knuckled grip, I clung to the jacket of my blue-eyed rescuer. He became a life raft. I refused to drown in fear without a fight, damn it. My fingers gripped him tighter as he cut the seatbelt and slid his arm around my waist. He tugged the strap away and counted to three.

I tensed a bit, but his firm hands held me safe. He dragged me from the car that teetered toward the ground. It was a wreck and so was I, even though I wasn't physically injured. *We all need to be grateful for the little things in life, right?*

Once on the ladder, Blue Eyes loosened his hold. We

descended to the base of the ladder truck from the edge of the abutment. When we stopped moving, he released me, and I looked around. I could see a dozen state troopers and Providence cops milling about on the ground below. Marcus stood among them, arms crossed as he waited for me.

Trooper Marcus Richmond came into my life earlier in the year and found a place in my heart. We sometimes disagree on my way of life, but mostly I think he accepts me for who I am.

Now his face seemed carved in stone. I was uncertain if he was angry over the accident or relieved that I made it in one piece. It felt like his hazel green eyes never left me as I clambered down the rear of the truck on shaky legs. On the ground, I leaned against the fire engine a moment while Marcus strode forward. Knees wobbly and skin moist, I waited for him.

"Where's my Margarita?" Marcus's softly murmured in my ear as he held me in his arms.

A hiccup sob escaped my lips, and I clung to his lean, muscled body. Tears slid down my cheeks. Strong hands stroked my back and smoothed my wild hair. I leaned away to stare into eyes that mystified me.

"I couldn't get out, and nobody could find me. It was awful."

"I know. We drove all over the place in search of the right bridge abutment. You left a trail, but then the tracks disappeared from view. Nobody knew where to look. I'm sorry we took so long, Vinnie." A tiny smile curled the corners of his lips as he held my face in his hands. "You scared the shit out of me, though."

His fellow troopers and cops looked on – a few of them familiar to me from my summer escapades. I nodded in their direction as Marcus escorted me to the rescue vehicle.

I perched on the edge of the step while a medical tech checked for damage, I took a look at the car suspended above. My eyes rounded, I gulped and stared.

"Damn, my car is junk." I stated the obvious and now knew what caused the look on Marcus's face before I descended the ladder. He probably had the same thought, but hadn't said so. I could have been crushed like a bug if the car had flipped over. I was saved by the grace of God. *Maybe church wasn't such a bad idea.*

"My mother doesn't know about this, does she?"

"Not as far as I know. The news people aren't here."

He nodded at cops as they headed back to do whatever they did. Fire and rescue personnel cleared up the car debris. A wrecker arrived to take away the crumpled metal that no longer resembled my gleaming, bright red car. I watched in a detached manner, my mind traveling at the speed of light, as the car was brought down from its perch and loaded onto the flatbed.

"This couldn't have been just an accident, who did this to you? Did you get a look at the vehicle or driver?" Marcus asked.

"No." I explained what had taken place. "I think it was just that, an accident. I haven't pissed anyone off lately."

"Is that right?" His eyebrow cocked a bit.

"Yeah. By the way, I'm late for class."

"There won't be any class for you today or tomorrow. I called ahead to tell them you wouldn't be in for a couple of days."

"Oh." Who would take over the Criminal Justice class for today?

A young EMT stepped around the truck and said, "You should have X-rays, Miss. I couldn't find any injuries, just your bruised clavicle. You'll be sore, though. Seat belts and air bags are necessary, but can cause unseen damage. Get checked out, okay?"

"Sure, thanks." *Not in this lifetime.* I'd had enough crap for one day. *There isn't a chance in hell I'd put up with doctors poking and prodding me like a guinea pig.* No – thank you very much.

The only car in sight belonged to Marcus. All the other troopers and cops had left. With a sigh, I walked toward the SUV that waited, alone on the street. Casting one last glance at my trashed Taurus, I slid onto the front seat of the messiest vehicle I'd ever seen.

A laptop computer sat suspended from the dashboard, piles of paper, booklets, and cop debris lay in a swath across the front seat, floor, and back seat. Nothing compact about an SUV, they are spacious. I guess it's so the officers can carry more junk.

"Are you taking me home?" I asked.

"It entered my mind, but you should get X-rays first." His intense gaze scanned my face.

"Nah, I'm fine. Just take me home. If I'm in pain later, I'll get checked out. I promise."

His expression may have been a bit on the doubtful side, I'm not sure. Sometimes Marcus is inscrutable, and I can't guess what his thoughts are. This was one of those times.

"If you say so. Take it easy today, and no jogging or any of that stuff, okay?"

"You're mothering me, Marcus. I'm fine, I said."

"I know." He smirked. "But you gave me quite a scare." He drew in a deep breath. "I would have a girlfriend who can't get from point A to point B without a catastrophe. You're a dangerous woman, Vinnie. Honestly."

"You've always said you liked dangerous women, haven't you, Trooper Richmond?" My attempt at humor was wasted.

"If you think of anything you might have seen, anything at all, just call me. I want this bastard, do you understand?"

His profile grim, I wasn't about to aggravate him. The best way to handle things would be to keep my ever-open trap shut. *Wrong again. Geez, I hate when that happens.*

"Do you understand?" He didn't settle for silence. The deadly undercurrent in his voice goaded me into answering him.

"Yes, I understand."

"Good."

The trip home from Providence didn't take long. We pulled into the driveway and I left the cruiser. Marcus was at my side in an instant to escort me into the house. He made a great bodyguard, an unnecessary one, but nice all the same.

In the kitchen, he set the coffee pot to perk and leaned against the counter in thought, his arms folded. This stance was common when something bothered him, and it caused me to wonder if I'd be in for a grilling session.

Cops are like pit bulls. They sink their teeth into a theory, rattle it around a while, and hang on until something shakes loose. When whatever that is, comes to light, they act on it. Sometimes that's a good thing and sometimes it's not. I was unsure of what Marcus was thinking at the moment. While I have an extremely curious nature, I wasn't inclined to ask.

Rhode Island State Trooper, Marcus Richmond had been on the force about fifteen years. Headquarters for this paramilitary group lay about a quarter mile from where I lived. Stationed out of that unit, Marcus cruised by my house often.

"Will you be all right here alone? Marcus asked. "Should I call someone to stay with you?"

Whatever he had on his mind would remain a secret until he decided to share it. Curiosity over needing to know his thoughts pressured me. I struggled hard to keep it under control.

"I'm fine, I don't need a babysitter. I promise to take things easy." My fingers crossed under the counter – I lied. To stay inside on a gorgeous day like this, even though I had a close call, would be foolish by any standards. After all, I hadn't been injured, other than my sore collarbone.

"If you're sure, then I have to get back on the road. The major will have a fit if he finds out I'm goofing off. Besides, I'm pulling a double shift and have to go to Newport tonight with the governor." He kissed me before he left the house.

After Marcus drove away, I puttered around the house doing odd bits of stuff until I could no longer tolerate being cooped up. With my jacket on, I headed up the street on foot. Walking was good exercise and surely I wouldn't get into any trouble doing that? My life is full of surprises, though, and there was nothing mundane about it.

Chapter 2

October in western Rhode Island is a splendid time. I realized it as I went through the village. Leaves from large elm and maple trees cluttered the yards of gigantic historic homes. Bits of their brilliant orange, rusty brown, rich red, and luscious yellow colors clustered on branches and snuggled around the bases of hundred-year-old trees. Lovely antique dwellings lined the main drag in the quaint village of Scituate, pronounced sit-chew-it. The two-story Colonial, bequeathed to me by my Aunt Lavinia, nestled among them.

It was quiet even though I knew the odd leaf peeper would be out. They must have all been shopping instead. The upcoming art festival, held on Columbus Day weekend, meant several thousand people would tramp through the village. They'd wander into yards and make a general nuisance of themselves. Those of us living here accepted the onslaught of city folk with a wry sense of humor, and hoped for the best.

These thoughts fluttered through my mind as I walked, breathing in the fresh, cool air of autumn. I walked a mile or so and passed the local fire station on the outskirts of town as I headed for home. The barbershop lay to my left. Several cars lined the street curb, and two more nestled together in the tiny parking area. One of the vehicles was a grey SUV, the usual patrol car of the Rhode Island State Police. A trooper was getting a buzz cut.

A battered old pickup truck slowed to a crawl and crept past me. At the edge of the barbershop's lot, I glanced at the truck, failed to recognize the driver, and kept on walking. The man pulled over and left the vehicle.

The scruffy-bearded, shaggy-mopped, raggedy-assed looking man called my name. I stopped mid-stride. Disbelief registered as I hesitated in front of the full glass window of the barbershop. Frozen in place by the sound of his voice, I turned to stare. My senses filled with apprehension when he moved toward me. His dark-eyed gaze roaming my body.

His brown eyes took in my long legs and meandered back to my face, stopping at my chest for a second. It took a moment to breathe normally as trepidation shadowed every inch of my being. For two years, I had managed to forget this creep. Yet here he stood, right in front of me. How much luckier could I get, a car accident and this creep, both in the same day?

"Hey Vinnie. It's been a long time. I can't believe my good fortune. How've ya been?" Tony's gravelly voice preceded a grin showing teeth that hadn't seen a toothbrush in a while.

I could swear he'd spit tobacco juice onto the sidewalk any second. Strange as it seemed, I was at a loss for words. *Yeah, I know that sounds impossible, but there it is.* My mouth gaped open like a fish out of water. Nothing good came to mind, so why speak?

"Well, aren't ya glad to see me?" he asked with a smarmy grin.

I swallowed. "I must say I'm surprised. I didn't recognize you right away. How have you been, Tony?" Surprise didn't cover the fact that I hadn't recognized this creep. It had been forever since Tony had crossed my mind along with the problems he'd created for me two years ago.

"You're lookin' great, but then you always have." Tony's gaze slithered over my torso once again.

I edged away from him as the barbershop door opened and closed. I heard footsteps and the voice of a man.

"Hi Vinnie, how are you?" The man asked as he drew near.

My glance slid toward him, and I smiled in relief at the state trooper. He smiled back and then turned toward Tony. It was an act of God that this man had been in the barbershop, even though I didn't know who he was.

"I'm great, how are you?"

Tony stood three feet away, taking in the scene. He shuffled a bit, but stood his ground. Apparently he had something else to say to me.

The trooper watched him a moment and then looked at me.

"I just spoke to Marcus. He mentioned you two are having dinner tonight. Maybe I'll stop by later, if you don't mind?" He lied really well, too.

I nodded and said, "Yes, please do. We'd be happy to have you." I glanced at Tony and then back at the trooper. "I'm sorry. I should introduce you to an old acquaintance of mine. This is Tony DeGreico."

The trooper dipped his hat-covered, buzz-cut head, and said, "Trooper Jonah Franklin."

Tony's glance slid between Jonah and me. His eyes narrowed. Neither man extended a hand to shake.

"Well, nice to meet you Trooper Franklin."

Unsure whether he realized I didn't know this trooper, or if something else went on behind those sneaky eyes, I waited to see what would happen next.

Jonah stood at my side for a few seconds after the introduction. "Things all right with you, Vinnie?"

"Yeah, fine. Tony just stopped to say hello, and I didn't recognize him right away. It's been a while since we've seen one another, isn't that right?"

"Yeah, we were tight a few years ago, but our friendship took a turn. We went our own ways, didn't we?" His smile, more like a sneer, caused me to shuffle my feet.

Anxious to keep him at a distance, I nodded.

I glanced into Jonah's eyes. They held a questioning look, but I didn't offer an explanation. His eyes held mine for a few seconds before he bid us goodbye. As Jonah entered the car, I felt my life raft drift away. It was then I knew I'd have to deal with this sleazoid alone.

A smile crossed Jonah's face and he waved as he pulled into traffic. The trooper ascertained there was no immediate danger and left me to handle things on my own. *Thanks a lot, buddy.*

Tony scuffed his feet in the gritty sand on the sidewalk as he scratched his scruffy beard. It entered my mind that there might be vermin in there, and stifled a shudder.

A grubby baseball cap rode the mop of bedraggled, matted hair. Again, I wondered what he'd been doing to let his appearance go to hell this way. The old Tony would never have looked, or smelled, this bad. Was that odor horse manure or a new men's fragrance?

"So, what have you been up to, Tony?" Not that I cared, but avid curiosity overcomes me at the worst moments. This was one of them.

"After I got out of the nut house I couldn't get a good job, so I went to work at a horse farm. I shovel shit now, thanks to you."

With a shrug, I stared at him for a few seconds. No sense to deny I had anything to do with his mental incapacity plea. He wouldn't believe me anyway.

"At what farm do you shovel this shit?" I asked, in hope that it was a farm far, far away, like on another planet. I knew there'd be no such luck.

"In Foster. There's a horse farm along Hickory Road and the owner needed some help. My social worker got me the job. I live there in the stable apartment. Big switch from my former life, eh?" His eyes turned fierce.

"Indeed. It's good to see that you're doing well, though." Sidling down the sidewalk toward home, I wished him well and started to turn away.

"Things could be better, Vinnie, and I haven't been able to forget how you helped change my life. I'll try to repay you somehow." He called, and cackled a bit.

Thank goodness Hickory Road was over ten miles west from my house. It meant the chances of running into the nutball would be next to none. Hickory Road, an agricultural section of the town of Foster, bordered the Connecticut State Line. I rarely ventured into that section of the town. The slim chance of any interaction with this man was a comfort.

In an effort to end the conversation, I hurried away, almost at a dead run. He gave me the creeps and I couldn't shake the sense that this wasn't my last encounter with the 'nutter.' Maybe my overactive imagination was on a rampage, but somehow, it didn't seem so.

I rushed across the street and into my yard.

The phone jingled its tune as I entered the house through the side door. I stepped to the counter and grabbed the receiver off the charger.

"Hello."

"Hi, it's mom. Where have you been? I've been calling for over an hour? Did your classes run longer than usual today?"

My mother, Bake Sale Queen and Chocolate Maker Extraordinaire, sounded a bit out of sorts. Now what had I done, or not done? Was this about the accident?

"No, they didn't. I took a walk and got waylaid returning to the house. What's up, is there a problem?"

"You're Aunt Mafalda is in a snit, and I need your help."

"Aunt Muffy? What's happened?" My aunt, the dater of mob-connected men, made life interesting for everyone except me. "Can you give me some idea of what the snit is about?"

"She and her new flame have been hauled to jail and she's called to see if you can get them out."

With a deep sigh, I paced the kitchen while I envisioned the possibilities. Without information, I couldn't help Muffy and hoped my mother would be more forthcoming.

"Why were they lugged?"

"It seems Antonio has been charged with racketeering and since Muffy was with him, she's been charged as well." Her voice hitched as she explained, and I assumed her stress level had reached the overflow mark.

"Where are they being held? What police station?" I asked, then dragged fresh jeans and a sweater from the dresser and charged into the bathroom to change.

"They're at the Providence Police Department. What can you do, dear?"

"I'm not sure, but I'll head down there now." *Good grief.*

Dirty Trouble

What was I, a miracle worker?

My mother uttered her thanks and hung up. I set the phone down, then changed my clothes. Somehow, my encounter with Tony left me feeling soiled.

My Aunt Mafalda, 'Muffy' Ciano was the divorced mother of four grown children. They had moved as far away from Rhode Island and Auntie as they could without leaving the country. Their father – bless his dead soul – was a smalltime hood from the Italian neighborhood of Federal Hill, in Providence. In the old days, the Hill had gained fame as the hangout of a major crime boss and his crew of cutthroats, hustlers, and enforcers.

Once the FBI and the state police cleaned up the neighborhood, Federal Hill became a tourist trap for those who got a thrill from sitting in a 'trattoria' on the Hill. It gave the fools a charge to visit a place where there had been a cold-blooded hit by mob enforcers. *Go figure!*

I called my best friend Lola, to ask if I could borrow her car. With a brief explanation of why I needed to do so, she readily agreed to let me take the MINI Cooper.

I was ready to leave when a knock sounded on the door. Aaron Grant, my upstairs tenant and an undercover FBI agent, strode into the house with a bag of sandwiches from the Salt & Pepper Deli on the corner. Lola owns the deli that serves the most scrumptious food imaginable. Aaron glanced at my face and stopped short.

"What's happened now? You have an anxious look on your face, Vin."

Dressed in jeans and a knit jersey, he looked as delectable as I knew the food was.

"My mother just called and said my aunt has been arrested by a cop from the Providence Police Department," I said while tying me sneakers.

Thick, dark, sculptured eyebrows shot up over warm chocolate brown eyes in the handsome face. He tossed the bag onto the counter. Aaron's professional wrestler-sized frame leaned against the door casing and he folded muscle-bound arms across his massive chest. His tan skin and dark hair enhanced his easy, sparkling smile. He reminded me of The Rock, a famous wrestler, turned movie star.

I stopped what I was doing and stared, "You know about this, don't you?"

"I didn't realize the woman with the 'perp' was your aunt. She's in trouble, Vin. Resisting arrest is a serious offense."

"You don't say?" I rolled my eyes. "She resisted arrest, huh? Just how did that happen?"

"When the officers attempted to take Antonio down, she stepped up and gave them a verbal beating. A real tongue lashing, from what I understand." Aaron chuckled a bit. "They tried to put her aside and she refused to allow it. The cops cuffed them both and took them to the station."

"Great, just what I need. My aunt, the Mafia Moll." I rolled my eyes. "Cripes, she's in her sixties for God's sake. I don't suppose you can help me out, eh?"

"No, I'm afraid it's in the PPD's hands at the moment."

"Well, in that case, I've got to go. Sorry."

"Right. Come upstairs when you get back. You haven't seen the place since I moved all of my stuff in. These sandwiches will wait, unless Marcus will be here tonight?"

"No, he's on duty in Newport with the governor. Save me some food, and I'll see you later."

"Sure, I have an important matter to discuss with you. By the way, where's your car?"

"That's another story, but I haven't the time to get into it right now. We'll talk when I get home."

In a hurry, I brushed past and left him to lock up on the way out. I scooted to Lola's deli, on the corner and down the street. Minutes later, I drove Lola's MINI Cooper to Providence.

Chapter 3

The two main men in my life, Aaron Grant and Marcus Richmond, are both gorgeous to a fault, arrogant, and involved in law enforcement. Marcus saved my life not long ago, and gets testy with me on occasion. Though I can't mind my own business, and I'm a thickheaded Italian woman, I think he's come to understand me. At least, I hope so.

My tenant, Aaron, a cool dude with a warm heart, never makes emotional demands on me. I consider him more friend than anything else, and never let his undercover FBI status interfere with my unconventional life and Italian family. Marcus, on the other hand, raises my blood pressure with just a glance and is always in my face about my behavior and my family.

I'm unfortunate enough to have an inner voice that screams at me constantly with dire warnings of the dangers of personal involvement with law enforcement agents. It rants on about how I'll only be hurt by a cop, a cop of any kind. For the most part, I ignore it. I was good about remaining romantically uninvolved with cops in the past, until I met Marcus.

It's been a challenge since I'm a Criminal Justice instructor at a local university and teach law enforcement officers of all types. Two Point Fives, 'flashlight cops', real cops that are called Five-O's, and 'wannabes' participate in my programs every day of the school year. The Two-Point-Fives and 'flashlight cops' – nicknamed such by real cops – are security personnel from all walks of life.

Real Five-O's patrol the streets to keep the American public safe. Wannabes are future recruits who further their careers in law enforcement through education while they wait for an opportunity to test for the police department. They're a gregarious group of people, men and women alike. Coarse, crude, funny, protective, and dangerous are the descriptive terms I use for them.

They share theories and get involved in classroom discussions to the point where yelling becomes a common occurrence. Sometimes things run out of control, but they blow over, and I breathe a sigh of relief. I often consider my job to be that of adult babysitter rather than an instructor of Criminal Justice.

As I cruised along the highway into Providence, I turned toward the huge police department complex. I lucked out when I pulled into the lot. One skinny slot stood open, and I squeezed the small car into it. An available parking spot was an incredible find.

Locking the doors, I edged sideways between the other cars to get out into the lot. It's a good thing I'm tall and lean. When I glanced back, I realized the passenger side of the car was nearly up against the cruiser next to it. With a shrug, I continued on into the police station.

Once inside, it was necessary to pass through metal detectors, where Officer Fernando Petronio stood guard. 'Nando', currently enrolled in one of my classes, grinned when he saw me. These guys never pass up a chance to act out, so I knew he'd put me through my paces. He'd go through my purse and probably search me if the alarm went off when I went through the detector.

"Step up and place your bag on the counter, ma'am." He grinned.

"Yeah, yeah. Hurry up, will ya?" I chuckled, even though I wanted to race onward and find my way to lockup.

"Walk through, Ms. Esposito." He waggled his brows as I went through the gate.

When the alarm didn't go off, I laughed at his crestfallen face.

"Sorry, Nando, you can't have everything."

"What brings you to the PPD, Vinnie?" Nando handed me

my purse.

"My mother called and said you have my aunt in lock up. Help me out here, will you? It's Mafalda. Mafalda Ciano."

He hauled a sheaf of papers toward him and scrolled down the list of names. "Go see Bellini in the interview rooms on the third floor. He's handling the investigation. Patrolman Dixon will escort you to his office." Fernando cocked his head toward a patrolman who loitered at a second metal detector, not fifteen feet away. He motioned the man over.

"Dixon, take Ms. Esposito to see Bellini. I'll call upstairs to tell him you're on your way. Good luck, Vinnie," he said with a grin.

Detective Bellini was a hard-ass in the detective division. I'd run across him on several occasions. We have a tolerance-type working relationship. He liked me when I didn't fail his fledglings. Sometimes, when one of them was on the brink of failure, he'd call, and we'd go three or four rounds on the phone.

For the most part, Bellini and I have mutual respect for one another. I don't tolerate his crap and he doesn't take any from me, either. If I had to choose someone to be on my side in a tight situation, his name would top the list.

In the elevator, Dixon glanced at me with disdain, as though I was a perpetrator. I glanced back and gave him 'the face.' It's the face your mother gives when you've done something that she isn't happy about. Usually it works like a charm to make someone change his or her attitude and this time was no different.

"Do you know Detective Bellini, ma'am?"

I really dislike that 'ma'am' thing. It makes me feel so ancient and I'm not, honest. There are times in life when good manners rub the wrong way.

"Mmm, we've been acquainted for ages." I also lie by omission and am darned good at it, too. It's a natural talent I received at birth, I think, a God-given talent so to speak. Bellini and I have known one another for a year or so – only our acquaintance is through the university and much discord. This cop didn't need to know that, though.

"Oh," he said, and fell silent.

The elevator door slid open and we left the confines of the cubicle. Dixon motioned me down the corridor on the right. Several interview rooms, or 'boxes' as they're called, sat to my left.

A hallway door opened and Detective Michael Bellini, a rugged man with a small roll of fluff lolling around his waist, stepped into view. His cropped hair was graying at the temples and his facial skin sagged a tad. His chest was headed south, and a rounded bulb tipped the end of his nose. He stood five feet ten and we were eye to eye.

Lean and leggy in comparison, I'm well-endowed breast wise, and hold my own in the looks department. Thanks to my Italian heritage, I have good skin and an attitude to match it. I'm also not Bellini's age.

"Ms. Esposito, come in. You can go, Dixon." Bellini's dark eyes measured me. He offered no smile or indication of friendliness.

His off-hand attitude indicated I might be in for a difficult time. I strode forward after thanking Dixon, and stepped into Bellini's office.

His brow arched. Bellini asked, "I'm told your aunt is in lockup?"

I would owe this man big time for any favors I requested. It irritated the snot out of me – but you gotta do what you gotta do, right? Family is family, after all. As an Italian, Bellini should understand that.

"Yes, apparently there's been a misunderstanding. My aunt is not, nor has she ever been, involved with racketeering. I'm told you may be able to assist me."

"Who told you that?" He smirked, aware that I was in a tight spot.

Should any of his primo students need to pass my classes, I'd have to relent and mark them on a curve. How big a curve remained to be seen. Family issues can be a real pain in the ass.

I swallowed my attitude and answered him sweetly. "Officer Petronio mentioned you might have some pity for my unfortunate aunt."

With a nod, he said, "I'll call lockup and have her brought in. We'll see her in a box down the hall. She's not dangerous, is she?"

He must be joking. The woman was in her sixties, not some punk-ass chick with a rap sheet as long as the interstate highway.

"Hardly, Detective. She's a mature woman headed toward her twilight years, who probably became extremely upset at the arrest of her boyfriend."

"Your aunt dates mobsters?" With a bark of laughter, Bellini dialed the extension for lockup.

It must have been the thought of a woman her age dating someone whose 'number was up' that caused his uncontrollable laughter. I listened while he ordered Muffy to be brought to Interrogation Room Three.

"She's my aunt. I know nothing about that aspect of her personal life." I lied. "I'm just going on what my mother has said. If I know my aunt, I'd say her smart mouth is what got her arrested in the first place."

"It must run in the family," he mumbled softly, as we strolled down the corridor and into another room.

Settled across the table from Bellini, I waited in silence for my mother's older sister to be brought in by the guard. Bellini flipped his ink pen over and over, and clicked the metal against the table until I thought I'd go mad. My instincts told me to be cool, but my nerves were ragged with pressure over what it would cost me to get Muffy out of the slammer.

A smirk lingered at the corners of Bellini's mouth, and I guessed he'd read my mind. He also undoubtedly enjoyed his position. Michael Bellini realized he could name the tune, and I'd owe him the dance. *Dang, it's annoying when that happens.*

The door opened, and we both stood at the same time. A lanky guard held the door while Muffy shuffled in. Her hairstyle askew and make-up smudged, she stood five feet tall and ramrod straight. Bodacious breasts were held up by a 'silver bullet' long line bra, and her round figure topped shapely legs. At her age, you'd have thought there'd be a ton of wrinkles, but Muffy had skin most women would kill for. From the look on her face, I guessed she'd made life hard for herself and everyone else involved.

The officer glanced at me, and gave a brief nod of recognition. A smirk trembled around the corners of his mouth and I knew my assumptions were on the mark. He settled against the inside door and waited for Mafalda to sit down.

"Auntie, sit here." I motioned to a nearby chair.

"Those bastards arrested me. Can you believe that Lavinia? I didn't do anything to break the law. You know I would never." She pointedly ignored Bellini as she ranted.

"Do you have anything to do with the charges against Antonio?" I asked in a calm voice and held her hand.

"No, I don't. Lavinia, I can't believe you're asking me such a question. These dickheads are just being ridiculous. Antonio isn't a racketeer. He's a *businessman*."

It was too much for Bellini to handle. He burst out in raucous laughter, and I have to admit I was hard pressed to keep a straight face.

"Mild mannered, just like you, huh?" he asked in a low voice.

"Right." I glared at him. "Detective Bellini, my aunt will apologize for her actions. Do you think I could take her home?"

His eyebrows shot upward. "She's got to face charges for resisting arrest, Vinnie. There's nothing I can do about that. She's not a flight risk, is she?"

"No, she'll show up. I'll bring her to court personally. I promise." I stared at Bellini for a moment. He appeared to enjoy this whole thing way too much – while I wasn't enjoying it at all.

"I could take some heat over this, but go ahead and take her home. I'll make it right with the captain." He turned to my aunt. "If you hadn't lost your temper, you'd have been spared this unfortunate situation, ma'am."

"Damned straight. If your men hadn't manhandled me, I'd have been spared more than that," she spluttered.

I put my hand on her arm and squeezed lightly so she'd shut her mouth. We rose from the table. I assured Detective Bellini all would be well. He smirked and said he'd be in touch. *My God, the things I do for family.*

I walked Mafalda through the station after we retrieved her belongings. In quite a state by the time we reached the car, her usually neat dyed black hair floated all over the place, leaving her totally disheveled. This just wasn't the way to see an aunt who normally took great pride in her appearance.

"Wait until I back the car out of the space, and I'll let you in, Auntie."

Muffy waited. I started the car, and tried not to sideswipe the cruisers parked on either side. It took some maneuvering, but I finally got the car out of the slot and unlocked the door. Auntie plunked into the seat with a sigh of relief and settled back in silence. For once, her mouth was clamped shut, and I wondered what thoughts ran through her brain.

"Take me home, dear. I need a bath. That station is a filthy pit, and only animals belong there. I can't believe they've kept Antonio – he's such a good man."

Yeah right. He probably had racketeering down to a fine science. It had fallen into a slump years earlier, when the mob was split and most crime family members were incarcerated.

Things had started to turn around, as most things do. I heard from my students that racketeers were alive and flourishing once again.

This slimy business covered a wide range of bad guy stuff. It had become more sophisticated, devious, and included everything from prostitution, to gambling, to smuggling and more. A visit by the 'bone breakers' wasn't an appointment at the local chiropractor's office. Instead, it was two big dudes who rearranged your kneecaps when you were in the shits for something.

I pulled into Aunt Muffy's driveway. After helping her from the front seat of the vehicle, we entered the house. The quaint, tastefully decorated bungalow was a perfect home for her. No crystal chandeliers or gaudy furniture. Instead, everything was clean lines and warm colors. Even the kitchen was streamlined.

With a promise to pick her up for the court date in Providence, I prepared to leave. Muffy made a cup of tea and managed to come to grips with the fact that she'd have to answer for her behavior – an unusual state of affairs, since she refused to answer for anything. Muffy said she realized she'd have to do so this time around. I finally left after she assured me she'd be fine and was happy to be home.

At least one of us was happy. I disliked owing anyone favors, and Bellini would hold it over my head for sure.

Chapter 4

With a glance at my watch, I turned toward home. While I covered the distance, I spoke to my mother on my cell phone.

"Muffy's out of the police station, and I took her home." I explained the charges and that I'd have to take her to court. Thoughts of that unpleasant experience filled my heart with dread, but nonetheless, it was a necessity.

My mother clicked her tongue against her teeth and sighed with resignation over the whole situation. It was apparent that she heartily disapproved of Auntie's dating habits, but had no control over them.

"Thanks for the rescue, Lavinia. Do you plan to come over for some dinner? I can have your father make you a dish."

"No thanks. I have a sandwich waiting at home. I was about to eat when you called. It'll still be good. Lola made it." My parents hadn't heard of my accident. What a relief not to have to answer a bazillion questions.

My father, a retired chef, had owned his own pizza restaurant until he took an early retirement. My mother managed it, him, and the books when they ran the restaurant. I ate at their house often and got terrific leftovers to bring home. Life is good in that way.

"All right then, dear. I'll talk to you tomorrow. There's a bake sale at the seniors' center, by the way. It's to raise funds for a trip to the performing arts center and I'm the chairwoman. I'll be home afterwards though, if you want to come down for dinner." She disconnected the call, and I pulled into the deli parking lot.

Not that my mother is old or anything. Lately, she'd become a champion to any and every cause concerning the elderly. I am proud of her for that, but sometimes it creates havoc within the family circle.

After returning the keys to Lola, I walked up the street, a breeze bringing the sweet scent of autumn swirling around me. Aaron's gigantic GMC Yukon sat in the driveway, kitchen lights from the second floor filtered over the yard. It wasn't late, but dark enough for lighting. The days were shorter with autumn underway, and I could smell the crisp, cool air that surrounded the decaying leaves and other foliage.

The side entry of the two-family Colonial I inherited this year, gave way to a rear staircase that led to the apartment above mine.

The upstairs door yawned open, and Aaron stood at the top of the stairs grinning. He beckoned me into the apartment with a crook of his index finger in a 'come hither' type motion.

"I just opened a couple of beers to go with the sandwiches, if you're still hungry," he said with a grin. "Lola called to tell me you were on your way home."

Anyone who knows me is aware that I never pass up a meal, especially when I can dine with a gorgeous man. I'm not stupid by any stretch of the imagination. I often act that way, but it's only an act.

With the long-strapped handbag slung over my shoulder, I hiked the steps two at a time and entered the kitchen. Lights blazed, and the food sat ready and waiting on the counter. Frothy beer sparkled in frosted mugs and my mouth watered. Yep, I was hungry.

His eyes crinkled at their corners as Aaron watched me dig in with fervor. I hadn't eaten since early morning and I'd worked that food off. My glance took in the generous smile. I chuckled with my mouth full.

"Not hungry or anything, are you?"

I swallowed the mouthful of food. Between sips of beer, I said with a grin, "I haven't had a minute to stop for a bite to eat since breakfast. This sandwich is great, by the way."

"My pleasure." Aaron studied me for a moment and then

asked, "How did things go at the PPD?"

"Do you already know the answer, or are you truly concerned?"

His hand went to his heart in feigned pain. "You wound me, Vinnie. Is there no trust between us?" Laughter rocked the kitchen.

"Yeah, yeah. All right, I'll take that to mean you're concerned. My aunt is determined that Antonio is just a common businessman. Detective Bellini couldn't handle that theory." I explained the interview room scene and how Auntie would be arraigned for her smart-ass attitude.

His eyebrows hiked when I made the remark about Muffy. I put my hand up in a stop motion. "I know. Don't say it. Bellini thinks it must run in the family, too. I bet good old Antonio is already out of jail. If he's a racketeer, he probably made bail, and left Auntie to rot in a cell."

"He was released within an hour of his arrest." Aaron shook his head. "The bum left her there. Imagine that?"

"If she finds out that's the case, then Antonio will probably need a chiropractic visit. Muffy has a wicked disposition, takes absolutely no crap. I wouldn't be in his shoes for anything." I chomped down the rest of my sandwich, followed by the beer, and then made a huge belch. Chuckling, my hand went to my mouth.

"Must be good food to produce that sound, Vin." He laughed, his white teeth flashing in the overhead light. "Tell me about Mafalda's penchant for mob men." He leaned back, his eyes on his beer mug.

"My family knows a lot of mob-related folks even though they don't have anything to do with them. When my parents were kids, they grew up in a neighborhood with guys who ended up on the wrong side of the law." I stopped and thought about Muffy for a minute, then said, "Sometimes women get into the 'bad boy' mode and become caught up with the so-called glamour of it. My aunt is one of those people. She married Benny 'The Stromboli' Perrano, and had a bunch of kids. When he got killed, she just went on with life and took back her maiden name."

"Tell me about the kids."

"They live as far away as they can without leaving the

States. All have good-paying professions and are law abiding, so far as I know. Why?"

"No reason, just want to get a mental picture of your family, that's all. Do your parents entertain anyone from the mob?"

"Not that I know of. My dad has an aversion to the way they do things. He drilled honesty into my twin brother, Giovanni, and me as we grew up. That didn't stop us from acting out of course, but we eventually listened to him. Unlike my two cousins, Frankie and Kenny, we're upstanding citizens."

"Indeed, Frankie and Kenny aren't happy about their living arrangements now, but they asked for it. You haven't suffered any ill effects from that debacle this past summer, have you?"

"Not really. I couldn't believe they were at the bottom of the gem smuggling ring. Well, I could believe it, but don't want to think they would hurt my mother."

My two cousins had smuggled high-end gems into the country by way of a ragtag group of people. My Aunt Lavinia, and namesake, found out they used her gift shop to traffic them. She tried to convince the two slime balls to stop their nefarious activities, but before Aunt Livvy could complete the convincing part, she died...under mysterious circumstances.

In an effort to retrieve the gems that she'd stowed away - and I found – the two dummies called and threatened my mother and me. My cousins were arrested, and they now reside as guests of the state prison system.

"You think Antonio is in the mob? How did you come to that conclusion?" Aaron's voice pulled me away from my thoughts.

My eyes narrowed a tad. "It's the trend Aunt Muffy follows. The last man she dated is now a guest of the Department of Corrections and she has moved on. Why are you so curious?"

"Like I said, I'm trying to get a picture. If I can help you out with the arraignment, then I will."

"That's good of you. I appreciate it." I stood, stretched, and yawned. Full of food and beer, exhaustion set in. I wandered toward the door and turned to thank Aaron.

Before I could utter a sound, he asked, "What was the

incident in front of the barbershop about today?"

"Um, n-nothing," I stammered in surprise. "A guy I know stopped to say hello."

"Are you sure that's all it was?"

"Why so inquisitive? What's going on?" I returned to the counter and waited.

"Really, there's nothing to it. Like I said, I want to get a picture of the family and Mafalda's relationship with Antonio. The thing in front of the barbershop was only a question. I have another one for you, too. Where's your car?"

"How did you find out about the barbershop thing?"

"I'd just pulled into the driveway when I saw you. Your body language piqued my curiosity. When the trooper stepped into the scene, I knew you'd be fine. That's all."

"Oh, well, it was nothing. But thanks for asking." I explained the accident. His face registered a look of concern while I wondered if he already knew the answer to the question about my car, before he asked it.

"I'm glad you're all right. If you need me, just give a yell." He hesitated as though he there was something else on his mind.

"What else?" I asked.

"My boss has notified me of a training course in Washington, DC. The course is a few weeks long, so I'll be away for a while." He tossed the sandwich wrappers in the trash.

This was interesting. What kind of training? Would he eventually leave me tenantless? *Well, shit.* This news capped off a real crummy day.

"When do you leave? And what kind of training is it?" I asked on a sigh.

"After I wrap up the ongoing investigation, I'll be leaving town. I can't talk about the program, sorry." He stared at me. "You won't evict me, will you?"

Wide eyed, I stared back.

"Not a chance, Aaron. You're a great friend, and I care about you a lot. You won't have to move to Washington, will you?"

"Not that I know of. I'm pretty well entrenched in Rhode

Island. As long as I don't piss anybody off, the likelihood of my staying here is good," he said in soft voice.

Rounding the counter, he stepped close to me and laid a hand on my arm.

"Besides, I wouldn't want to leave you here."

"Oh." I wondered he realized where my heart truly lay. He was obviously hoping that he could win me over somehow.

He cleared his throat and said, "I value your friendship, Vinnie."

I nodded and turned toward the door to scramble down the stairs before things became complicated, family wise, mob wise, and otherwise. Aaron's career was headed in another direction. Thank God he didn't plan to move away. I was fond of him and enjoyed his presence in the house.

I considered his inquisitiveness. It was a sure bet his investigation included Muffy's boyfriend. Jeez. As long as it wouldn't dredge up old crap like Tony, I was happy.

When the lock on the doorknob of my apartment clicked, I slid the bolt home. I'd taken up this habit when the apartment was ransacked over the summer. After a run-in with an intruder, I'd become more cautious. I even took a Rape Aggression Defense class as a common-sense mode of protection.

Tossing my purse on the counter, I kicked the sneakers off my feet. In the living room, I flopped on the sofa. My head was full of questions with no answers – a situation that happened often, I might add.

The possibility of Muffy's involvement in some illicit business would send my mother off the deep end. When that happened, it wasn't a pretty sight and meant complications in my life. Mom would insist I look into the situation unbeknownst to my father. Yikes. The only thing worse than that, would be if my twin brother, Gio, decided to move home from Nebraska. I'd taken the fall for him once too often when we were kids. He would come up with some scheme or other that I would get blamed for. As twins, we never told on one another, either.

The phone jingled a lighthearted tune. I snatched it off the hook.

"Vinnie here."

A charming, smooth voice echoed in my ear. It brought a smile to my face and a rush of heat to other parts.

"What are you doing? Are you lounging around in the nude?" Marcus Richmond's voice oozed across the miles.

"Why do you want to know, Trooper Richmond?"

"If I can't be there to see it, then I need to imagine it. This detail with the gov is big time boring, and I'd like to be there with you. You're on the sofa, aren't you?"

"How did you know?"

"A wild guess." He chuckled. "What have you been up to while I'm stuck here in Newport? Did you rest, like I asked?"

"Not quite."

With a deep breath, I launched into the PPD episode and Aunt Muffy's arrest. Since he'd met her this past summer, he had a grip on my dilemma.

"Uh huh, does she know that Antonio was sprung from the PPD before she was?"

"Not that I know of. But she will. And then, if there's a homicide concerning Antonio, it's a safe bet she got to him before anyone else could. The man took his life in his hands when he failed to spring her at the same time as he got out."

"So what else is new? Have you seen Romeo?"

Marcus and Aaron Grant are constants in my life. Don't ask me why, but they are. In his attempt to tolerate the fact that Aaron is my tenant and friend, Marcus calls him Romeo. It's the only indication that there may be a spot of jealousy that niggles at him.

With a grin, I said, "As a matter of fact, I had supper with him tonight. I think it was a working supper, though. All he did was ask questions about my family and Muffy's connections."

"Got to watch those FBI guys, you know. They're sneaky."

"Yeah, as if the state police aren't. Who are you trying to kid?" Soft laughter accompanied the remark.

"I didn't say we weren't capable of clandestine activities." He laughed. "So what else is going on?"

He asked the question a few times too many and I realized

[38]

he knew about the barbershop incident too. I guessed that Jonah Franklin had been on the phone with Marcus the minute he left me on the sidewalk.

"An old acquaintance popped up today. He stopped me outside the barbershop and Jonah Franklin was there. Is that what you want to know?"

"Jonah did mention it when I called headquarters. This guy, is he a creep or what?"

"What makes you think he's a creep?"

"Don't be cute, Vin," he said with a resigned tone. "I know he's a creep and wonder why he was so quick to approach you."

"It was a chance meeting – that's it."

"Uh huh, if you say so. How do you know him, anyway?"

"I met him a few years ago."

"You don't want to share any information with me, do you?" Marcus made a *tsk* sound. "I'll find out for myself, then."

"Be my guest. You know Marcus, it would be nice to have you here with me right now," I said, in what I hoped was a sultry voice, wanting a change of subject.

"Mm, it would be nice to be there, but unfortunately, I won't be back until late tonight sometime. I'll see you tomorrow then."

I agreed and said goodbye. It would only be a matter of time before he figured out my association with Tony. With a deep sigh, I leaned back on the sofa and tuned in to a murder mystery on the television.

Chapter 5

The heavy front door closed with a *thunk*. Knuckles rapped against my apartment door. Reluctantly, I slid off the sofa and realized I'd dozed off with the television on. It was morning and time to get up anyway.

Stumbling across the room, I rubbed my eyes and flipped my hair back from my face.

"Who is it?" I asked while I flexed my sore shoulder.

"Lola. Open up, Vin."

I slid the lock back and opened the door to admit my petite, gregarious friend with the Julia Roberts' smile. She waved a bag under my nose and scooted past me into the kitchen. It smelled delicious. Curious, I followed her into the sunlit room and started to brew coffee.

Plates from the cupboard clattered across the counter before Lola opened the bag. She slipped flaky pastries onto the dishes. Lola was at it again, baking the most delectable foods imaginable – with me as her guinea pig. If I liked them, it was a safe bet they'd sell like crazy.

I poured two cups of strong brewed coffee and grinned. "You're in experiment mode again, aren't you?"

"It's true, I made these with you in mind. I thought you'd try them out for me. How do you feel today?" She gazed at my wrinkled clothes, and grinned. Her gorgeous set of pearly whites glistened in her infectious smile.

"Not too bad. My shoulder is sore, and my muscles are, too. I'm fortunate I wasn't seriously injured. Thanks for asking."

"Been sleeping in your clothes, huh? Marcus must be away."

"Yeah, he went to Newport with the governor." I munched the buttery pastry and sipped coffee. "These are wonderful. My waistline will never stay the same if you keep this up."

"Uh huh," she said. Then she asked, "What's the thing with Tony DeGreico, Vin?"

"Jeez, am I the talk of the town, or what?"

"I heard that you ran into him yesterday. What was that all about?"

After I explained the chance meeting, I started a second pastry. I could see the wheels turning as Lola eyed me.

"I thought he was still in the looney bin. When did he get out?" she asked, studiously twiddling the spoon in her cup.

"He didn't say when he got out, but he said he couldn't thank me enough for screwing up his life."

"Do you feel threatened by him?"

"No, and don't let your imagination run wild either."

"He could have hurt you badly two years ago, you know that. His actions were those of a deranged person."

"Yes, but his act in court was that of an Oscar nominee. Tony pled insanity because he hoped he'd get a lighter sentence. He just didn't realize what the looney bin would be like, is all." Anger simmered just beneath the surface, and I struggled to control it. I'd believed that part of the nightmare was over with, but I was mistaken.

"He had a wonderful future with Maria until he blew it with his drug dealing. Then he blamed you for their break up. The worst of it was that nobody could get through to him. Stalking you and setting fire to your apartment was way past any sane limits, Vin. There was a time when I'd have found it hard to believe he'd hurt you." Lola shook her head. "He proved that he was a loser when he refused to stand up and take the punishment like a man. Instead, he claimed he'd been under duress which caused him to act irrationally." Lola watched my reaction.

"What makes you bring this up now?" I asked.

Elbows resting on the counter, she gazed out the French doors for a moment. Then she turned that dark, liquid gaze toward me, and said, "He's back in the real world again, and I'm not sure you're as safe as you think. Besides, his drug supplier was never found, you know."

"Did your brother tell you that?"

Lola's brother is a cop, and a good one at that. She often got the inside scoop on stuff that nobody was supposed to know.

She shrugged a shoulder, saying nothing.

"Well, Tony now shovels manure on a horse farm in Foster, and that's where he'll probably stay. You know, with the animals."

My appetite fled. I leaned back from the counter and sipped the coffee. The silence in the apartment lengthened. I noticed Lola's eyes held concern for me. It wasn't necessary, but it was nice to know she cared.

"Please don't worry about me. I'm certain that Tony won't bother me. After all, I wasn't the rat who gave him up to the cops, even though he thinks so." I toyed with the crumbs on my plate, pushing them around with my fingertip. "I was nervous when he stalked me because the cops were crawling up his butt with a microscope. Where he got the idea that I was behind his arrest, still hasn't surfaced."

"It was a nightmare for you, and it won't hurt to be aware of any unusual occurrences. That's all I'm saying." A worried frown wrinkled Lola's freckled face, a face that was surrounded by a huge halo of deep auburn hair. Italian by birth, an Irishman had gotten into the mix somehow.

"I know. Thanks for caring."

As Lola slid off the chair and away from the counter, she pushed the plate toward me with a smile.

"Maybe you should share these with the hunk upstairs."

"Why don't you run up there with them and see what response you get?" I chuckled, knowing she had a serious crush on Aaron.

"Good idea." She grabbed the plate and dashed out the door.

High-heeled shoes clattered up the rear staircase and I heard her rap on Aaron's door. Muffled words were exchanged as Aaron greeted her, and the upstairs door closed. With a grin, I headed into the shower.

After I cleaned up and smelled human once again, I dressed and headed into my office. An enclosed central staircase that led to the upstairs apartment separated the two front rooms in the house. One of the two rooms was my living room. The other, I used as a dining room come office, where I ate with family or guests and used the table to plan programs for classes.

Teaching was a real kick. The cops who lined up to take my classes were some of the smartest streetwise people I'd ever seen.

The fare I offered included fingerprinting, crime scene investigation, and the psychology of crime. I enjoyed my job and the stories shared by the students. Some tales they share seemed too surreal to be true, though I knew they were. We often had laughs, and occasionally I had the opportunity to ride along with a few of the cops. They're funny and willing to talk until the shit hits the ground, then everything's strictly business.

This week's schedule lay before me as I stared out the window, lost in thought. My laptop computer sat to the right. With reluctance I pulled it closer. The keys clicked under my fingertips, and reports written by the class participants rapidly surfaced. After reading the homework assignments, I typed responses to everyone and sent their e-mail grades off to them.

Unable to settle on the next workload, I figured exercise might lighten my down-swung mood. Lola's words echoed in my ears. While I'm not the bravest person in the world, I act like it. I hoped Tony wouldn't be my next challenge.

Exercise usually removed the cobwebs from my brain. Though my muscles whined over the thought of a workout, I slipped my sneakers on and left the house. I walked past Lola's MINI Cooper still parked in the yard. A smile flitted across my face as I considered her attempt to woo Aaron.

My Italian grandmother, Nonni, always said the only way to get a man was to feed him well. *I heartily disagree, but hey, I'm not married, so who am I to say she's wrong?* Nonni, still a strong-willed woman, had ruled her household with an iron hand, or wooden spoon, whichever came first.

Even my father conceded when she entered a conversation, whether he agreed with her or not. If one disagreed with Nonni, a lecture was sure to follow, along with no dinner, or maybe a smack with a wooden cooking spoon. The worst part was that she was usually right about stuff.

I left the house and noted the street lined with cars. A hearse was parked in front of the church. *Must be a funeral.* The Catholic Church sat on the corner opposite Lola's Salt & Pepper Deli. As a Catholic, I feel it's a good thing for others to go to church, but not necessarily for me to participate.

Nonni and my mother disagree with that idea, but I live more than ten minutes away from them, and that's my saving grace. In Rhode Island, if you live more than ten minutes travel time from someone, likely you'll never be on his or her visitation list. I often refer to this as the unwritten ten-minute rule. The likelihood of 'no visitors' doesn't faze me at all. I relish privacy.

As I crossed the street, the fresh autumn smells of crisp leaves wafted over me. The hint of a chill made me shiver. Tendrils of my hair fluttered around my face in the breeze. My thick sweatshirt and jersey sweatpants seemed appropriate now that I was outdoors.

I rounded the block and passed the fire station as a huge bay door rolled up. The gravelly voice of Bill MacNert, the oldest member of the fire company, carried across the launch pad.

"Whatcha' up to this mornin', Vinnie?" He smiled and came toward me. His gait hitched with every step.

Bill MacNert was a longtime friend of mine and Aunt Livvy's during our life in Scituate. He had handled some of my problems earlier this year. He and his wife lived in this neat village that lay west of Providence. They claimed that though it was only a stone's throw from the metropolitan area, coming here was like entering another world.

When I had the gem smuggling issue during the summer, Bill was first on my call list. Though he gossiped like an old woman, his heart was pure gold.

"Just shaking the cobwebs from my brain, Bill. How's the

fire-fighting business?"

"Well, it's been slow this season. I was wonderin' if you might have somethin' comin' up that would take the edge off our boredom here at the station?" He cackled, as only senior men do.

"Saw you talkin' to Tony DeGreico yesterday. Nothin' good about that bum, so you just watch yerself. Okay?"

Lordy, was everyone aware of my business or what? Nonni and my parents would be the next ones looking out for me. Geesh. With a mental eye roll I tried a confident smile.

"I'm certain there's nothing to fear. Thanks for the advice though."

Sidestepping the conversation, I moved toward the reservoir on the edge of town. Waving my hand, I walked away from Bill's inquiring stare. A glance over my shoulder revealed him turning back into the station.

Was there no relief from these do-gooders? By the time I reached the softball field, a quarter mile from the village, my nerves evened out. Cars lined the lot next to the field and along the road. A preschool kids' ball game was in progress.

Stationed outside the chain-link fence, my fingers curled into the diamond-shaped openings. I watched the little players step up to the plate, their bats larger than they were. They were miniature pros. I envied their ability to hit the ball and focus on the game. Swarms of mothers cheered, proud of the players' efforts to win.

After a few strikes, I moved away and headed back to the house. My mind still stuck on the Tony thing, I wondered why everyone was so nervous about him. It seemed I was the only one who didn't see a threat. Was that dumb or what? Only time would tell.

Arriving at the house, I wandered out behind the huge Colonial and sat on the deck that stretched across the kitchen and my bedroom. Tubs of geraniums still bloomed, and while I'd planted warm-hued fall mums, the flashes of the bright colored geraniums were pleasing to the eye.

It wasn't but a few minutes before I heard loud caterwauling and searched for the origin of such a noise. My gaze settled on a ratty looking tomcat whose tail crooked at a permanent angle. It appeared he'd been in one scrap too many. Rubbing his body against the rail post, he eyeballed me. A ragged left ear sported scars from past fights. I guessed his weight would put him around twenty pounds or so – a husky brute at any rate.

He strutted across the deck, lifted his leg, and sprayed the flowerpot. A rank odor wafted past my nose as he lolled on the deck as though he owned it. It occurred to me that the beast probably thought he did.

My eyes narrowed as my nose wrinkled at the acrid smell. I scrambled into the house for a bottle of vinegar. Wine vinegar was stored in the closet. I grabbed it and proceeded to douse the pot and deck. To reclaim my territory, I lectured the beast.

"Who do you think you are, anyway? This is my house and my deck." If he answered, I'd have been thoroughly surprised. With a stamp of my foot on the deck, I hoped the miserable crumb-snatcher would get his sorry butt out of my yard and head back to his own. *I dislike being wrong, truly.*

Not only did the arrogant beast stay put, apparently, he'd taken on worse than me and lived to tell about it. With an evil glance, he stretched and yawned, displaying fangs the likes of which I'd only seen on lions. Was he half mountain lion or just a smaller version? As he flexed wide paws, claws sprang forward, gleaming in the sunlight.

Sprawled on the sunniest patch of wood at the top of the step, the beast purred – at home, as though this was his right. I studied his multi-hued coat of grays and black, with a smudge of white thrown in for good measure. His face held full puffy cheeks and the most beautiful eye makeup imaginable. Only nature could produce that perfect eyeliner, I envied him for it.

Content in the sunlight, he lounged as I went in search of something for him to eat. Don't ask me why I thought he might need a meal. A solitary can of tuna sat in the cupboard. Opening the can, I pried the top off, slopped the fish into a bowl, and set it outside the sliding door. The beast jumped it in a flash. I watched him wolf the fish down like it was his last supper.

He ate, flopped into his former spot of sunlight and started the grooming process. Perched on the edge of the top step, he washed the wide paws, rubbing them over his face. One paw stretched open, and his long, sharp-hooked claws protruded, reminding me never to mess with him.

A chuckle floated down from the smaller deck suspended from Aaron's apartment. I stepped outside the French doors and glanced up.

Aaron's handsome face smiled down. "You'll never get rid of him now, you know. That Italian habit of feeding everyone has made you the new owner of that ragged beast."

"I know, but he looked hungry."

"He's the size of a dog, for heaven's sake. How can he look hungry?" Rich laughter scrolled across the yard. "And what is that horrid smell?"

"Well, he marked the flower pot as his own. I soaked it with vinegar, but I don't think it worked."

With a shake of his head, Aaron moved inside his apartment. I heard feet rumble down the back stairs, into the hallway outside my kitchen door. He strode into my apartment and joined me on the deck. "He's a bruiser, isn't he?" Dark eyebrows rose as he stared at the cat.

"Yeah, an over-sized feline, if you ask me."

A chuckle followed, as Aaron leaned toward the cat. The animal puffed up to twice his size and a testy growl rolled from his throat.

"Safe to say he doesn't like men. Have you tried to pet him yet?"

"No, I only fed him."

I stepped toward the cat and leaned forward with my fingers extended. He sniffed them with disdain and gave me a haughty glare before meandering off into the yard. *So much for warm and fuzzy.*

As we watched him wander into the woods behind the house, I turned to Aaron. "How did you like the pastries from Lola?"

"She's a great cook. It would be difficult to eat her food daily and stay in shape. Nice woman – tiny, but nice all the same." He looked appreciatively over my long legs and height. I stood only a half head or so, shorter than him.

Aaron's wrestler-sized body stood over six feet tall, his dark good looks were enticing and the brilliant smile he sported, nearly irresistible. If I weren't so enamored with Marcus, this man would be at the top of my wish list. A true gentleman, but a lawman all the same.

Beware. The silent voice in my head screamed like it always did when I considered a cop.

Marcus stood nearly the same height, but his craggy features and hazel eyes hooked me. Fit, and somewhat arrogant, as most state troopers are, we butted heads on occasion. It's inevitable since I'm a confident woman, and Italian.

Needless to say, sex played a part in the happy equation. Marcus and I sleep together on occasion, and we seem to enjoy the relationship we have established. The conversation has never turned toward marriage and we all need to be grateful for something.

"What's on your agenda for the rest of the day?" Aaron asked with a smile.

"I'm headed to my parents' for a meal. Lola's going to lend me her car again. She's working late at the deli to prepare for the Columbus Day weekend crowd. Want to join me? My mother always has plenty of food." I offered the invitation without thinking ahead.

"Thanks, but I have some work to finish. Make sure you lock up when you leave, in case Tony comes around."

"You're not going to go on about this Tony thing, are you? I suppose that Little Miss Dynamite mentioned it when she brought the pastry upstairs this morning."

"Yeah, she did. She's worried about your safety."

Flailing my hands in the air, I shook my head in disbelief. "The man stops to say hello on the street, in broad daylight, and now suddenly he's a stalker and megalomaniac? God help me." I rolled my eyes and shook my head.

"Okay, okay. Don't get upset." Aaron smiled and raised his hands in mock self-defense. "I only said Lola's worried about you."

"Fine, I get the message."

As we entered the apartment, he moved toward the hallway door shaking his head.

"If you have any problems, I'll be around. You might not hear from Tony again, but just be aware that he's a free man now."

"I'll keep that in mind." With a mental roll of my eyes, I watched him leave.

Exasperated, I strode toward the bedroom to get my wallet. My hands shook as I tucked money and my driver's license into my pocket. Maybe Aaron and Lola *were* on target? Was Tony stalking me? Was the accident on the highway more than that? Was it an attack of some sort? I hadn't really considered that possibility until now. With a heavy sigh, I locked up before I left for the deli.

Chapter 6

Rolling down the sunlit country roads from Scituate to Cranston in Lola's car, life's challenges swam through my head.

My parents live in a suburb near Cranston Stadium where my twin brother, Giovanni Esposito, played baseball when we were in high school. We always camped out in the bleachers. My mother would second-guess the umpire, often using Italian adjectives that burned my ears, and brought comments from the other parents. I'd learned from her.

The closer I got to the house, the more Gio lingered in my mind. My brother and I had been on the wild side during our teenage years. Gio was the thinker, and I was the doer. The doer gets blamed all the time, so I was always the fall guy – or girl. Needless to say, when I christened him Saint Giovanni, there was good reason. I adore my twin, but I enjoy the fact that he lives in Nebraska and practices medicine out there, in corn country.

I pulled into my parents' postage stamp-sized yard as a pang of guilt hit me. It was a bit unfair that I lived here and Gio lived away from the family. My mother missed him a lot. My father, well, he never lets me forget that Gio is the man of men. When Gio chose to attend medical school, my father became ecstatic about his decision. My career choice hadn't been heralded as the best direction I could take. My father believes I should never have taken on a man's job.

While I am the woman of women, I am still *only* a woman. A woman who should bear many children, stay at home, be a soccer mom, and cook spaghetti. Yikes, perish the thought. *I enjoy children, as long as they're someone else's. Thank you very much.* The Giovanni guilt pang passed quickly. I unfolded my long body out of the car and strolled into the house.

Plates and flatware lined the table. Dinner for four lay spread out, and I wondered who'd be joining us. My mother handed me a glass of wine while my father stirred the pot of pasta. Nobody uttered a sound. My gaze, filled with question, danced between my parents. I didn't have to wait long for the answer.

"Your friend is joining us for supper tonight," my father said with a dark-eyed, suspicious sideways glance.

"Marcus is coming here?"

"No, your other friend. The tenant guy. Have you been up to something we need to know about?"

"Dad, I haven't been up to anything other than working. Why do you ask?" My father and I butt heads often. Now would be no exception.

"Why would he call and invite himself to dinner, unless you're up to something, Lavinia? What does he do for a living, anyway?" He looked at me, suspicion in his eyes. "You're not pregnant, are you, Lavinia?"

My given name is Lavinia, and usually only my parents use it. My brother issued me the nickname of Vinnie when we were in school, and it stuck. Marcus only uses my formal name when he's in the throes of aggravation. Aaron calls me Vinnie all the time.

"No, I'm not pregnant, nor am I sleeping with Aaron. What could I be up to? I have no time now that the semester is in full swing. And Aaron works for the Rhode Island Gaming Commission. That's it, plain and simple."

It occurred to me that Aaron had realized his mistake in refusing the dinner invitation I'd extended. Coming to dinner would offer him the perfect chance to check out my family. While Aaron worked undercover for the FBI, and the Gaming Commission was his cover, he could use his job to his advantage. He was free to roam around and stick his nose into everyone's business.

"Why would he want to eat with us?"

My father, the pit bull. Once he got his teeth into something, it became nearly impossible to open a different dialogue.

"I invited him to dinner, but he said no. Maybe he reconsidered." I shrugged. "Perhaps he thought he'd enjoy your cooking. Ever think of that?" How silly to consider that argument might work, but it was worth a try.

"Yeah, right. By the way, Lavinia, you're not thinking of doin' anything foolish, like investigating Antonio or Mafalda, are you?"

"No, and where did you get that idea?" My hand snuck to my hip while my father stared at me with cold, hard eyes. Oh, yeah, we were about to butt heads all right.

Mom, peacemaker extraordinaire, stepped forward. She glanced at my father and then at me.

"I might have mentioned that you got Muffy out of jail. I also might have said that Antonio is being investigated by the cops. Sorry, Lavinia."

"I still don't see what this has to do with me." I glared at my father, as he turned away from me.

"It better have nothing to do with you. That's all I'm sayin' here. You don't need to get involved with something that's none of your business, like the gem thing last summer." His flat, dark-eyed glare swung toward me. I glanced away.

My father inhabits the old school of thought. He figures all women should be married and mothers – not be policewomen, not be criminal justice instructors, and not be anything else. He has respect for my education, but there's always that old school way of thinking that sneaks into our conversations.

With a sigh, I sipped my glass of wine and turned at the knock on the door. My gaze followed my mother as she answered the summons. She and my father had never met Aaron, which meant this should prove an interesting meal. I was most certain of it.

A bunch of flowers came through the door prior to the sexy hunk. Aaron grinned in that suave way he had, and my mother stood awestruck. As he handed her the flowers she smiled from ear to ear, stepping aside so he could enter the room.

Aaron's size dwarfed everything in the compact room. My father turned toward Aaron after he set the cover on the kettle. With bated breath, I waited to hear what would issue from his mouth.

"So, you're the tenant, eh?" He looked Aaron up and down before he extended a hand in greeting.

Crinkle lines appeared at the corners of Aaron's eyes, and he nodded. It was plain to see he wasn't any more intimidated by my father than Marcus was on his first meeting. Undoubtedly, it was a guy thing.

As the two men shook hands, I expelled pent-up breath and stepped forward with introductions all around. My focus strayed to Aaron and then back to my parents. My mother seemed to have fallen under his good-looking and well-mannered spell, while my father, well, that remained to be seen.

Soon the flowers sat on the table, clustered in a vase of water. Across from them my mother poured Aaron a glass of heady red wine. My father settled a plate of tempting aromatic meatballs, sausage, and mushrooms on the table. The pasta boiled, and dad returned to the job at hand without a word. I watched Aaron's reactions and wondered why I'd issued the invitation in the first place. Maybe Aaron reconsidered his refusal when he realized dinner with my family offered him the perfect opportunity to snoop into our affairs. Only God knows what he expected to find.

From the looks of things, my mother would think of Aaron as marriage material and start with wedding noises. My father would give me the third degree. He'd say nothing good could come from marrying a cop, any cop. This meant Marcus, of course, because they had no idea of Aaron's true occupation.

Since they didn't know that, the wedding noises would be two-fold. Gosh, who even considered marriage here? Maybe I was a bit ahead of myself. It was just the way my parents' thought patterns worked.

Aaron slid into a chair at the table, leaned back in a relaxed position, and sipped his wine. I hid a smile as he and my mother conversed about the care of the flowers. There was a moment when

Aaron's attention was on me, and I caught the delighted twinkle in them. He was working my mother, I thought. This visit had to do with Muffy and Antonio, for sure. Geez.

A bowl heaped with pasta followed a dish of antipasto salad that filled the center of the table. Proscuitto and chunks of hard Provolone cheese, which smelled like rotten socks and tasted tangy, nestled within the salad greens. Black olives clustered among roasted red peppers. My mouth watered. I inhaled the heady aromas and waited impatiently to start shoveling this tasty fare down my gullet.

My father took a seat at the table next to my mother. His dark-eyed stare lingered on me for a few seconds before he served up the meal. His gruff voice filtered across the table as we sucked down the excellent food.

"Tell me about Mafalda and what you did to get her out of jail?" Dad said.

"It just took a promise that I'd be the one to take her in for arraignment. I was extended a professional courtesy. Why do you ask?"

"She called earlier this afternoon and mentioned how you wrangled her way out. Don't get involved in this matter, Lavinia. She also knows that Antonio was released quickly and left her there. She's not happy about that either."

Aaron stared at me, a smile tickling the edges of his mouth.

I knew he realized my father didn't care for the curiosity that drove my lifestyle, and I could see where Aaron would get a chuckle from it. I shrugged, and we went back to our meal.

"There's no way I'd become involved with that. Don't worry about it, okay?"

"Sure, you say that now, but I know you. Just stay out of it, understand?" Dad's voice was gruff and loud.

There was more than an underlying message here. My father was trying to tell me that I wouldn't be lucky if I stepped into that arena. The mob didn't like women who tried to mind their criminal business. I got the message, loud and clear. With a nod, I dug into the salad.

The conversation wasn't lost on Aaron, since he'd drilled me about the family and Muffy's connections. He slid me a curious look, and I smiled before passing the salad to him.

"Try the antipasto, Aaron. It's unbelievable."

He grinned and heaped a healthy portion onto his plate. Interested in my father, he asked, "Did you know that Tony DeGreico met up with Vinnie yesterday?"

My fork slipped from my hand and clattered to the floor. Dang. He would bring that up now. Great, my parents would be all over me about it, and my mother would insist I move home. My father, well, he'd just be all over me. It's awful to be right sometimes, but....

Shaggy eyebrows drew together as my father grimaced across the table.

"That bum is out of the nut house?" he roared. "You didn't say he was on the street again. Where'd you meet him, Lavinia?"

I kicked Aaron under the table as I spoke to my father. "He stopped me on the street. He's working in Foster on some horse ranch, shoveling manure. That's all that happened, honest." I didn't stammer, but close to it. *Aaron would pay for his inability to keep his trap shut.*

"Maybe you should move home, dear." My mother's voice was filled with worry.

"He's paid his debt to society, Mom. He isn't about to violate any laws, or he'll end up back where he was. He just stopped me to say hello – end of story. I'm not moving home. Besides, Aaron lives upstairs from me now, so I'll have protection. There's always Marcus to consider."

My father grunted and tore a chunk of Italian bread apart. He mopped up the thick red pasta sauce on his plate with the bread in *a la zuppa* fashion and looked around the table as we all watched.

"What's the other hand for?" he grumbled.

"Bread," I uttered, in unison with my mother.

Aaron broke into a grin, watching me follow suit with the crusty Italian bread. He joined in, and I was certain he'd rarely, if ever, eaten with an Italian family before.

Between dipping the bread, and eating it, I asked, "What made you change your mind about dinner with us, Aaron?" I still smarted from his tattletale DeGreico thing. Maybe a little torture would be good for him.

With a smirk he said, "I just couldn't pass up a great Italian meal with you and your family. Besides, who wants to do paperwork? I get enough of that during the day."

Such bullshit. I barely restrained grimace. Nonetheless, I smiled to hide the fact that I didn't believe his line of crap for a second. My father caught the look. His bread stopped in midair.

"What is it you do for a living?" Dad asked with a cool stare, even though I'd told him. It was the same flat-eyed stare a shark has. When my dad gives it, well, you don't want to know what he's about. Let's just say it isn't a trusting look.

With a serious and earnest expression, Aaron told my father about his position with the Gaming Commission. He even outlined the job – with a lengthy explanation of the system in Rhode Island. It was such a well-played lie that even I was tempted to believe him.

Gosh, he wasn't only professional wrestling material – he could have won an Oscar for that performance. Who'd have thought, eh? But then, he'd fooled me last summer, and it was only halfway through the gem investigation that the truth came out about occupation. I was sworn to secrecy and kept my mouth shut.

My mother jumped into the conversation every once in awhile with a question about gambling laws and such. When she did, I could see Aaron sum her up for a brief second as he answered the query. Dinner with my family was never going to happen again for Aaron. I should have known better than to issue the invite after he grilled me about Aunt Mafalda and her connections. Too late now.

Warm apple crisp topped with real whipped cream was the *dessert du jour*. I ate my usual – more than I should have. Replete from the meal, I unbuttoned my jeans. Mom and Aaron stared at me. Aaron had a wicked twinkle in his eye. My father smirked and grunted, that which passed for humor. I smiled, belched, and gazed around the table.

"Lavinia, excuse yourself." My father's dark glare was back as he waited patiently for the words.

My fingers in front of my mouth, I muttered, "Excuse my bad manners." With that, I reached across the table for one more crumb on the dessert plate. A rap on the knuckles, from my father's fork handle, was my reward for this wayward behavior.

"Lavinia, you've been hangin' with those bad-mannered cops again, haven't you? They eat like slobs and have no manners to speak of." His gruff voice boomed.

With an inward sigh, I nodded and licked my fingertips. I took in Aaron's wide grin, rose from the table to clear the plates, and loaded the dishwasher.

He and my father started talking about the pizza business. Oh, yeah, Aaron Grant was a fisherman of the worst kind. Whether he fooled my dad was another thing altogether.

Later, with a bag of goodies from dinner, and dessert, I headed for the door. Aaron stepped close behind as we said our goodbyes. My mother had a hopeful gleam in her eye. I heaved a sigh of resignation. Dad shook Aaron's hand and issued an invitation to join them again. Wow, Dad never invites anyone back for dinner.

My inquisitive nature falls into play more often than it should. I suspected there must be more to the invitation from my father. As unlikely as it seemed, Dad liked my tenant.

It was obvious Aaron relished the invite. He quickly agreed to the invitation. I knew without a doubt that he had convinced everyone he was what he said he was. The fact that Dad thought he wasn't a cop might have a lot to do with the return invite.

Apprehension skittered along my spine. I was this would be the beginning of a potential marriage battle. If they only knew about Aaron's true reasons for his interest in the family, my parents wouldn't give him the time of day.

With a wave of my hand, I made a beeline toward the car. The goody bag landed on the front seat.

I turned to Aaron and snapped, "You do realize you're going

to pay for the DeGreico thing, don't you? There was no reason to shake my parents to their roots, you know. Did Lola tell you the whole story?"

His eyes widened at my change in attitude. He hemmed and hawed for a second and then stood there with his hands extended, palms up.

"If I'd known the response it would bring, I wouldn't have mentioned it. I'm sorry if I spoke out of turn. Lola just said this guy had harassed you and that he might do it again."

"Well, it was more than that. I'd appreciate you minding your own business in the future."

A humorous sparkle entered his eyes. "Does this mean I can't come to dinner anymore?"

A smile teetered on the edge of my lips, and I gave in.

"You can, as long as you keep your trap shut."

He held his hand against his heart. "Wow, that hurt."

"My parents are good people, and DeGreico scared the bejeepers out of them. It's bad enough my father doesn't give me a break about my job and living alone. You did see that, didn't you?"

"I did. He's just concerned for your welfare, though."

"Oh, yeah, I get it. The guy thing." Aaron wandered toward his truck. My hand rested on my hip.

"My father is the epitome of male chauvinism. Do you understand? I don't need a babysitter, a hero on a white steed, or any of the rest of that shit. I'm a woman who's quite capable of taking care of myself. Understand?"

"Yeah, I understand. Maybe better than you think." Aaron backtracked toward me with a tense attitude.

I'd hit a nerve.

"What I understand is that those two people in there care deeply and worry about their only daughter. The same daughter caught up in the life of criminal justice. A life they don't begin to comprehend. Try to consider that, will you? I think you give your father a bum rap."

"Think what you want. I've lived with them a long time and of course, I know they care. I also know how easily they'd run my life, if they could." I sighed and shook my head. "Sorry about the tirade, but I'm well aware of my parents and their conniving ways. You have no idea."

He drew nearer and ran his warm hands along my arms in the chilly night air. Goose bumps layered my skin. "I think you're overreacting to the fact that I've been invited back. It's no more than a simple extension of hospitality, I'm sure.

He didn't know my father the way I did. He also wasn't aware that if my father knew Aaron was FBI, there would be no further invitations for anything. Even Marcus walked a thin line with my dad.

This was a no-win situation. I realized Aaron was blind to the ways of Italian parenting. To end the argument, I nodded in agreement and forced a smile to my lips.

He smiled back and said, "I'll see you later. I'm headed into Providence for a bit." His lips brushed my cheek, and he was gone.

As I settled into the front seat of Lola's car, I buckled the seat belt. I backed from the driveway after Aaron pulled away from the curb. My mind a muddle, I knew there would be hell to pay with my parents. They'd taken a liking to this guy, and it made me nervous.

Chapter 7

Sunlight waned as I covered the distance from my parents' house to the deli. I returned the car keys to Lola and walked up the street to the house. A Dodge Ram pickup truck glided into the driveway as I neared the door, my goody bag in hand. Marcus parked his truck and strolled in my direction.

His walk neared a swagger, reminding me of a pirate ship captain. My imagination had run away with me again. It must be his craggy good looks that brought me around to this way of thinking.

A slow smile crossed features, hiking my pulse and warming my heart.

"Is that a bag of food from your mother?"

I should have known he'd be interested in the food first.

I chuckled. "Yeah, are you starving? Didn't you eat yet?"

"There wasn't that much time today. What's in the bag?" He reached over and uncurled the crimped edges of the brown bag. A rich aroma wafted out, and he turned to me with that wolfish grin.

"Come on in and I'll share with you."

"Dessert, too?" Dark brows waggled as his grin widened.

"Don't tell me, you have to have dessert, too?"

"It depends on what you have to offer."

I ignored the remark, unlocked the doors to the house, and entered the kitchen. I set out a plate while Marcus unloaded the goody bag. I rounded the counter and he wrapped his arms around my waist, nuzzling my neck.

Succumbing to his lips, my knees weakened, and my mouth

found his. To hell with dinner, I thought while my inner voice started its usual low-keyed scream of *Beware, beware, he's a cop. He'll break your heart.* I ignored the rant and let Marcus have free reign.

A while later, we wandered into the kitchen. I was happy, and Marcus looked pretty happy too. I chucked dinner into the microwave, set the timer, and straddled a stool at the counter. Across from me, Marcus picked at the apple crisp and then asked, "What's been happening with DeGreico?"

"Nothing, though everyone seems worried."

"Who's everyone?"

"My parents, Lola, you, and Aaron."

"Your parents know he's out of the looney bin?"

"Yep, and my mother thinks I should move home. Good grief, as if that would ever happen."

"Want to tell me the whole story? I'm a good listener, you know."

"Honestly, I'd rather not relive that particular experience, if you don't mind." My look pleaded with him to stop the interrogation.

He gave a small nod.

"Whatever you say, Vin. If you ever want to discuss it, let me know."

This was way too easy. If I were a stupid, gullible sort I'd have believed that tripe. However, I know Marcus better than that.

"You've undoubtedly done a preliminary search for information on this guy, Marcus. Don't play me, okay?"

"No search, no prelim, no nothing," he said with a sincerity that I didn't believe for a moment. "If you want to tell me, you will. If not, then don't."

Uncertain if this new attitude was real, I nodded and changed the subject.

"What's the scoop on the racketeering charges against Antonio?"

Laughter erupted from Marcus, and then he sobered. "It seems that Antonio, the businessman, has been shuffling more than his share of stolen goods. He's into high-end merchandise, and, unbeknownst to him, the stupid ass dealt these goods to an undercover FBI agent, the same agent who lives upstairs."

"Get outta here," I exclaimed in surprise. "Aaron never said it was his investigation and that he was the agent involved with the arrest. It makes sense, though, now that I think about it."

"He wasn't. The police and FBI set up a sting with Aaron as the buyer. Antonio made the deal, and the whole thing was taped. The arrest wasn't made at that time. The fool did another deal on the way to pick up your aunt. When they were leaving her house, they both got arrested."

"That's when my aunt shot her face off, right?"

"Right. She was a firebrand. Huffing and puffing like the old dragon she is." Laughter rolled from Marcus.

Humor tickled the corners of my mouth and I gave it to laughter. Aunt Muffy had always been a dragon. Her candid attitude was legendary in our family and among friends. Much to my mother's dismay, Muffy drew the worst of the bad boys and loved every minute of it. If this were the 1930s, my aunt would undoubtedly be considered a 'Gun Moll' for the mob. I smirked at the thought.

When Marcus raised a brow in question, I explained my thoughts. We shared the humor of it.

"What do you think will happen to Auntie?"

"She'll probably get let off with a warning from the judge, and maybe some community service – if she keeps her dragon attitude to herself."

"I'll make sure she doesn't turn the courtroom into a circus. Lord, I don't know how I get dragged into these things."

"District Attorney Kincaid might try to use her against Antonio, you know. It wouldn't be the first time the DA's played that particular game, tough bastard that he is."

"She'll have an attorney. I won't allow her to be used by anyone. What do you know about Kincaid? He has a nasty reputation among the cops, but then, who doesn't?"

"Kincaid is a climber." Marcus turned toward me with an arched brow and a cool stare. "You know what that means. He'll step on anyone, anywhere, at anytime to get his foot up another rung on the ladder of success. He's about as ruthless as they come. If I were you, I'd make sure Mafalda has the best attorney money can buy."

"All I said was that I'd take her to the arraignment, not all the way to the Supreme Court, for God's sake." I ran a hand across my brow and flipped the mop of hair off my face.

He stretched his hand across the counter to run strong fingers over mine, which then tightened into a squeeze.

I glanced into his warm gaze and smiled.

"Why did you have to protect the governor yesterday?" I asked. "Doesn't he have a regular trooper to do that? Someone who's assigned to him?"

"Yeah, the trooper was on vacation. He and his family went to Disney, and I caught the last day. It's not unusual for that to happen, but it's not a job I care for. Standing around looking like a boob, while the governor shakes hands and has dinner, is boring as hell. I even had to eat in the kitchen with the help." Marcus stretched and yawned. "At least they were good company." He smirked as he rose from the counter.

"Leaving already?"

"Yeah, tomorrow is another busy day. I'll stay in touch, though."

This was said as he ran his hands along my arms, up to my shoulders. A finger traced the neckline of my scoop-necked jersey. He pulled it open a tad and glanced down the front, a gleeful smile on his face.

"Don't start something you can't finish, Richmond."

"Who says I can't finish it?"

"Me."

With that, he backed me into the bedroom again, toward the bed. He started to pull my jersey up when the phone jingled. I sighed. He sighed. And I answered on the second ring.

"Vinnie speaking."

A long silence met my greeting. I waited another few seconds, repeated my name, and then hung up. My fingers tapped the surface of the phone as I tried to figure out who called. Caller ID listed the caller as unknown.

"Who was it?"

"Nobody, probably a wrong number." I shrugged and moved toward Marcus.

A buzzing sound filtered through the material of Marcus' trousers. I glanced down and then looked at him, a smirk on my face.

"Your pants are buzzing, Marcus Richmond."

"Shit." He withdrew the small unit and read the text message. "What?"

"I have to report to headquarters. Sorry." He grimaced.

"No problem, I knew you couldn't finish what you started." Humor filled my voice, and I chuckled at his look. One point for me, and zero for Marcus.

We walked to the door as Marcus tucked his shirt into his uniform pants. After a lingering kiss that promised he'd be back again, I watched him leave and then locked up.

The truck spun out of the driveway and I heard it roar up the street. Whoever paged him better have a good reason, I surmised Marcus wouldn't be kind to anyone who yanked his chain.

Extinguishing the lights, I entered the bedroom as the phone jingled its tune again. The clock on the bedside table had just climbed to ten o'clock, and I wondered who'd call this late. Not another family emergency, I prayed.

"Vinnie speaking," I said on a sigh.

Silence met my words once again. I disconnected the call and checked the phone for the caller's number. The read-out showed unknown, which left me a bit annoyed and apprehensive. I slipped the phone into the cradle, set up the coffee pot for the morning, and headed to bed. One dead-air call was fine, but two in a row could be more than coincidence.

The house was secure, though I hadn't heard Aaron return. I knew with his stealthy maneuvering I wouldn't hear anything but his truck. With that realization, I snuggled under the covers and awaited sleep. To toss and turn all night was not my idea of a good time.

An hour later, I still lay wide-awake, the covers in a jumbled mess. Cripes, I needed to be clear-headed for class or the cops would harangue the daylights out of me. It isn't easy to stay one step ahead of people who work on the streets everyday. Earlier, I'd considered how I would manage to get to class without my car. I couldn't continue to borrow Lola's, though she didn't mind. A sigh escaped me as I thought of the students again.

These people had more street smarts than I'd ever have, but I had more expertise in areas they rarely worked. That was my one advantage when they snickered over my inexperience with 'upfront and personal' crime. When push came to shove, these cops, Two-Point-Fives and real Five-Os, grudgingly gave me credit for teaching them something they didn't know, and a good time was had by all.

After another hour of flopping around like a beached fish, I sat up in the dark. The pillows bunched behind me. I slumped against them with chagrin. What was bothering me? I ticked the list off in my mind.

Aunt Muffy's arraignment for resisting arrest topped the list. My mother might start making marriage noises. Aaron would undoubtedly grill me about my family and their connections due to the fact he was investigating Auntie's new flame. My father was worried I'd get involved in a mob investigation. To top it all off, 'Tony the Slimeball' had left the looney bin, and my family was frantic about it already. All I needed now was for Nonni to enter the picture. *Cripes.*

I tried to relax in the soft darkness of the room and listened to the noises outside. A hearty wind rattled crisp leaves, while tree branches grazed against the house. I slipped from beneath the covers and drew the drapes against the sound. A chill scuttled along my skin. I hunkered back under the blankets and considered Tony DeGreico.

He'd been a charming guy who had been engaged to a bright, cheerful woman. Maria had been in high school with me and we stayed in touch. Early on in my career, I lived in a small duplex in Cranston, not far from her florist shop.

An elderly retired couple, which migrated to Florida from

November through April, owned the duplex. That left me on my own. I checked their apartment and watered the plants while they were gone. Once in a while, I managed to kill a plant and would replace it with healthy look-alike from Maria's shop. The couple never caught on to the fact and I was most grateful.

While in her shop, Maria Grimano, my old school chum and Tony's fiancé, introduced me to Tony. His charm was a bit overdone, but then again, I didn't find him as dashing as Maria did. We met often, since I was a regular customer of Maria's cubbyhole-sized business.

Dressed in flashy clothes, with lots of bling hanging off his wrists and neck, Tony seemed to have nothing but time on his hands. He hung out at the florist shop and became what I considered to be a nuisance.

Tony got in the way of customers until Maria took him aside and explained in the kindest way she could that she needed to attend to business. That was when I overheard him tell Maria she never needed to work because he had enough money to care for her in style. He said she needn't grub around in the dirt for a living.

The bling glittered and so did his eyes as he stared at Maria. I stood aside and pretended to peruse the flowers but kept an eye on him. Where did the gold jewelry and fancy clothing come from? He didn't seem to work, and my father said he didn't come from money. Dad knew the family from his childhood.

These thoughts rambled on in my head until eventually my eyelids shuttered, and I slept. It wasn't until the alarm sounded that I realized I'd managed a few good hours of rest. Still sore from the accident, I slid from bed and headed into the shower before my usual cup of java.

Coffee at my place is most always on automatic. I set the pot up whenever it's empty, especially at night before I head to bed. I started the habit when I first moved into my own digs.

Selecting clothes from the closet, I quickly dressed. If I didn't get rolling now, I'd never get across the George Washington Bridge before the traffic slowed to a crawl. It was inevitable that some fool would smash into another every morning, and the traffic would come to a screaming halt.

A knock on the outer door caught my attention. With a quick step, I opened it to find Lola on the doorstep.

"I knew you'd need a ride, so I'm going to take you to pick up a rental. My cousin Arty has a place on Killingly Street, in Johnston. He has a car ready for you to pick up, okay?" She gave me the irresistible smile that made men fall at her feet.

I hugged the slight woman and grinned. With a tall stainless-steel Starbucks coffee mug filled to the brim, a package of crackers, and my bulky book bag, I trailed behind Lola. She backed into the traffic and we drove east.

Within minutes, we arrived at Arty's used car lot. *Oh, my God. Where did he get these wrecks?*

Lola took one look at my face and promised to take me car shopping later. We left the MINI Cooper and entered the office. Arty, red-bearded and bald-domed, stepped forward, his hand extended. I shook his hand and he set the keys on the counter. His potbelly spoke of good food, and the short stumpy legs wobbled when he swung toward the front window.

"Take the Volkswagen Beetle over there on the corner." He pointed to the yellow car squatting by the curb. "Just bring it back in one piece, okay? It's the best of the bunch."

No doubt there, I thought, as my gaze swept over cars that had seen way better days. With a smile, I turned to him. He must have heard of my penchant for the unexpected. I nodded and thanked him as I signed rental papers. He ran my credit card and winked at me while he did so.

Lola left for the deli and I swung onto the highway, headed east toward the university. Hopefully, during this trip, my luck would hold. The car coughed, puffed smoke, but didn't break down.

With bated breath, I crossed the G.W. and made the exit to the university. In a matter of moments, the car chugged into the parking lot. My glance rested on the other cars parked nearby. No one. No drivers sat behind the wheels of the cars that I could see. It wasn't until I crossed the open space between the car and the college that I knew I wasn't as alone as I thought.

Dirty Trouble

A motor revved, tires squealed, and a dark-windowed sedan sped in my direction. I dropped the book bag and ran back to my car. It was closer than running to the sidewalk outside the building.

Reaching the car, the toe of my shoe caught on the tire of the Volkswagen and I sprawled flat on the ground. I heard the car race past and the sound recede. Apparently, the jerk wasn't about to stop and check to see if I was still alive.

I was shaken. Fear and anger mingled and pulsed through my system. I sat up and checked my hands. Scraped skin and tiny pebbles were embedded into the heels of my palms. It was the only damage I could see. I stood up, dusted off my clothes, and streaked across the lot, retrieving the book bag on the way.

Reluctant to report the attempt on my life, I stood on the sidewalk shaking like a leaf. There was nothing to tell really. Since I hadn't seen the driver, and I didn't know the make of the car – or any other pertinent information – the cops might think I finally lost my marbles.

Before entering the building, I viewed the grounds for the car, driver, or any stranger that appeared suspicious, but the campus was quiet. *Could the driver have been Tony or someone he knew, someone who would be happy to run me down for a little extra cash?*

I stepped into the rest room before going to class. Locked in a stall, I sat on the toilet and took several deep breaths, trying to calm my shattered nerves. I checked my watch and knew I needed to get moving. The students would be waiting.

Uneasy about the incident, I started the lecture on a shaky note, though nobody seemed to notice. Hours passed with no surprises, arguments, or problems. Everyone listened while I explained the homework assignment. A subdued group, they left without any wisecracks or loud discussions. I sighed, relieved to have been given this slight reprieve.

Chapter 8

The car puffed back to the village. I parked in front of the garage next to the Dodge Ram truck Marcus leaned against. From the look on his face I figured something untoward happened. Hopefully he wasn't aware of my run-down experience this morning.

With a mental head slap I knew he couldn't know because nobody knew. I'd been smart enough to keep my mouth shut.

With a wide smile – though I felt far from smiling – I asked on a cheerful note, "Hey, what are you doing here? Got the day off?" What an actress, huh?

"No, but I wanted to stop by before I reported to headquarters." His eyes wandered over the rental car. "Where did you get that rattletrap?"

"Lola's cousin rented it to me so I could get to work today."

"You couldn't take another day off, could you?"

His eyes gleamed. I wondered why.

"I felt well enough to go to work. I'm sore, but that's all." I beckoned him to follow me into the house and set the coffee to perk.

"Tell me about Tony," he stated in a flat voice as he settled at the counter.

"Not that again."

"I want you to tell me what happened in the past between you two."

"Fine." My hands flew up in the air. "Just relax, will you? You're making me nervous."

"Nothing makes you nervous. Just explain what happened with Tony back then." Marcus leaned his elbows on the counter and waited for me to explain.

Marcus is good at interrogation – I'll give him that. He didn't get into my space and he appeared relaxed, with his hands folded lightly in front of him. He even spoke in a soft voice to lull me so I'd spill my guts.

"Two years ago, I lived in Cranston." I explained the location of the duplex and about the owners. Marcus just nodded every now and then, but he never uttered a sound. He let me step back in time.

"Maria Grimano, a friend from high school, owned a florist shop where I used to buy plants. Tony hung there all the time, totally enamored with her. He never seemed to work, but he had lots of gold jewelry hanging off his body and fancy clothes, stuff like that. Anyway, one day I overheard him tell Maria she needn't ever work for a living, that he could take care of her in splendid fashion. While I was replacing a plant I'd managed to kill, I listened as he went on and on about the life they'd have."

I rose and filled coffee cups with the fresh-perked brew.

Silent, Marcus waited for me to continue.

"During the conversation, I wandered around the shop and listened. I wondered where he got the bling and clothes. He sure didn't have the hands of a workman and his family didn't have money. Needless to say, I became more than curious, and then started questioning a few of the cops I knew."

"What did you find out?"

"It was weird, really. Nobody knew much about him. No warrants, no traffic violations, no arrests of any kind. A squeaky-clean kind of guy, you know? It just didn't add up. I decided to mind my own business until I ran across him doing a deal at the flower shop. Maria had a dentist appointment, and Tony ran the shop while she was gone. I went in to get some fresh flowers for my mother and caught him finishing a drug sale to some scumbag. He tried to appear nonchalant and innocent, but I knew what I saw."

"What happened when you approached him about it? I know you must have – you can't help yourself." Marcus smirked a bit but continued to watch me.

"I asked him what the hell he thought he was doing. He tried to play it down, but I wouldn't have it. So, he got mad and told me I'd better mind my own business, if I knew what was good for me. I said I would and left it at that."

"I can't believe you'd do that."

I shrugged one shoulder. "I watched and waited, and a month went by. He was in the shop again and the same thing happened. This time we got into a heated discussion over what this would do to Maria if the cops ever found out he used her shop as a drug dealership business. He just grinned, bluffed, and said she knew and didn't care." A headache coming on, I massaged my temples with my fingertips.

"It was a slap in the face for me, but I suspected he was lying."

The coffee had cooled as I told the story. I sipped and talked while Marcus listened and said nothing.

"One day when Tony wasn't around, I mentioned drug dealing to Maria – nothing pointed mind you, just in general. She immediately said that all drug dealers should be killed. Her brother had been hooked on prescription drugs. When he couldn't get them from the pharmacy anymore, he'd turned to street dealers. It nearly cost him his life." I sighed and continued the story. My collarbone started to ache.

"I realized Maria would never go along with any drug deals, in or outside her shop, so I told her what I'd seen. At first, she didn't believe me, so I challenged her to set him up and watch from a distance with binoculars. Reluctant at first, Maria finally agreed to it. We parked down the street in my father's car, facing the store with a clear view right into it. It must have been hard on her since she was engaged to him. We all know love is blind."

"She watched him deal drugs?"

"Yeah. She cried, and I felt like crap. Maria waited a week or so and then broke it off with him. I got blamed. Rightly so in Tony's mind, and he began to stalk me. Tony couldn't bear the thought that Maria wouldn't listen to him." Anger crept into my voice. "After all, he was all and everything, ya know what I mean?" My forgotten fear and uneasiness of the past resurfaced in full force as I relived the events, and I was uncomfortable.

"Then what happened?"

Refreshing our coffees, I said, "This stalking thing went on for quite a while. Worried, I went the legal route to get him off my back with a restraining order. We all know that restraining orders don't help when someone is hell-bent on getting even with you." I leaned back in the chair with a sigh and rubbed my neck. I hadn't realized how tense I'd become. I wanted to change the topic.

"You're going to tell me what happened next, right?" His eyes bore into me.

Could he read my thoughts? Squirming in the chair, I stared at the counter top. The napkin beside my cup was scrunched out of shape in my hand. I methodically smoothed it out while I summoned the courage to finish the story. To be stalked is frightening enough, but to have someone set fire to your home, while you're asleep in it, that's a different matter. It leaves a lasting impression. Goosebumps crawled over my arms. I rubbed them away.

Marcus waited in silence, his face expressionless. This man could outwait me, and I knew it. I took a deep breath and blew it out slowly.

"One night I got home late, exhausted. I'd taught all week and covered extra classes for a professor who was sick. I fell asleep as soon as I hit the pillow. Around two in the morning I awoke, choking on smoke. My bedroom door led to the kitchen and was cracked open a bit. I could see flames. If I hadn't awakened, I'd have died of smoke inhalation."

"How did the cops link the fire to him?"

"The jerk left the evidence handy. The cops figured Tony may have been scared away or something of that nature. Anyway, later they traced the gas can he left behind back to him and locked him up. He pleaded mental duress, and, because he had no record, the judge sent him to the looney bin for evaluation. Tony did such a good job of convincing everyone he was a nutcase that they kept him for the duration of his sentence, with a parole option attached. That's the whole story."

"You must have been frightened when he stalked you." His voice, not so soft now, sounded curious.

"It wasn't the highlight of my life, I can tell you that. I never thought he was unhinged enough to act so irrationally, but he blamed me for the split with Maria, and the fact that he was caught in an arson. Tony never did confess to the drug thing, though the investigators harassed him for information. He wouldn't give up a name, and the supplier was never found."

"Are you worried about him now?" Marcus asked, as he refilled the coffee mugs once more.

"No, I think he's paid his debt and that's it. Why the insistence on the story, Marcus? Surely you don't think he was behind the car accident? He shovels shit for a living. I'm sure he has better things to do than skulk around pushing my car off the road."

"Stranger things have happened. We do know how you draw accidents like a magnet."

I snorted as I stared at this chic magnet. I shook my head in denial.

"I know I'm an accident looking for a place to happen, but I don't think Tony had anything to do with this. Let it go, Marcus."

"If that's what you want." He shrugged.

Okay, if I weren't a suspicious sort, I'd have believed Marcus. However, that's not the way my mind works, so I just stared at him. My face must have registered disbelief.

"Really, if you want me to let it go, I will," he insisted.

The statement sounded sincere, but I was skeptical at best.

"Good, then this is the last I'll hear of it, right?" I asked.

"You got it." He slid from the stool and rounded the counter. His hands smoothed the skin on my arms as he drew me into an embrace. "I'm glad you're all right. It was difficult to see you suspended, up in the air like that. Whether it was an accident or not, I wanted to rip someone's head off and stuff it up their butt. Good thing nobody stepped up to confess, huh?"

A chuckle escaped me. It wasn't funny, but in a weird way it struck my offbeat sense of humor. I kissed Marcus full on and then walked him to the door.

[73]

Dirty Trouble

He left for work, and I turned to answer the ringing phone.

Chapter 9

Lola's familiar voice crossed the distance between us. I smiled and knew she was about to take me shopping for another car.

"Hey, Lola. What's up?"

"Just wondered if you wanted to go shopping later?" Her voice held humor. My guess was she'd been horrified at the car I'd driven today.

She chuckled. "I guess you made it past the G.W. Bridge today, since you are home."

"You know how awful that section of the highway is. Every man for himself and all that. I never knew what hit me and I lost control of the car. By the way, thanks for the loaner car. And for setting up the rental, such as it is. I do need a new one."

"Anytime you're ready, give me a holler and we'll go shopping. Are you hungry? I can scoot something up to you from the deli."

"Would you? I'm sore and energy depleted. The morning's activities left me on empty. My shoulder is aching from seat belt strain, too." *Was I whining or what?* In search of sympathy, that's what.

"Don't go anywhere. I'll be right up," she promised and hung up.

I started to turn away, when the phone danced off the hook again. I checked the number and realized my mother was on the line.

"Hey, Mom," I said, flexing the shoulder.

"Dear, I just saw a replay of the latest news stories. Was that your car?" She gasped. The concern in her voice was unmistakable. "You never let on when you came to dinner."

"Yeah, I lost control of the car. I'm fine, though. Marcus brought me home." There was no sense in explaining the whole thing. She'd only get paranoid about it.

"It was an accident?"

My eyes rolled toward the ceiling. "Yes, it was only an accident. The traffic that area is always chaotic, Mom."

"All right then. I'll have your father bring you some dinner around five tonight. What will you use for a car now, dear?"

"Lola's cousin rented me a loaner. She's taking me shopping for a new one later. I have to call my insurance man and get that squared away. It's safe to say the car is a total wreck."

"Mm, hmm. If you need anything, just let me know, dear." With that, she ended the call.

A most extraordinary mother – she would hover if I let her, and it would do no good. Then she'd insist I move home, and that would start another issue. Yikes.

A knock on the door announced Lola's arrival. When I opened the door, I saw she carried a brown bag filled to overflowing. Her glance took me in from head to toe, and she started to grin. "Okay, okay, I get it. You're just tired. Let me see the shoulder."

My shirt slipped sideways as I gave it a quick yank. The bluish-purple bruise lay exposed. Lola shook her head in dismay and handed me the bag of wondrous goodies. Delicious smells emanating from these treats made my mouth water.

In a hurry to unload the scrumptious fare, I took them to the counter and slid the contents onto the surface. A sandwich wrapped in foil, a couple of pastries, and a container of macaroni salad were the fare. I sniffed each in turn.

"Dig in, friend. I wasn't sure what you'd want, so I brought a variety." Lola fetched a plate from the cupboard.

"My mother called. She's sending Dad up with supper. Want to join me? We can shop for a car after dinner, depending on what time we eat and when Dad leaves. Mom said he'd be here around five, but who knows if he'll be on time."

"Sure, that would be great."

Being friends for many years, I knew Lola Trapezi's friendship was a sure bet. My father taught us both to cook. Lola took her experience one step further and opened up the deli down the street from my home. The residents of the town knew a good thing when they saw it, and her business flourished.

Lola didn't need to work year-round, but she did. She could afford to take the winter months off, but instead she worked and used the slow season to originate recipes. This year, Lola decided to write a cookbook. Her proposal to an editor earned a phone called request for a manuscript. I figured that as her guinea pig, I'd get to taste all the treats she'd write about.

While I ate, Lola outlined our car shopping plans. If I wanted, we could head east toward Johnston and revisit the car dealership where I bought the Taurus. With a heavy dose of perseverance, I had managed to grind a great price from the salesman when I purchased the car a few months before. In agreement with the plan, I nodded.

My first car was stolen. Then I'd inherited Aunt Livvy's dilapidated, ancient Volvo. I'd used that until my cousin torched it while it sat broken down on the side of the road. My latest car, the Taurus, had just been crushed. Not a great track record.

When I finished eating, Lola rose to leave and agreed to return when my father brought dinner. I promised to call her, and watched her MINI Cooper roll out of the driveway.

Alone, I hunkered down on the sofa in the living room. I flicked through TV channels and realized daytime television sucked more than during primetime. With a sneer and *tsk* of my teeth, I clicked the off button and rose, intending to go outside.

My shoulder throbbed, and I realized this was a prelude to what life would be like for the next however long. My whole body hadn't hurt until today, and the minor aches bothered me. Stretching my arm and neck, I heated a cloth in the microwave and applied it to relax the tightening muscles before I stepped through the sliding French doors outside.

Crisp, brilliant-colored leaves littered the deck and furniture.

Dirty Trouble

There might not be many good-weather days left to enjoy before the cold set in. I kicked leaves away with my foot and plucked several others from the plant pots.

The art festival, scheduled for the coming weekend, would team with thousands of gawkers, interlopers, and city dwellers. Yard sales would abound from end to end in the village, and kids would sell cookies on the sidewalks outside their houses.

For three long days, artists would crowd onto the village green, into the community house and then spread out over the lawn of the church grounds in their booths where they would exhibit handcrafted artistic treasures. The place would be full of crowds, traffic jams, and folks hawking their wares.

I was interested to see who showed up on my doorstep for a pee break or to ask if they could park in the driveway. Since a bunch of friends would probably stop in, I considered a refreshment list for the occasion.

A movement caught my eye and I glanced sideways. The huge cat from the day before peeked from under an evergreen. Leaning near the garage, the scraggly tree looked as ragged as the cat. It too sported frayed branches that bent in odd directions, similar to the cat's tail and ears.

The beast stepped forward on tentative paws. Huge, silent pads covered the distance from the tree to the deck. At least he didn't lift his leg and spray anything this time. Instead, he slunk onto the deck and paused, giving me a baleful glare. If I were superstitious, I'd say it was the evil eye. He stared and took a tentative step forward. A low, rumbling growl issued from his throat as he crept closer.

My hand stretched toward him, the beast rubbed his head on my palm. We were making progress, I guess. His glance roamed the deck in search of something. I wondered if he was hungry. There were leftovers from Lola's fare, and I went in search of a paper plate to toss the remnants on. I slid the food onto the dish and nudged it forward for the monstrous animal. He sniffed the offerings from end to end.

Fangs gouged the sandwich while sharp claws shredded the bread, holding it firm. He chowed down and wiped the plate clean with a pink sandpaper tongue. Moments later, the beast sat washing his face and paws. He seemed to enjoy the bounty I'd given him. When he finished his ablution, he stared at me with disdain.

His ears twitched as he listened to my murmured words of welcome and again when I asked questions that would never be answered. I glanced at the evergreen tree and then at the cat. He just stared at me without a sound and flicked his tongue to lick his fat cheeks.

"I'll call you Evergreen."

The baleful stare moved away from me as Evergreen stretched his massive body. The cat sprawled in a patch of sunlight on the deck and purred. There was a moment when I thought he'd fallen asleep, but the rich green eyes weren't quite closed. Evergreen was aware of every movement around him. If he were human, he'd have been a survivalist, I was sure.

The day was well into the afternoon when I rose from the chaise. Across the street from my house, the small post office held my daily allotment of mail. I rounded the corner of the house and waited for traffic to cease long enough to cross over.

Cars and trucks came to a halt. I stepped onto the asphalt. By the time I crossed to the other side of the street, traffic had resumed. Horns blew, and I waved without a glance, assuming it was someone I knew. Everybody knows everybody in a small town. When I had a bomb scare last summer, I'd become a public figure. I'd just finished a bomb course and I over-reacted when an unmarked package was left on my doorstep. That package became big news and eventually led to arrests, not at all related to bomb making. Go figure.

Today the mail in my post box overflowed. Advertisements filled the small space, but there wasn't much else of interest. I tossed the junk mail into the recycling bin and headed out the door just as Herb, the middle-aged mailman, came around the corner. He waved at me, and I stopped to chat.

He grinned. "In the news again, eh, Vinnie?"

"Yeah, it hasn't been the best week of my life – but not dull. Where did you hear the news?" I said, curious about the coverage since I hadn't seen any news cameras on the scene of my accident.

"The announcement was made on the afternoon news. No camera coverage though. I bet you were in a panic, huh?"

"You could say that," I said and started to walk away.

"Was it an accident, Vin?"

"Sure was. The cars make the turn like they do at Daytona. Someone hit my car, and I was off the road and out of control. Why do you ask?"

"Just wondering. Since you've had car troubles in the past, it occurred to me that this might be more of the same." His bright-blue eyed gaze roamed the parking lot filled with vehicles.

There wasn't much space to park, and everyone tried to make enough room for the next guy who came along. The lot only held six vehicles. Since parking was at a premium, the street usually filled up around this time of day. SUVs and smaller vehicles huddled in the lot. Expensive new cars parked next to older models riddled with dents and dings in the fenders.

Just as I turned back to Herb, the post office door opened, Tony DeGreico strolled out. His watched me for a moment. Herb noticed him, and we waited together while Tony approached us.

Dressed in a pair of clean tan workpants with a red v-neck sweater and casual shoes, he looked dapper. A real switch from the last time I saw him. Even his hair was under control and the beard trimmed.

"Gee, Vinnie, you had a close call on the highway, eh? Never know when bad things will happen. It must have been scary for you." His nearly black eyes took in my entire form, stopped at my chest, and then met my own dark eyes.

"Everyone has accidents. You never know what life will bring, do you, Tony?" I said in a wise-ass sort of way.

Herb shuffled his feet but stayed put. If there was some action, I was sure he'd want to have a ringside seat.

"That's true enough. Just look at me. Once I was a man of means, and now I work on a horse farm. Just never know where life will take you, huh?"

I nodded and wondered if the remark held a double meaning.

As I turned to Herb, he seemed a tad nervous. His eyes flicked back and forth between Tony and me. Whatever caused him to shake in his shoes I couldn't imagine, but I determined that Tony's reputation had made the rounds by now. *Shit.*

"See ya around, Herb," I said and gave Tony a slight nod.

Halfway across the parking lot I heard Tony call out to me. "You might want to be more careful, Vinnie. You might not be so lucky the next time."

In an effort to escape the creep, I turned, shrugged, and stepped off the sidewalk into the parking lane of the street. Cars stopped, and I crossed the street with long, quick strides before entering the gated path to the house.

My nerves were shot by the time I closed the foyer door. *Was that a threat? Was Tony just rubbing in the fact that I couldn't get from point A to point B without a catastrophe?* Maybe Marcus was right – I'm a disaster magnet.

Forget it, I thought. Tony wasn't in a position to do anything to me without returning to the psych ward for it. "Who would be that stupid?" I spoke the question out loud and pushed my thoughts away from the possibilities.

In the office, I sat and scribbled a list of snacks for the weekend. That numerous friends would be running in and out of the house was more than a possibility, especially now that I made the news. I'd be number one on their agenda before anyone hit the art show.

Off duty cops, their wives or girlfriends in tow, my cousins and other relatives would stop in. They had in the past, and this weekend would be no different. The house is on the main drag. Most folks walk right by it to get to the village green where the festival is held.

I settled into the luxurious padded folds of the leather chair. The windows faced the street, and one smaller window faced the driveway on the western side of the house. A tide of people ebbed and flowed in their daily routines as the sun drifted further west and daylight faded.

Chapter 10

A car turned into the driveway, and I watched my father maneuver along the side of the house. He always drove under the speed limit, which sent my mother to Jupiter every time they were out together. My mother has a heavy foot, a habit we share.

I heard the car door slam. I called Lola at the deli as I rose from the comfort of the chair to greet my father. I hurried to open the doors for the tasty fare he probably spent the afternoon cooking. Stepping aside, I made room for him to enter.

Gino Esposito, my father, is a rugged man. Square-shouldered, olive-skinned, and heavyset, he sports dark hair peppered with white. He was a handsome devil in his youth and is still a looker now. At least, all my friends tell me that. He has charm, they say, while I wonder where they got that idea. All I get is lectured.

The still-hot casserole accompanied a loaf of bread, warm and crusty, that nestled inside a foiled wrapper. It wasn't Italian food, but it didn't matter. My father made it, and that was good enough for me. From the largest bag he slid a scrumptious cake, smothered in white butter frosting.

"Is that a chocolate cake?" I asked, pointing at the confection.

"It is, your mother made it for you. She knows you like it with white frosting." He settled onto the stool as though to stay.

With a sense of foreboding, I fiddled with the casserole and pulled a couple plates from the cupboard.

"What's with the accident, Lavinia? Why didn't you mention it last night?" he asked, his gruff voice soft, as he stared at me.

My hands stilled, and I glanced at him. Dark brown eyes took in my appearance as Dad waited for an answer. Not some trumped-up story, not an excuse for my stupidity, but the God's honest truth. *Did I dare tell him what I thought? Would he get berserk and start yelling at me? Hmmm.* I opted for the stupidity angle.

"It was only an accident, Dad. That section of the highway is always a nightmare. You know that. A racecar driver couldn't handle it any better than we all do everyday. I just lost control of the car." As I tried to make light of the situation, I realized how cowardly I was.

"Lavinia, did you see who did this to you?"

My father's face held a somber look. I took a deep breath and shook my head.

"The car hit me from the left rear. I never saw it coming. Why?"

"This thing with Mafalda, it might be more than Antonio hustling stolen merchandise. Have you stuck your nose where it doesn't belong?"

"No, I promised I wouldn't. You know, Dad, I got the message loud and clear at dinner. Aaron didn't understand what you were inferring, but I did. I won't mess with the mob, honest."

Earnest eyes and a solemn expression met mine, and he nodded. *Wow, this is big. No yelling, no recriminations, and, best of all, lots of food. Yeah, my dad loves me.*

The door swung open after a single knock, and Lola strolled in. She gave my father a big hug and kiss on the cheek. When she hitched onto the stool next to him he smiled in a benevolent manner and asked how she was.

"Hungry, that's how I am. How are you, Mr. E?" Her Julia Roberts smile was in place, and my father succumbed to it, as all men do.

With a roll of my eyes, I pulled flatware from the drawer and laid out napkins. I glanced at my father with a silent question, and he shook his head no. Apparently he wasn't about to eat with us. Just keep us company while we sucked down the meal.

"Are you sure you won't eat with us, Dad?" I asked.

"Come on, Mr. E. Have some dinner and tell me what you've

been up to," Lola pleaded with another smile and won the day.

It's tough when others have more control over your family than you do – but whatever works, ya know?

A smile curled the corners of my lips as I set another plate on the counter. I hauled the wine from the fridge and poured three glasses while my father dished up the fragrant casserole. With a gleam in her eyes, Lola peered at what he scooped from the casserole dish and started questioning my father about the spices he'd used.

Nothing about the accident was mentioned, and after we finished eating we readied to leave. Before going to his own car, my father walked us to the MINI Cooper and chuckled when he saw it.

"A petite car for a petite woman," he said with a grin at Lola.

"Yep, it's a neat little car, Mr. E. Goes a bazillion miles an hour, too. Zero to sixty in a second flat."

"I'm sure," he said, a wry smile on his lips.

Now if I'd made that statement, there'd have been a lecture on speeding and how I'd managed to crash my car. But since Lola was not a family member – and with her killer smile – she could get away with it. That's life. Ain't it?

We climbed inside the car, the engine revved, and Lola swept from the driveway. She glanced around at the house, in search of something. I figured she was searching for Aaron.

"He's not home yet," I said with a smirk.

"I can see that. Is he out on business this late?"

"Yeah."

We followed behind Dad's car, then scooted along the four-lane roadway, after my father turned toward Cranston. We hit the Johnston town line in no time. Within a few seconds, we pulled into the car dealership and stopped at the front door.

The salesmen were inside, gawking through the windowpanes. Ah, look, potential customers, their hungry faces said. I bet their pulse rate hiked to abnormal proportions and they salivated. Car dealers are a bunch of sharks circling any poor slob stupid enough to come in off the street. Their craft is known as the art of the hustle.

Three reps approached us as we entered the building. Circling, bobbing, and ogling us, as though we were aliens from another planet, they smiled. God help me, I thought and turned toward the salesman I'd beaten down the last time.

His face held a resigned look as I approached him with a wide smile. Rising from the desk, he left the safety of his glass cubicle. A hand outstretched, he shook mine and we turned toward the rows upon rows of gleaming cars outside.

The suit he wore was in better condition than the last one I saw him wear. It had also seen better days. His shoes were scuffed, a frayed necktie lay knotted around his collar, and the shirt had a green booger attached to it. Wait, that wasn't a booger but was dried up hamburger relish. Ugh!

"I wondered if I'd see you again," he said. "How's the Taurus running?"

Apparently he hadn't heard or seen the news. I remembered to be thankful for the little things in life. Unable to relate the story one more time, I smiled and said, "Fine, but I'd like to purchase something newer."

"We could take the Taurus in trade, you know," he offered.

"No, that's okay. The book value is probably too low. So, what do you have that's good on gas, relatively inexpensive, and fairly new?" If he ever saw the condition of the Taurus, I'd get about a dollar ninety-eight, and a smirk, as a trade in value.

We'd entered the danger zone now. The salesman's smile faltered as we ambled down the rows of overwhelming car confusion. I'm not a car shopper, and my eyes glaze over quickly with too many offerings to choose from.

"This Altima's a great car, economical, and sporty. This model might fit your needs. Step over here, Ms. Esposito." His eyes took on a gleam, and I knew the price would choke a horse.

The pale blue sedan glistened beneath the overhead lamps. These lights could illuminate New York City with no problem. The car lot was brilliant, and even though it wasn't real dark, the lighting allowed for no guessing as to condition, on the part of a potential customer.

I stared at the smart-looking vehicle. Love at first sight, you might say, until I glanced at the list price. *Way over my budget.* Well, maybe not way over if I could schmooze the salesman. I looked around for Lola and saw her step quickly toward us.

The booger-shirted salesman glanced at me and then at Lola. He must have experienced *de'ja vue*, because his smile dimmed and a look of dismay replaced his previous expression. A fleeting pang of guilt hit me, but it only lasted a second. Hey, business is business after all.

"I'll take her for a spin, if you'll get the keys," I said with a wide, enthusiastic grin.

Lola's smile matched mine, and we hung around until the man showed up with keys and a dealer license plate. He slapped the plate on the car, and we took off at warp speed. There were things on the dashboard that glowed in neon colors. A speedometer, odometer, and lots of other inconsequential stuff glared brightly inside the dark interior. The new car smelled delicious, and the leather seat molded, soft and pliable, under my body.

We cruised along at a breakneck pace until flashing lights caught my attention. *Dang. Where did those come from?* I was about to receive a speeding ticket on a car that wasn't even mine.

Disgusted, I eased the car into the break down lane, stopped beneath an overhead highway lamp, and waited as I slid the window down. Lola chuckled and I sighed, resigned to the fact that this was a crappy way to end an already lousy day.

"Ma'am, do you realize you were driving in excess of eighty miles per hour?" the trooper said in a familiar voice as he shined the flashlight into the car.

I glanced up to see Marcus Richmond staring down at me. His eyes opened wide. He reached for the car door.

"What the hell do you think you're doing, Lavinia?" he yelled. "Out, now." He yanked the car door wide open and motioned for me to step out of the car.

"I'm not getting out of the car, Marcus. Just give me the damned ticket."

"You nearly got killed this week and you're tempting fate

again, so soon? Are you nuts?" He leaned down to look inside the car, his eyes rested on Lola. "And you've dragged Lola into this?"

"Marcus, I can explain—" I began, but he wouldn't let me finish.

"For God's sake, go home. You said you'd get some rest." His tone sounded exasperated, his temper volatile as if he barely controlled it. "Lola can drive since you can't keep your shit together for five minutes. This could have waited a few more days, you know."

"I'm fine and I'm not going home. Since I need a car to get to work, I may as well get one now."

His anger high, I figured he was beyond reason. I knew this from prior experience. Maybe Lola should drive. It would get him off my case, I thought. I turned and mumbled to Lola, who nodded.

I stepped out onto the pavement as Lola left her seat and scooted over to mine. I glared at Richmond and marched around to the passenger side of the car while trying to figure a way to get past this encounter.

Marcus held the passenger door open as I turned to enter the car. His hand snuck onto my arm and tightened. I glanced at him and waited.

"This wasn't a good idea. You were speeding, Vin. Don't let it happen again." He bit the words out.

"I know, Marcus, I know." Meek and mild has never been my strong suit. However, I know how to play cards. This was one time I needed to fold, especially if it kept my butt out of jail.

His eyes gleamed and narrowed. Yeah, like he believed my act for one second. The campaign hat dipped when he nodded, and I could have sworn he hid a smirk. When Marcus glanced up at me again it was with a straight face, so maybe I just imagined it.

"Is this your new car?"

"It will be if I can beat the salesman down on the price," I said with a smirk.

"Poor bastard."

"Yeah, but business is business, ya know?"

He glanced inside the car and said to Lola, "Go straight back to the dealership and keep it to the speed limit. Understand?"

"Sure thing, Marcus." She smiled the Julia smile, and Marcus got that stupid look on his face – the one most men get when Lola flashes those pearly whites.

With a nod, he closed the car door and headed back to the cruiser. Lola and I glanced at each other with a shrug and a chuckle before she zipped into traffic. The nearest exit was a mile up the road. We turned off, swung back toward the highway, and headed to the car lot. Marcus followed us until we hit the Johnston Town Line before he disappeared.

The Altima handled like a charm, rode smooth as a dream, and felt perfect. This car fits me, I thought. Even if the salesman wouldn't give much on the price, I was determined to have the car.

Our return to the dealership was met with hungry anticipation. The man knew I liked the car and he'd made a sale. We haggled over the price, and though I didn't get exactly what I wanted, it came darn close. He pulled my previous file and set the paperwork in motion. The car would be ready for pick up in the morning.

After the hour-long wrangling, Lola and I headed to the donut shop for coffee. My body had wound down and I knew I'd pay for all this activity. Why is it that muscles don't react immediately but wait a while and then become stiff? The accident happened two days ago. Things should be fine now.

With coffee in hand, we turned toward Scituate and chocolate cake smothered in white frosting. I sipped my latte and leaned back against the seat.

"Marcus is worried about you, huh? Man, he got hot under the collar," Lola said with a smirk.

"Yeah, he forgets that I'm inclined to action, rather than inaction. It causes him some anxiety when he can't control me, I think." My chuckle matched her laughter as we buzzed along the highway toward home. "I mean, did he really think I'd be able to lay around day after day with nothing to do? Get real."

"Exactly. Men just don't realize women are stronger than we're given credit for."

The car slowed and we shot across the road into the driveway. Lola pulled up beside Aaron's SUV and cut the engine. Her eyes strayed upward toward the lights emanating from the second floor. She glanced at me and smiled.

"Why don't you throw on a pot of coffee and I'll invite Aaron to join us for cake?" Her eyebrows waggled up and down.

"You just want a piece of him, never mind the cake." I laughed.

"Mm, hmm. Be right back."

I strode into the apartment as she ran up the stairs. I heard her knock on the door and Aaron's greeting. Two sets of feet trampled down the steps, and the couple tumbled into the kitchen. Coffee perked and I turned with a smile.

"My mother made a chocolate cake. We figured you might be in need of a snack."

"Glad you asked. By the way, did I hear something about you getting a new car?" Aaron's dark eyes roved my face.

"Yeah, we just went out for a test drive. Car runs nice."

"Really? That's not quite the story I heard, but if you insist." Aaron's face registered what I thought might be skepticism. I wondered what he'd heard, and from whom.

Lola reached over and uncovered the cake. She spread the plates out, along with flatware. I watched her efficiency and tried to ignore Aaron's continued stare.

It would seem that Marcus had been on the phone to Aaron. This meant he'd question me later. There was no doubt in my mind. Another person who figured I needed to be controlled, I thought. Huh, pain in the butt men.

We munched cake while Lola explained my shopping trip for a new car. She kindly left out Marcus and the speeding incident, though her eyes sparkled with mischief when she glanced at me.

"Vinnie beat the guy down on the price. It'll be ready tomorrow. I won't be around since I'm meeting with an editor and that lasts most of the day. Can you give her a ride in the morning, Aaron?"

Eyebrows hiked as he glanced toward me and nodded. "Sure, I can do that. How are your muscles reacting after the accident?" A tiny curl at the corners of his lips brought a smile to my own.

"My shoulder is sore and my body protests a bit. Other than that, I'm good."

A short while later, I found myself alone and ready to call it a day. The MINI Cooper had zipped eastward toward the Salt & Pepper Deli after Aaron returned to the upstairs unit. Quiet encompassed the apartment and I yawned. Time to hunker down for the night.

Changing into sweatpants and a t-shirt, my cool-weather sleepwear, I padded barefoot into the living room. I turned on the lamp and slid down into the sofa. The lightweight, hand-woven designer blanket slid over me as I tugged it from the sofa ridge. The only thing on television – other than commercials enticing viewers to thin down using drugs, or to enjoy their sex life more with drugs – was violence. Either way, it was all about drugs, so I flicked the tuner to the stereo and listened to music.

Chapter 11

Fists pounded on my door, and the incessant rattling of the doorknob woke me. In a sleepy state of mind I shifted beneath the blanket. Someone stood outside in the front entry and wanted in. *What time was it?* Bleary-eyed, I glanced at the clock on the end table and sighed. Midnight. I'd only been asleep for a couple hours or so.

"Who's there?" I called. Stiff-legged, I rolled over the edge of the sofa. Were these my legs, the same ones that carried me running for miles? Muscles cramped when I tried to rise.

"It's Marcus and Aaron. Get up Vinnie. Now!"

The pounding resumed.

"All right, all right, I'll be right there. Geez. What's the hurry?"

I slid the bolt back and turned the door handle. When the door started to open, it pushed inward with force. I stumbled back, caught my foot on a pair of sneakers and lost my balance. My arms flailed in the air as I went down like the Titanic. A resounding thud accompanied a loud *woof* from my lungs when I hit the floor.

The two men struggled to enter the room at the same time. Well, that didn't work – they were just too wide-shouldered. I lay sprawled on the floor, gaping at the two hulks towering above me.

"What's up, guys?" I asked with raised brows and raging muscles. It seemed that as my body relaxed, muscle pain set in. *Dang, that's inconvenient.*

The two men got through the door and hauled me off the floor. I moaned and groaned over the effort and tried to figure out their motive for waking me in the middle of the night.

"I asked you, *What's up?"* My annoyed voice was a tad louder this time.

"We need to get you outside. Come on." Marcus dragged me toward him and through the hallway with his hands under my armpits.

"Why?" I asked, as he hauled me through the outer door, with Aaron following.

The street was filled with flashing lights, fire truck tankers, and neighborhood people who milled around on the sidewalk. Smoke filled the air. I sniffed and glanced around, curious to see the origin. An eerie orange glow filled the sky above the house. With a sudden movement, I disengaged Marcus' hold on my body.

"Marcus, what the hell happened?" Scared, I yelled at him and turned toward Aaron. My eyes popped wide open when I caught sight of the flickering light behind the house. Smoke billowed into the dark sky from my backyard.

"Damn it." I headed toward the driveway but Aaron caught me by the waist and lifted me off my bare feet.

Together, the two men dragged me further along the post office parking lot. I struggled against their strength. Aaron held on tight and spoke some words that I didn't comprehend until we reached the end of the parking lot.

"Stop, Vinnie. You can't go back there. The garage is on fire and the firefighters are doing their job. There's no place for you over there." The Hulk-sized body barred my retreat on one side, as Marcus blocked the way on the other side.

"I didn't hear the sirens."

Aaron shook his head. "We told them not to use any. I was working late and went outside to get some papers from the truck. It was then that I smelled the smoke and saw flames coming from the garage. I'm sorry, Vinnie, but at least it didn't reach the house." His hands rubbed my arms. I glanced into the handsome face above me and nodded numbly.

In disbelief, I turned to Marcus. He stepped forward, threw an arm around my shoulders, and pulled me close. His lips pressed my temple and I leaned into his hard body while I stared across the street. *What happened? Who set fire to the garage?*

A few possibilities crossed my mind while I watched firefighters move back and forth from the tanker to the back building. Maybe Tony wanted to make a statement. A reminder of what he thought I deserved. But why hadn't he torched the house instead of the garage?

There was always the mob to consider. They might be sending me a message about Antonio? Nah, they'd just get in my face instead of burning down my building.

God's wrath was another consideration, but I hadn't done anything outrageous, so I dismissed that idea completely. Why was I always a target? A disaster magnet, that's what Marcus called me. My shoulders slumped and despair hummed along my nerves. Aunt Livvy, God rest her soul, must be watching from above, shaking her head.

"Would someone explain what happened here? I'm still confused."

Aaron's warm brown eyes appeared black in the shadowed light as he faced me. He said, "After I saw the flames, I reported the fire and asked that no sirens be used. I didn't want the whole town awake, but by the look of the crowd, that consideration was useless."

Aaron's glance traveled the groups of bystanders, gawking at the show. "I ran down the back stairs and tried to wake you, but you didn't hear me and then I heard Marcus pull to the curb.

Marcus picked up where Aaron left off. "We stormed the front door and woke you. I figured you might be in the living room on the sofa when Aaron said he couldn't wake you."

"Thanks for that. I was so beat I never heard a thing. How did the fire start? Any idea?"

"No, MacNert is handling the scene and will have information for us later. The fire marshal has to look the scene over, too. Right now we should get you out of here. Why don't you go to headquarters and wait for me?" Marcus asked.

"Good idea, Vinnie," Aaron said. "It makes no sense to stand out here in the cold. You're barefoot and aren't even wearing a jacket. I'll catch up with you in the morning. The fire chief won't let us into the house until everything is clear."

"I think I'd rather go to Lola's house, if you don't mind. She lives close to the barracks." I'd started to shake and knew it was imperative that I get my act together. No sense in falling apart in front of these two macho men. It was bad for my independent image.

Marcus gazed at me and nodded to Aaron. "Take her, would you? I'll stay here until things are under control."

Several troopers and local cops stood in the street. Traffic was nil at this late hour. Anyone who tried to get through the village was redirected to an alternate route at the corner traffic light.

Trooper Jonah Franklin stood several feet away and gave me a nod. His eyes turned toward Marcus. A silent signal sent Marcus toward the man. Their conversation was so quiet I wondered if they used some type of Boy Scout code. In my mind, troopers are similar to a secret society. They have little to say about many things and ask a ton of questions all the time. A secret club, where few women were allowed. It piqued my curiosity, and we know that curiosity leads to trouble.

With a hand on my elbow, Aaron guided me toward the SUV parked at the nearby corner. He held the door as I climbed in, my muscles groaning with the effort. Before he could close the door, Marcus stepped into view.

"Headquarters has notified Lola that you'll arrive shortly. Vinnie, try to get some rest and stay put, will you? I'll stop by later this morning to see you." He leaned in and kissed me.

The warmth of his lips felt good on mine, and I wanted nothing more than to fold myself into his body. Maybe the strength of Richmond's arms would save me from this overwhelming sense of doom. My life held one calamity after another. I needed a break from it.

With a nod of agreement, I leaned back in the seat and Marcus closed the door. The motor started and purred like a giant cat as we slid the car from the curb onto the street and headed west. Aaron's truck sported tinted windows and a black interior that matched the exterior. A stealth truck, I thought, as my eyes slid toward the broad-shouldered man.

"Thanks, Aaron. I mean that. If you hadn't been there, who knows what would have happened?"

"My pleasure. We were lucky I was awake. With my bedroom in the front of the house, I probably wouldn't have seen the flames or heard anything either."

The truck slowed as we approached the road facing the state police barracks. Aaron turned left and we headed up the dark, winding lane toward Lola's house. I indicated the driveway as we approached, and Aaron whipped into the yard. After he parked in front of the garage we hiked up the multitude of steps toward the house.

Lola's house was a neat affair perched on a stone ledge that overlooked the road. The house, grey with white shutters, had a screened-in porch that faced two flights of stairs that were staggered from the ground to the entrance. The building appeared compact until we arrived at the front door. Appearances can be deceiving as was the case with this adorable cottage.

The front door swung open, and Lola rushed toward us wrapped in a chenille robe with bunny slippers on her small feet. She embraced us both in turn though her face was a map of concern.

"I'm so glad you're all right," she said ushering us inside. "Tell me what happened. The trooper who called gave me no information at all."

With a swift explanation, Aaron summed up the latest incident in my fiasco-prone life. At least there's never a dull moment. I needn't ever worry about a mundane existence. It appears my life is just one huge happening – nothing more and nothing less. Ah, it's good to be alive.

The coffee perked and we drank decaf brew while Lola insisted we both stay with her for the night. Aaron glanced around the house with interest. I stifled a chuckle. The house was just the right size for Lola, but Aaron dwarfed the place.

Dirty Trouble

Towering over six feet, Aaron Grant was well muscled and toned. When he moved into the apartment above mine, it occurred to me that he'd fit better in a monstrous mansion with Italian tile, high peaked windows, and vaulted ceilings. Instead, he was at home in a Colonial registered with the historical society that featured low-ceiling rooms and uneven floors. You just never know about people.

Once we agreed where Aaron would stay, we turned in for the night. Aaron slept on the sofa, his feet dangling off the end. I bunked in with Lola. I tossed and turned for a while, but managed to drift off.

Several hours later, footsteps sounded in the living room. I yawned and stretched a body that complained. It would be safe to say I wouldn't run my usual miles today. However, inactivity wasn't on my agenda either. With mild muscle pain, I rose from the soft confines of Lola's bed and headed to the bathroom.

As I passed the door to the living room, I caught the sound of voices. In an instant, I realized Marcus and Aaron were in conversation.

"House is fine. The rear of the garage isn't. Fire Marshal Fred Kinsky was on site at first light, inspecting the scene so he could work up his report," Marcus said.

The knowledge that my house escaped ruin eased the fact that my garage might be a charred nightmare.

In the bathroom, I faced the mirror and dragged a comb through my wild mop of hair and I wondered what started the fire. Was my life a single pile of manure, or what? I checked the bedroom, but Lola wasn't in there, and I could smell food. I listened to the soft voices for a moment longer before I strode back into the bathroom.

An extra toothbrush lay on the shelf in the cabinet. I ripped the package open. After a quick scrub of my teeth, I rambled toward the kitchen. Come what may, I needed coffee – and not decaf either – pure caffeine, unadulterated, and strong. I couldn't start a day without it.

The threesome sat at the kitchen table. It was covered with

food. Lola served omelets, grilled toast, and sausage patties. Chunks of fresh fruit filled bowls that nestled alongside each dish, and the smell of coffee permeated the air. Life was good.

Men always look great in the morning. A woman always looks like a shipwreck. *Why is that?* Pasting a smile on my face, I hobbled toward the table, exerting an extreme amount of effort to appear as though I wasn't stiff. *Is that considered showmanship?* Probably.

After one look at me Marcus glanced at Aaron, and a smirk quivered on his lips. Aaron chuckled outright, and I gave in. The effort it took to pretend wasn't worth much, and I succumbed to my aches and pains. Marcus leaned sideways and pulled a chair from the table while Lola poured a mug of rich, dark brew and set it in front of me.

"So tell me what started the fire," I demanded.

"Good morning to you, too." Marcus rolled his eyes.

"Sorry. Good morning. What time did you get finished at the house? How bad is the damage?" I tempered the questions with a touch of patience. It was tough, but I managed.

"We left around four and the Fire Marshal hasn't made a determination yet. He's still working on it. The house isn't damaged at all since the fire started on the rear, western side of the garage. It does appear to have started at the lower corner of the structure, though. Curious, isn't it? An arsonist doesn't usually do things that way."

"Have you guys started questioning anyone?" I meant had they questioned Tony, but I wouldn't say so.

"Just some preliminary questions to the neighbors. Do you have anyone in mind?" Narrowed eyes gleamed at me as Marcus scanned my features.

"No, I just wondered." *Evasion is a wonderful tool at any given moment, don't you think?*

"By the way, you're taking Mafalda to her hearing this morning. I was at your apartment getting your clothes when your mother called. She left a message that you need to be in court by eleven o'clock this morning. An attorney, John Schmuck, will meet you there around quarter of. You're to go to Superior Court on South Main Street. If you get dressed, I'll give you a ride."

Handing me a gym bag, Marcus grinned and I could only imagine what a great time he had in my underwear drawer. When I searched the contents, I saw he'd included a filmy bra with panties to match. Slacks and a sweater set accompanied a pair of shoes. My purse lay at the top of everything. *The man has clothes sense.* I smiled.

A wide grin met my eyes as I rose from the table to shower and dress. Time was short and I needed to get a move on in order to make it to court on time. Reaching inside my purse, I retrieved the cell phone. I grinned at Marcus and went toward the bathroom.

My mother answered after the first ring. She explained that Muffy would meet me at the courthouse on the first floor. I could only imagine my aunt going through the security system set up just inside the entry. She'd probably get lugged if there were an issue with her purse, jewelry, or anything at all. I agreed to meet Muffy there and stepped into the shower after the call ended.

Hot water coursed down my body, and the soreness of my muscles melted away. I knew the feeling wouldn't last, but for the moment the reprieve was most welcome. After I dressed, swiped make up over my pale features, and added lipstick and mascara, I swung through the doorway, ready to take on the world. Well, maybe not the world, but Aunt Muffy at least. *How do I get involved in these issues?*

Ready and waiting at the door, Marcus looked me over. I imagined he envisioned my underwear rather than the outerwear. A smile hovered around his mouth and before he broke into a wide grin. The wolf grin, I thought. He nodded his approval of the choices he'd made for me.

Before we went to the courthouse I glanced around for Lola, but she'd disappeared. Aaron explained she'd be gone all day but would call me when she could. He said he'd straighten the house and meet me back at the Colonial. I nodded and left with Marcus.

Chapter 12

As we maneuvered through the traffic in Providence, I sat in silent contemplation of what would happen with Muffy in court. The woman, a harridan on a good day, wasn't afraid to take on anyone. After all, she hung out with mobsters, right? The attorney's name wasn't familiar to me, and I had no idea what to expect from him. Frayed nerves stretched, and I let out a sigh.

"Are you worried about Mafalda or everything in general, Vin?"

With a quick glance at Marcus, I hauled in a deep breath. "I guess it's everything, though I never know what to expect from Muffy. She's quite a character, to put it mildly."

"Things will work out, I'm sure. If you need a ride home, just give me a call. I'm off today, but I have a detail tonight. The governor is holding a bash, and I have to be there."

"Lucky you, hanging out with the brightest and best again, huh?" I asked.

"Yeah, it sucks, but the money is good."

Marcus swung the Dodge Ram truck around the corner and pulled to a halt in front of the courthouse. The Grecian-styled building was an imposing structure, columned in the front with a set of wide swinging doors for entry. It appealed to the artist within me.

Swinging the truck door open, Marcus grasped my hand and pulled me toward him. His lips met mine and I hovered there for a moment, wishing I didn't have to exit the vehicle. His warm lips played over mine once again and sexy hazel eyes met my dark brown ones.

"Call me if you need to. I'll be around all day, Vinnie."

"Sure thing. Thanks for the ride. Get some rest. You look tired."

"I am. By the way, I like your underwear drawer. Very nice stuff. Maybe you should model some of it for me, huh?" His smile gleamed.

I grinned before sliding from the seat. With a wave of my hand, I headed into the courthouse. Scores of people milled near the entrance while attorneys, cops, and criminals hustled through the huge doors. When I entered the great hall I glanced around the foyer. Veined, cream-colored marble covered the floors and walls and shimmered in the sunlight.

A huge set of gateways and security conveyor belts squatted in front of me. People with swipe cards were allowed to enter the inner sanctum of the structure without so much as a glance from the Capitol Police who guarded the courthouse. I, on the other hand, shuffled into a line of people who had to enter through the conventional means of search and seizure.

Mafalda stood near the gateway, and it wasn't until I stepped forward in line that I fully noticed her short frame. She looked elegant dressed in a classic black suit with a diamond brooch and her neatly styled dark-hair. Her eyes stared into the crowd. She scanned everyone, while seeking me, her life preserver. At least, I think she sought me.

With ramrod straight shoulders, Mafalda approached a middle-aged man with thin brown hair scraped across his dome. A bald spot shone like the sun on the crown of his head, and a loose suit hung off the slight frame. I took in his appearance in one swift glance.

He was likely the attorney, Mr. Schmuck. A worn leather valise hung from his left hand as he reached out with his right to shake Muffy's extended hand. Muffy stepped closer to him, and they started to speak.

By this time, the line closed in on one of the security ports and I was near enough to hear Muffy and her attorney. I stepped forward, and since they stood with their backs turned toward me, the opportunity to listen presented itself. Without shame, I leaned my head in their direction.

Muffy listened intently as Schmuck explained what to expect in the courtroom. It was unusual for her to be so calm and collected, especially because she just didn't get arrested every day. Judge Alibaster was the *Judge du Jour*, and, though I never met the man, his reputation was exemplary. If my aunt didn't shoot her mouth off, she'd be fine. I'd heard the judge was a nice man with a terrific sense of humor. In his line of work humor was a much-needed commodity.

With a nudge, someone behind me pushed forward. Sometimes Rhode Islanders are so darned rude. I touched Muffy's shoulder as I caught up to her.

"Auntie, let's get through the security line," I said, getting her attention.

The look on her face sent chills along my spine. Was I in for a day of days? Was that vengeful glare bent towards me, or was it just a look of surprise? These were questions that needed answers prior to entering the courtroom.

The attorney and my aunt stepped in front of me and slapped their belongings onto the conveyor belt. The guy behind me moaned and mumbled about people cutting the line. I sent a nasty glance in his direction, but he'd turned away and knelt to tie his shoe. We all moved a step forward as Muffy went through the metal detector doorframe.

The super sensor didn't make a sound and I breathed a pent-up sigh of relief. Muffy stepped into the inner sanctum of the courthouse. No guns, no knives, no bombs in her purse. *Life is good.*

The attorney went next and I waited for my turn. The guy behind me mumbled under his breath for a few more seconds. I tried to ignore him.

The security cop motioned me forward. When I didn't move as quickly as the person behind me thought I should, I received a shove. My purse flew toward the conveyor belt, and I heaved forward in surprise, and tripped over the floor pad within the metal detector frame.

Flat on my face with the rubber mat for support, I heard guffaws from the crowd. The security cop hauled me to my feet and asked if I was all right. I nodded and turned toward the jerk that pushed me. It seemed a gleam of satisfaction entered his eyes as I realized Tony DeGreico stared back.

With a swift rush of anger, I tried to return through the detector frame. The cop caught my arm and turned me around. With a negative shake of his head, he handed over my purse and said, "Move on ma'am. No need to get angry." He smiled in a kind way, probably to defuse the situation.

I nodded back and thanked him as I shot Tony a nasty look. It's a look worse than the one your mother gives you, kind of like a look of promise, a look of bad things to come. It's not in my nature to be vindictive, even though Tony was a thorn in my side that refused to go away. If there'd been no one around, I'd have enjoyed kicking the shit out of him, but it would have to wait.

Together once again, Schmuck, Muffy and I wandered through the marble-lined corridors in search of our courtroom. We'd gone two floors up by the time we found the right place. When we entered, the spacious room was empty of anyone other than the bailiff and secretary. They both glanced up with curiosity.

Schmuck stepped past the bar and approached the secretary. He mumbled some words. She checked the docket and glanced over Schmuck's shoulder toward Auntie and me. Her eagle eyes rested on Muffy for a fraction of a second before she turned back to Schmuck and mumbled something unintelligible. He nodded and thanked her, then returned to us.

"The judge will see us in chambers. He's not holding court today, but he has agreed to speak with us privately. This is very unusual, Ms. Ciano."

"Who else will be there?" I asked.

"Just us, the bailiff, and the judge – no DA or anyone else. Like I said, this is unusual. I'm not sure what to make of it, quite frankly." His pale features wrinkled as his eyebrows rose.

The bailiff left the room for a moment or two and then returned. The brawny man motioned us toward the office behind him. We lined up like wooden soldiers outside the judge's chambers and waited until the door opened to allow us access.

Charged nerves tightened, but I gave what I hoped was a confident smile to Aunt Mafalda. She stared at me for a moment, and said nothing. Foreboding marched along the frayed nerves and sore muscles of my body. I envisioned shackles and handcuffs on her ankles and wrists after she assaulted not only the bailiff, but the judge as well. *Okay, so my imagination was in overdrive again.*

The bailiff ushered us inside and the judge turned toward us in greeting. He wore a suit – not robes – and I relaxed a bit. Black robes are a tad daunting, especially when they accompany the mega power that judges hold within their hands.

He stretched his hand out, motioning to chairs lined up in front of the massive desk. A black leather blotter covered the majority of the desktop, and the remaining mahogany gleamed from years of polish.

Judge Alibaster's character-lined face showed strength. His eyes sparkled with humor as he welcomed us to his sanctuary.

"As you've been told, I'm not holding a court session today, but I've agreed to speak with you as a courtesy." The brilliant blue-eyed stare held Muffy's own as he spoke.

I gaped in awe. It dawned on me that Muffy not only knew the judge but was probably also listed in his little black book. *Dang, the woman gets around.*

Attorney Schmuck listened as the judge expounded on the incident in the file before him. Judge Alibaster glanced at Muffy every so often and tried to hide the humor within his gorgeous eyes. Eventually he stopped speaking and just stared at her.

Schmuck said, "Ms. Ciano is not the type of person to break the law, Your Honor. She was taken aback by the rough handling she received from the officers. I'm certain my client regrets the incident."

"I'm sure she does," the judge said with a tiny grin. He leaned back in his tall leather chair, cupping his jaw between the thumb and index finger of his left hand.

"Tell me, Ms. Ciano, how do you think we should handle this?"

Until this moment, Mafalda hadn't uttered a sound. She crossed her legs and smiled at the judge.

"I would be happy to apologize for my behavior if I thought I'd done anything wrong. However, those cops were beastly to me. I didn't warrant their rough handling. I'm not a woman who breaks the law, you know. I'm an upstanding citizen who pays taxes, and I've worked hard for a living all my life."

"Be that as it may, this is a serious charge, Ms. Ciano, one that needs to be addressed. Would you consider doing community service? It is better than jail time," the judge said.

My aunt, on the front seat of a bus, headed to the Women's Correctional Facility? It was beyond comprehension. I squirmed in my seat as the Judge turned his attention to me. A smile hovered on his lips. I wondered if the jail time threat was a ruse.

"Did you have something you might like to say?" he asked me.

"My aunt could work with the senior citizens at the center near her home as a community service. There is always a shortage of help, especially with coordinating functions. I'm sure Mafalda would be happy to assist, Your Honor." My foot met Muffy's under the chair leg, and she nodded. My head pounded from a headache. I guessed stress to be the cause of it.

"Indeed, that is a wonderful idea," Muffy added.

The jail time suggestion loomed in both our minds as an impossible solution, I guess. She'd be lucky to get off so lightly, and we both knew it. We turned toward the attorney and watched him fumble in his valise for several papers.

"Your Honor, it appears Ms. Ciano is amenable to this arrangement." Schmuck handed the documents to the bailiff, who passed them to Judge Alibaster.

The judge skimmed the pages and slid them into the file. He glanced at the three of us, sitting before him. Stiff as bowling pins, we waited for the ball to knock us down.

"That's a fair solution, and I think seventy-five hours of community service in a seniors' center of your choice will be sufficient. You'll be responsible for contacting the administrator of that facility, who in turn will report to me. If you do not follow through on this, I will be forced to have you arrested and sent to the Women's Correctional Facility for three months. Don't disappoint me, Ms. Ciano." His harsh words softened with a tiny smile.

Was he serious about the three months of prison time, or was that threat to keep Muffy in line? I didn't know, but I was curious – as ever. The judge nodded to the bailiff. We were finished, and we rose in unison.

"Thank you, Your Honor," I murmured with relief.

He grinned back at me and then turned to Muffy, a sparkle in his eyes. I watched the attorney stuff papers back into the leather bag and head toward the door. I stepped behind him and realized Muffy wasn't moving.

I halted and stared at the judge and Muffy. He inclined his head toward her, and she stepped away with a smile on her features. I wondered what that was about, as we strode from the room into the people-filled corridor outside.

Schmuck moved ahead of us and disappeared into the crowd. Astounded, I watched his bald crown bob away, adrift in a sea of people. Muffy grabbed my arm and we hustled through the courthouse, onto the sidewalk of South Main Street.

"My car is parked right up the street. Let's stop for lunch at my favorite restaurant on the Hill, dear," Auntie said.

Stunned, I watched Muffy's self-satisfied face and had the urge to strangle her. The courtroom scene felt like a set-up. The judge was likely an old flame, and the attorney probably worked for the mob. As these thoughts raced through my brain I realized it was a sure thing. I scrambled to catch up to this squat, mature woman as she approached her green Toyota sedan.

"Auntie," I demanded, as I reached for her arm. "Don't tell me that was a scripted scene?"

"Lavinia, I'm sure I don't know what you're talking about," she said as her dark eyes darted around the street.

With hands outstretched, palms up, I pleaded with her.

"Auntie, what the hell is going on here?"

"Lavinia, get in the car and we'll go have lunch. Just damned well do as I say." Black eyes glittered and her head dipped toward the car.

Am I stupid, or what? The sixty-plus woman would answer me once we were in the car – not before. I stumbled into the front seat and buckled the seatbelt. The pounding in my head beat like a set of drums. The last thing I felt like having was lunch, especially on Federal Hill.

Once upon a time, Federal Hill, the neighborhood located on the outer edge of downtown Providence, was a hangout for the mob. Social clubs still exist, and the inhabitants aren't friendly folk. The FBI, state police, and local cops keep a close eye on the activities of the people that frequent those establishments. I knew little of the places and cared about them even less, until now.

The Toyota crossed the Providence River and headed west, through the city. We careened around corners and I held tight to the dashboard. My glance slid toward the woman at the wheel. I saw her determined chin jut forward as we pulled into the Ristorante Da Ravioli. *Oh, boy.*

In the parking lot, we sat in silence for a moment until Auntie turned to me with a serious face. She stuffed the car keys into her designer purse and licked her lips. It seemed as though she made an inner decision, so I waited.

"You deserve an explanation, Lavinia, and I'm going to give it to you. However, I must ask that you not speak about it to anyone else."

"Okay, Auntie," I murmured.

"The judge and I dated when I was younger. We had a wild affair but parted company when he was forced to marry a woman of wealth. His parents considered an Italian woman without a college education beneath him, and that was that." Muffy paused, stared out the windshield and then turned back to me. "The attorney doesn't know this, and I'd rather it stay that way. Your father pulled strings to have Alan, Judge Alibaster, handle this case. Gino knew I'd get off with a reprimand, and handled the whole affair with finesse. Your dad knows how to get things done, Lavinia. He's a wonderful man."

"There's no question about that, Auntie, but you could have warned me," I snapped.

My aunt turned to me, wide-eyed at my snippy remark. "I don't think I like your attitude, my dear." Her voice was calm, though laced with steel.

"My life has been an incredible pile of shit lately and without the ability to know the workings behind the scene, it's been a bit unfair," I whined.

Again Aunt Muffy glanced at me with wide eyes. "Tell me about this so called pile of shit, honey." Her tone changed, softened somewhat – held a hint of curiosity.

In turn, I stared at the old dragon. Could I trust her not to squeal to my parents? Would she fail me? I remembered how Aunt Livvy always kept mum about my sorry-ass life. With a deep breath, I gave Muffy a brief rundown of my affairs.

"These are most unfortunate events. What can I do to help you, dear?"

She managed to make me feel warm and fuzzy inside. *How did that happen?* Muffy was a tough character, holding her own against the world. She'd been forced to, from day one, though her connection to the mob was just a little over the top as far as I was concerned.

I begged her. "You've got to keep this information to yourself. If my parents find out, they'll have a conniption fit. They worry enough about my lifestyle as it is."

"Never fear. Everything will work out, and I won't say a word to anyone. Now, let's go have lunch."

Unable to refuse, I slid from the seat and walked alongside her short, stiff-backed form. Muffy was up to something – I could feel it in my bones. Besides, there was a certain gleam in those sharp eyes that boded ill for someone.

Chapter 13

The restaurant's reputation was an outstanding one. Advertised in the best magazines, wannabes and real film stars often frequented the place. Filmmaking was on the rise in Rhode Island. It wasn't unusual to see show biz folks, directors, actors, and actresses hanging out on the Hill.

We strolled through the columned front door, and entered a high-domed area. I could hear the low buzz of voices from diners engaged in conversation over lunch. We waited for an escort to seat us in the dining room.

My gaze traveled around the luxurious walls of tinted Tuscan plaster. A warm, rich golden hue on the walls, burnished to a textured sheen, complemented floors of glossy veined marble. Soft leather chairs in various shades of red, rust, deep orange, and rich mustard yellow, were placed around the oval foyer. Giant potted ferns accompanied these chairs. The restaurant overflowed with ambiance.

Dressed in a starched white shirt, black bow tie, and black slacks, the man turned to us with a smile. His even white teeth glowed brilliantly in the soft lighting as he greeted my aunt. He knew her by name. That was the first sign that lunch would be interesting.

"Ms. Ciano, it is such a pleasure to have you with us today. Are you meeting someone or is it just you and your lovely friend?" His eyes swerved toward me, and I beheld the rich green eyes of an undercover cop, about my age, from one of my past classes.

With a chuckle, my aunt turned and introduced me to the man.

"Lavinia, this is Andre Messino. He works here and is a handsome devil, don't you think? This is my niece, Lavinia Esposito."

Smiling in acknowledgement, I reached out to shake his hand. His eyes never registered recognition, but he as an undercover cop – acting was one of the first things taught in his training.

"Glad to meet you, Mr. Messino," I said with a nod.

"Andre, please. I am so glad you could join us here at Da Ravioli today. Our luncheon menu is quite wonderful, and I'm sure you'll enjoy it. Have you been here before, Ms. Esposito?"

Now, I know he's an undercover cop, probably a narc from the narcotics squad, but he was fishing for information. His name was definitely not Andre Messino either. It tickled me to take the bait from his hook.

"No, this is my first visit. My aunt thought it would be a nice treat, didn't you, Auntie?"

She grinned and nodded. I wondered if she realized this man was a policeman. In light of how she felt mistreated by the PPD, the probability she knew was slight, to none. We followed Andre to the booth where he left us to peruse the menu.

My appetite perked up at the tasty fare offered. While I glanced around, Aunt Muffy mentioned a few things she'd ordered before. Other diners were ushered in. Among them was Antonio, the businessman. The same man who left my aunt to rot in a jail cell while he made bail. And I knew, she knew.

The appetite I'd just found, now fled. My mouth dried out, and my glance swung to Muffy. I knew Auntie would undoubtedly play for the lunch crowd. Good Lord, I thought, and then did a mental eye roll.

Antonio stopped at the table. His eyes rested on me for a second and then on Muffy. The wicked gleam in her black eyes caused my armpits to sweat. Shit, here it comes, I thought. Act One was about to begin.

"Mafalda, how are you, sweetheart?" he murmured.

"Very well, no thanks to you. How could you leave me in that place with those beastly cops? I fought for you, and look where it got me." Muffy's voice rose. "You should be ashamed of yourself, leaving me to the likes of them." Bright, razor sharp eyes pierced him. The smoke nearly curled from her lips as my aunt, the dragon lady, threatened him. "So, I'll tell you what I'm gonna do. I'm gonna make you so sorry you'll wish you were never born. I'm gonna make you pay, you slimy son-of-a-bitch."

If Muffy were a witch, she'd have given Antonio the Mallorca Curse and pointed three fingers at him. He'd probably have shit his drawers, since most Italian Mafia men are superstitious to a fault. As it was, his features tightened, and his face paled.

This was the last thing he expected, I thought. Served him right that Muffy was on his ass. After all, he abandoned her in a time of need. Every rat for himself, and all that.

I saw Andre grinning in the corner, his shoulder leaning against the wall. It was an enjoyable moment for him and an embarrassment for me. Dang, I do hate when that happens. Not for one second did I acknowledge that he was watching or that I was embarrassed. I stuffed my head in the menu and tried for invisibility.

The invisibility thing wasn't happening today – no, not for a second. Uh-uh, not for me.

Mumbling that he was so sorry for any harm Muffy may have sustained, Antonio, the businessman, tried to move away from the table. Auntie reached out with blood red claw-tipped fingers and snatched his wrist up in a steel-trap grip.

Here we go, Act Two, I thought, and slid down in the seat. I knew better than to interfere.

"You think you can simply apologize to me, and that will make everything all right? You really believe that? Could you be that stupid? Let me tell you, Antonio, you are a complete asshole, and you will pay big time. Now get the hell out of my sight."

The other men with Antonio moved on when Auntie started her tirade. However, they kept an eye on developments when Auntie hoisted her handbag onto the table and started rummaging around in it. The room became quiet as a tomb.

Wide-eyed, I stared, and from of the corner of my eye I saw Andre straighten up and tense. Antonio, already gaunt in appearance, paled to paste white, and started to sweat. He stood cemented to the spot. I waited to see if Auntie would pull a .38 Special from her bag, and shoot him right there. *God help me.* I prayed.

Tipped sideways, her hand withdrew something from the designer bag. She turned it over. A cell phone filled the palm of her hand, and she dialed a number. Her other hand shooed Antonio away as though he were inconsequential, which I'm sure he was. The phone flipped closed as the bum walked away from us.

I heaved a sigh of relief.

"The line was busy," she stated and shrugged. "Order your lunch, Lavinia. I refuse to leave without lunch. The ravioli is splendid. Have some, it will do you good. You're looking a little peaked and in need of a good meal."

A good meal? That's what I needed? Good golly! What I needed was a psychiatrist, a savior, anybody please. My mind frayed around the edges. I damn near fainted from relief that Muffy *hadn't* shot the mobster in front of his cronies, half the Hill, and me. Cripes. How did I end up in these situations?

Andre hustled over and stood in front of us with a smile bursting at the seams. He glanced at Muffy and then at me. I got a wink and then he asked for our order. He didn't have a pad to write on, and I wondered if he was good enough that he could remember every order, of every person he waited on. Do they teach that in cop school? I don't teach it in my criminalistics classes.

We ordered pasta, salad, and wine. I figured I might get some of the food down my throat, barring any further outbursts or dramatics from my wayward aunt. I never should have agreed to lunch – but there hadn't been much choice. Maybe the wine would bring my blood pressure back to normal. If I were lucky enough, there wouldn't be a homicide while we were in this chic restaurant, either.

When Andre brought our lunch, I left the table and headed toward the Ladies' Room. Sure I'd be waylaid on my return, I dawdled a bit, hoping to avoid Antonio or his goons should they be waiting for me. I hung out in the spotless little room for a few moments longer than necessary, and then headed back to the table after peeking out the door.

Several tall potted palms with fanned fronds were clustered together near the end of the corridor. A hand reached out as I approached the plants. Someone hauled me into a small closet and closed the door. My first reaction was to reach up and touch someone rather hard with my fisted knuckles. I glanced up at the owner of the hand and realized it was Andre.

"Don't do it, Lavinia. I just need a word with you," he said under his breath, his hand enclosing my fist.

He grinned when I stepped closer and whispered, "What the hell are you doing here? Moonlighting?" *Dumb question, huh?*

"Not likely," he mumbled softly. "What would a nice girl like you be doing here?" The emerald green eyes held my gaze.

"My aunt insisted we come here for lunch. Why?"

We whispered as heavy feet sounded on the carpeted corridor nearby. Andre put his finger to my lips, reached out, and shut the light off. Nervous doesn't come close to what I felt. The day continued to worsen instead of getting better. At least it wasn't mundane.

I heard a man turn the corner and utter Italian words to someone with him. The man grunted an answer. Their voices faded and Andre turned the light back on. I glared at him for a second. *What the hell was going on?*

"Have your lunch and get the hell out of here. The FBI has the place staked out. We're waiting for one false move, and its goodbye to these thugs. Don't get involved with these people, Lavinia," he whispered.

"Okay, okay. I'll get Auntie out of here right after lunch. I promise." Quickly, moving away from him and the cramped space, I left the confines of the closet. At the end of the corridor, I scooted toward the dining room.

"Is everything all right, dear? You look a bit upset," Auntie remarked when I slid into the seat.

"Everything is fine, Auntie. Let's just eat and head home. I've got so much to do." Anything was better than sitting amongst the mob, waiting for a hit. My imagination once again moved like a freight train. I was hard pressed to stop it.

Each time Andre Messino ushered someone into the room, I waited for an incident to take place, an incident where my aunt would haul off and slug someone. Instead, she merely nodded as mobsters passed our table to join Antonio.

My fear continued to climb as fast as my curiosity. What did these gangsters talk about while eating plates of pasta? Did they compare notes on upcoming slayings? Or was their conversation more on the humdrum side where they talked about their prostate problems. None of them were young – or virile, for that matter. At least I didn't see them as virile.

We finished lunch, drained our coffee, and fled from Federal Hill. I waved to the invisible FBI folks as we left the restaurant. Either they were holed up in an apartment across the street or in a van nearby. It didn't matter, since I would never come back to Da Ravioli again, and didn't want to cause anyone grief. FBI agents aren't always the friendliest of folks, and they have absolutely no sense of humor in these instances.

Auntie dropped me off at my parents' house, at my request. A black Yukon SUV, with license plate HIRLLR, sat in the driveway. *Why was Aaron here?* I strode up the driveway and quietly entered the house.

The kitchen, empty and silent, held no signs of the occupants whatsoever. Voices issued from the living room, though, and I sidled up near the door to listen. I know it's rude and one never hears well of oneself in an eavesdropping situation, but my curiosity got the better of me. If Aaron had the nerve to interrogate my mother, I wanted to know what it concerned.

"So you see, Lavinia has worked hard to become successful. Her brother did, too, though my husband made things easier for him," Mom said.

"I see. Does Vinnie have any issues with this DeGreico character?"

"He did give her a terrible time, but I think that's behind them now."

Bless her soul, my mother thinks well of everyone. She hesitated to say anything bad. Unless it was at the umpire at my brother's baseball games in high school, that is. I stood silent and waited.

Aaron's deep voice continued, "It's a shame Vinnie endured such torment from him. She's a lovely and high-spirited woman."

"She is. You know, when Tony haunted her, Lavinia never uttered a sound to us about it. It wasn't until her apartment was set on fire that we found out. Gino was beside himself. He wanted to set the young man straight, but Lavinia would have none of it. She told him to let the law handle things."

"How did Mr. Esposito intend to accomplish that, Mrs. Esposito?" Aaron asked.

I decided now was the time for my entrance. I stepped through the door and said, "Hey, you two. What's going on?" The wide smile pasted on my lips assured everyone that things were fine. However, things were far from it. Aaron was here using my mother to gather information, and I didn't like it – especially that last question.

"Hi, Lavinia, what are you doing here?" My mother glanced at her watch and stood up. "Oh gosh, I'm sorry to say it, but I'm going to be late if I don't leave in a few minutes." She glanced at Aaron and me.

Aaron's gaze rested on me as I leaned against the door casing, hand on my hip. He smiled and rose from the armchair in greeting. His lips brushed my cheek.

"Auntie dropped me off, and I thought you could give me a ride home," I said to my mother. "It's a good thing Aaron is here since you're going out, isn't it?" I smiled.

"Sure is, dear. Sorry, I have a function at the 'elderly housing' complex shortly and can't give you a ride. Your father is out with his Knights of Columbus friends arranging some type of fund-raiser. Since you and Aaron live in the same building, I'm sure he can drive you home." Her glance leveled on Aaron and she smiled. "Can't you?"

"Certainly, Mrs. Esposito, I'll be happy to take Vinnie home," he said.

Did he realize I overheard the conversation? If he did, he showed no sign of it. Did he care? I figured those would be two of the questions I'd ask, among others, on the ride home.

I turned to him once again and nodded. "Thanks, I appreciate the lift. I'll meet you outside. I need to speak to my mother – alone."

Dark eyes peered at me for a moment before he nodded. His long stride took him through the house, and outside. When he was out of earshot, I leaned toward my mother. I whispered to her about court and the actions of my aunt at the restaurant. She chuckled when I told her how Antonio blanched and sweated when Auntie reached inside her bag.

She whispered back, "That's an old trick she used when we were young. One time she pulled out an apple and threw it at Johnny Mulroney. Then she started carrying a loaded squirt gun. When she got a hard time from anyone, they got soaked. It earned her a reputation." She glanced around and then back at me. "Why are we whispering, dear?"

"I don't need my neighbor knowing everything about our family, Mom. So watch what you tell him in the future, okay?"

"All right, dear – if you say so. We were just talking about Tony DeGreico and your job, things like that. Aaron is a personable and charming man."

I recognized that wishful look on her face again and knew it was time to flee. I said my goodbyes and left the house.

Outside Aaron casually leaned against the truck, long legs in fitted jeans stretched out before him. A burgundy sweatshirt fit his muscled upper torso like it was made especially for him. He was a handsome hunk, but also an FBI agent on the hunt. My anger must have shown, since Aaron was quick to explain his visit to my mother.

"I happened to be in the neighborhood and thought I'd stop in to see your mother," he said all innocent-like, when we climbed into the truck.

"I'm sure," I answered with sarcasm. "This street is far out of anyone's way. You just happened to fall into the neighborhood, right? That's your story? You're sticking to that, are you?" My voice sounded testy even to me. So far, I had a trying day, my head ached, and his visit to my parents' house hadn't made things any easier.

"Why are you so upset, Vinnie? Has something happened?"

Dark eyebrows rose in concern as we left the neighborhood and started the drive toward Scituate.

"What happened?" I faced him with a look of incredibility on my face. "You went to visit my mother, probably knowing full well that my father was out. You worked her for information about me and our family. Why is that, Aaron?"

"It isn't what you think," he began.

"How the hell do you know what I think? Do you ask? No, you don't. You just start digging around in places you have no business going. In the future, if you want to know something about my family, or me, you damned well better ask me instead of my mother. Got that?" I guess my temper was on the rise, since my voice echoed off the truck windows.

We reached the Scituate Reservoir land, not far from the village. Aaron pulled the Yukon over to the side of the road. He cut the engine and leaned against the side window, his gaze wandering over my face. The silence between us lengthened while I glared at him.

"I can see it's been a tough day, Vin. I'm sorry if you're offended that I went to see your mother. This fire incident concerns me greatly, and I'm trying to figure out who's behind it. The car crash was bad enough, but with the fire added to it, well, it seems more than coincidental. That's all, nothing more."

"Fine. Just remember in the future, if you want any information, ask me and not my mother. Got that?"

"Yeah, I got it. Loud and clear." His eyes took on a twinkle.

I stared.

"Does this mean I can't go to dinner there anymore?" A chuckle followed the question.

It was too hard for me to stay angry, so I sat back and smiled. I'd suffered another overreaction attack, which had become a bad habit. *Maybe I'd read him wrong once again and didn't that make me feel a tad foolish?* Uh, huh.

"I guess you can go to dinner. Just don't go without me, that's all. Okay?"

"Sure thing." He chuckled, started the truck, and took me home.

Chapter 14

Aaron parked on the street in front of the house, and we walked back toward the garage. The rancid smell of charred wood filtered through the breeze from the back corner of the building, which lay in ruins. What the fire hadn't destroyed, the firefighters had. I walked around the old structure, inside and out, taking stock of the damage.

When I stepped outside, Aaron rounded the other corner. He peered into the garage and shook his head. We turned and wandered toward the deck on the back of the house. The poor evergreen was fried to a crisp, the branches charred. The ground at the base lay covered with ashes from the burned greenery.

"I guess that evergreen tree is done for." I said on a light note. I wasn't really in a lighthearted mood, mind you.

"I'd say so. The garage can be repaired though," Aaron offered. "I know a guy who does this sort of thing for a reasonable price, if you're interested."

"Sure, just give me his name, and I'll call him. Have you spoken to the fire marshal?"

"Not yet. Maybe Marcus has a preliminary report. By the way, did you want to pick up your new car? I totally forgot about it."

With a grin, I glanced at the handsome brute. "I did. It's been a long and nerve-wracking day, but I do want to pick it up. Can I hitch a ride?"

"Sure thing, ma'am." His eyebrows waggled while his smile brought a wide grin to my face.

"Sorry I lost my temper earlier. I get overprotective of my family, especially after last summer."

A muscular arm swung over my shoulder as he leaned in close and kissed my brow.

"No problem, beautiful. I understand."

This was a term he'd never used before and it brought a smile to my face. While Marcus was forthright with his feelings and overtures, Aaron used a more conservative approach. There was no doubt in my mind that he found me attractive and wanted a relationship. However, Marcus won my heart, hands down.

The French door slid sideways after I unlocked it, and I turned to Aaron. "Give me a few minutes and I'll be ready to pick up the car. I just need to get some paperwork and my checkbook."

"Sure, I'll check my messages and be right down. Okay?"

With a nod, I sauntered into my office and shuffled through a load of paperwork from the car dealership. My cell phone jingled when I turned to leave. The number displayed was Richmond's, and I answered on the second jingle.

"What's up, Marcus?" I asked.

"I got the report from the fire marshal and also from the body shop where your Taurus was taken. Do you have a minute?"

"Yeah, are you coming by, or do you want to give me the bad news over the phone?" My heart thumped against my ribs as my stomach churned.

"I'll be by in a few minutes. I'm leaving headquarters now."

"Okay, I'll wait for you," I said with dread, and disconnected the call.

The call ruffled my feathers. I started to tremble and sat down abruptly in the leather office chair. Smoothing my hair away from my face, I cupped my chin in my palm, staring out the window.

The grey SUV pulled to the curb, and Marcus stepped from it. I watched him swagger toward the house and went to let him in. He was a hot babe in that uniform. My heart fluttered at the sight of his craggy features and well built, toned body.

Marcus stepped into the foyer and then the apartment. Turning, he took me into his arms, firm lips covering mine in a long kiss. He took my breath away and I warmed at his touch.

Could life get any better than this? I wondered. *Well, yes. You could fall for someone other than a cop.* I ignored my inner voice and enjoyed the kisses Marcus rained over my face and lips.

"The news must be bad if you're priming me this way," I uttered, my blood pressure on the rise.

"I've been waiting for this all day. The news has nothing to do with it." He leaned back with a wolfish smile.

"Even though this is wonderful," I said, "tell me the news. I can't stand waiting."

"Ah, yes, that impetuous and curious nature." He walked toward the sofa and sat down. He patted the seat next to him and waited for me to sit.

Good Lord, I thought, it must be horrible news. Nervous, I scrunched up on the end of the sofa, turned to face him, and folded my legs underneath me. Fidgeting was a dead giveaway and I wanted Marcus to think I was calm, so I folded my hands in my lap.

"So, tell me. I can't stand the suspense."

"The fire was set. Burnt matches were found near the base of the tree. It appears that the garage caught on fire after the tree was set aflame. The person responsible is being sought. That's all I can tell you about that."

Questions spread across my mind like wildfire. No pun intended. If he wouldn't tell me anything else, it meant there was a suspect or suspects. Huh?

"Okay, now what about the car?" I asked.

"Gary, at the garage, called to say they'd given the wreck a once over. The car was damaged underneath from the landing. However, the rear bumper and fender were scraped, and black paint left behind." His eyes never left my face. "Since your car was red, chances are we may be able to find the vehicle that pushed you off the road. It's a slim possibility, mind you, since the other vehicle may not have sustained enough damage to report to a body shop."

"That's better news than I anticipated, Marcus. I was nervous that you were going to deliver the worst news I could imagine." I sighed and leaned back against the pillow on the end of the sofa.

Eyebrows hiked and questioning eyes watched me. He asked, "What kind of bad news, Vin?"

"I can't think of what it would be, but I dreaded whatever it was. Maybe it's just wrinkled nerves on my part. I don't know."

A smirk tickled his lips, and I smiled. Ridiculous as it seemed, I was pleased at the news. My garage lay in ruin, my car was totaled, and I felt pleased. *Imagine.*

The back door opened with a holler of greeting from Aaron.

"Are you ready, beautiful?" he called.

"You got a date, *beautiful*?" Richmond's eyes widened as his smirk vanished.

I stared at him for a moment. Was that jealousy I saw? *Nah, must be my imagination.* Couldn't be signs of proprietorship, could it? *Nah.*

"Not a date, exactly," I began.

"Oh? Well, *beautiful,* why don't you tell me exactly what it is?" His emphasis on the word told the whole story.

Ah, he was jealous, and 'Was I just a bit pleased at that,' you ask? 'Indeed,' I answer.

"I'm hitching a ride with Aaron to get my new car. Lola's away today, remember?" I grinned with pleasure. Marcus never said how much he cared, and I considered this reaction a good sign.

Aaron strode around the corner and stopped short. He took in my Cheshire Cat grin and Richmond's chagrin as he stepped into the room. The large frame settled against the door casing.

"Is everything all right?" he asked, and nodded at Marcus.

"It sure is," I said smugly.

"Good. Well, we should get going if we're to pick up your car." He checked his watch.

"Okay." As I stood, my muscles protested a bit, but not as bad as earlier in the day. My headache nearly disappeared. There was hope for me yet.

We trooped out the back door after I locked the front door. Suddenly my life didn't feel like such a pile of shit, and Marcus was the reason. A lighthearted sigh escaped me as I turned toward him.

A question shot across his face, and I grinned like a fool. Leaning toward the handsome brute, I laid a kiss on his lips, darting my tongue out for good measure. When I leaned back, I could see a smile forming and knew all was well once again. I guessed the jealousy part was over for Marcus.

* * * *

Aaron turned the truck eastward toward the car dealership. Ahead of us Marcus turned onto the highway, while we continued on. As we entered the car lot I stared up and down the rows of cars.

"Is your car among any of these?"

"No, it's probably out back," I said as we pulled up to the front door.

Aaron parked the Yukon and we went inside the dealership. I glanced around, looking for Mr. Snot Necktie, but I didn't see him right away. As I turned to Aaron a man approached us with a shark-like grin, and introduced himself.

"Hi, I'm the manager. Justin Scuzzi. You must be Ms. Esposito?"

Extending a hand to shake his, my glance took in the shiny suit and gleaming shoes. His shirt was crisp white and the tie pure silk. Ashen-colored skin accompanied the slicked-back brown hair on his egg-shaped head. I could smell *parfum du cigar* smoke on his clothing, even though I wasn't standing close to him. Ugh.

"Yes, that would be me. I've come to collect my new car." The prospect of owning this classy new vehicle excited me, even though I had liked my Taurus a great deal.

"Sure thing. Come this way and we can get the remaining paperwork out of the way," he said.

I turned to walk alongside him, and then glanced back at Aaron.

"You needn't wait. I can manage from here. Thanks for everything."

"That's all right. I'll hang around until you take possession of the car." His gaze roved around the room before landing on me again.

The hair on the back of my neck stood at attention as I glanced around quickly, taking his cue. *Was anything wrong? Did I miss something?* The showroom was quiet, as far as I could tell. Maybe Aaron thought I couldn't stay out of trouble for a moment. I shrugged and nodded at him.

"Okay, we'll only be a minute then." I smiled and strode after Scuzzi.

With the check and paperwork signed, and handed over to Scuzzi, I accepted the car keys along with the registration papers. Curious as to what happened to the regular salesman I dealt with, I turned to Scuzzi with the question on my lips.

Before I could open my mouth he smiled and said, "Mr. Beducci has the day off. That is what you are curious about? Am I right?"

"Yes. He has been most helpful to me in both my purchases, and I wanted to thank him." Actually, I was just wondering where the man was.

"Well, I'll be sure to give him that message," Scuzzi said with a smile. He ushered me down the hallway and into the showroom where Aaron awaited my reappearance.

He stepped forward and grinned when I jingled the keys at him. Excitement coursed through me as we exited the glass doors toward the pale blue Altima. I proudly strode around the car with a grin the size of Montana on my lips.

Laughter rumbled after me as I sped around the car twice.

"Are you going to circle this car all day, or drive it home?"

I giggled, opened the driver's door, and slid behind the wheel. I slid the key in the ignition. The new car smell enveloped me like a fur coat. *Wow, what a smell.*

A rap on the window reminded me that Aaron stood outside looking in. I glanced at the dashboard, found the window button and pressed it. The window slid downward in silence.

"What?" I asked.

"I'm headed into the city for a bit. Are you going straight

home?"

"Yeah, I have some work to do for class tomorrow. I need to report to the insurance company as well."

"All right. Go straight home. No stops and no shenanigans, understand?"

"Yeah, yeah," I said.

"Promise me."

"All right, then." I promised, but my toes were crossed the whole time.

Reaching into his pocket, Aaron handed me a small strip of paper. The name of a builder was printed in his bold script. I scanned the phone number and realized the guy lived in Scituate.

"I'll call this number when I get home. Thanks," I said.

The car purred when I turned the key further. After fastening my seatbelt, I headed from the parking lot. The smooth ride convinced me that everything in my life would turn around. Why I was that naïve, I can't say. Maybe it had something to do with the new car smell.

The Altima scooted along and I reached the house in no time at all. Parked at the back door, I wandered around the garage once again in search of the cat, Evergreen. He'd slipped my mind until I stared at the woebegone evergreen trees at the edge of the property.

Several ragged trees needed replacing, but the one at the side of the garage was toasted to a crisp. I scuffed the dirt with my toe and stared around at the landscape. No sign of the cat or anything else for that matter. No birds sang and no caterwauling from the ragged beast.

On a sigh, I returned to the house and rummaged through the fridge for a few scraps of food. Tossing them onto a paper plate, I thrust it outside the back door and waited in hopes it would draw the cat out of his lair – a lair that used to include the garage.

When Evergreen didn't show up right away, I left the French doors and headed into the office. Messages from the university, and also from my mother waited for me. I sat at the desk and fiddled with a pencil, lost in thought as I listened to them.

Chapter 15

The school wanted to know if I would carry two more classes next week. My mother's message was urgent, she said. She needed a return call right away. Good God, now what? I rolled my eyes and heaved a sigh. I only left her a while ago.

The slip of paper holding the builder's number lay on the desk in front of me. I called, left a message, and hung up. Dialing the number for the university, I spoke with Margy Gluck, Secretary of All and Everything. She asked if I was well enough to teach an added class or two. I assured her that things were fine but that I couldn't manage the other classes. Margy said she'd take care of things. I thanked her and ended the call.

Sliding away from the desk, I rose and checked the plate of food on the deck. It was empty, but no there was sign of Evergreen. I turned away and made a pot of coffee before returning to the office.

It doesn't take a rocket scientist to figure out that my procrastination level was at an all-time high. I'd stood and waited for the pot to finish perking. I folded paper napkins, threw a load of laundry in the washer, and checked the deck once again – for Evergreen.

With a cup of steaming brew in hand, I finally dialed my mother's number. She answered on the first ring. Dang, I thought. She must have been next to the phone awaiting my call.

"Hey, Mom, what's up?"

"Dear, I just returned from the seniors' center. You'll never guess who I ran into." From the conspiratorial sound of her voice, I could only imagine it was someone I'd rather not know about.

"Who was it?" Reluctant as I was to ask the question, curiosity factored in.

"Antonio, the businessman. That's who. What do you think about that?"

"Get outta here," I said in a state of disbelief. "What the heck was he doing there?"

"He wasn't visiting anyone, I know that much. He came out of the business office as Nonni and I left the arts and crafts room. A thug was with him. Do you think they were shaking someone down?"

"Mom, it's not likely. Who would they shake down at a seniors' center? Besides, Antonio isn't a shakedown artist. He's got bigger business to handle."

"What kind of business, Lavinia?"

"I'm not sure, Mom," I lied. I wanted to spare my mother the worry of my aunt's involvement with a true-to-life badass gangster. She knew he was a businessman for the mob, but she didn't know the rest. Far be it from me to enlighten my mother at this juncture.

"Oh, well, I thought I should tell you in case one of your law enforcement friends might be interested. I'll call you if I run into him again. What do you think he was doing there, Lavinia?"

"I have no idea, Mom. If I hear anything, I'll let you know." *Yeah, like that was gonna happen.* "Are you sure he wasn't there to visit someone?"

"I really don't think so, though you never can tell. Maybe you're right and it was innocent. Nonni wasn't impressed with him in the least."

Right, innocent. The man wasn't born innocent, I thought. He'd always been a mob guy and was probably born with that tattooed across his forearm. You know, something like, 'Antonio, the Mob Businessman' or its equivalent. So far as my grandmother being impressed, well, she was kinda like my dad in that area. He wasn't an easy man to impress either.

With a goodbye, my mother rang off. I went in search of the mail. Across the street, I entered the post office. My box was full of junk mail, a few bills, and a small envelope addressed to me, Vinnie Esposito. Not Lavinia.

I tossed the junk mail into the recycle bin on my way out the door. With the bills tucked under my arm, I tore open the Vinnie envelope. My hands shook a bit since there was no return address and the postmark said Providence. This meant it could have been mailed from anywhere in the state.

Renoir's artwork covered the shiny surface of the card. I flipped it open and scanned the bottom of the page for a signature. There wasn't one. Dammit. My eyes scrolled up to the top of the card and I read the brief message inside.

The pounding of my heart reverberated in my ears as I read the words. The note said I was to consider myself lucky to have lived through the accident. It stated that I might not be so fortunate the next time, and wouldn't that be too bad. The note ended at the bottom of the page with the words *Best wishes that you may rest in peace.* That was all there was to the note.

The words were cut from a magazine and pasted on. No handwriting to analyze, and probably no fingerprints either. My students were currently working on fingerprinting in class. The note would make a great project for one of the superior detectives in the class. I knew which one I'd give it to, since he had the reputation of keeping his mouth shut. Not like that blabbermouth who lived upstairs from me. Boy, for an FBI agent, he sure did shoot his mouth off to my family, and Marcus, a lot.

I crossed the street and entered the house. Flinging the mail onto the kitchen counter, I marched straight to the French doors and opened them. I slouched down on a deck chair, wrapped my sweater tighter around my torso, and rested my head against the cushion.

A chilling breeze swept past and an ungodly caterwauling began. I glanced around for the origin of the noise and saw Evergreen slink toward the deck. His fur matted, he appeared as unkempt as ever. I had wondered if he escaped the garage unhurt by the fire, and he had.

The heavyweight animal mounted the three steps to the deck

and wandered toward me. He never missed a beat as leaves swirled around and crossed the surface. Scraggy-edged ears pricked forward at the rustling sounds of crisp, dead foliage, but he kept moving. Evergreen arrived at my chair and sat back on wide haunches. The pouched cheeks of his scarred, but still handsome face, sat below green eyes that never left my own.

Tentatively, I reached out to the beast and played my fingers across his head. No growl this time. The purr sounded like a jet engine readying for takeoff. I was sure this cat was part mountain lion. A paw reached up and tapped my hand as his pink sandpaper tongue scraped across my wrist. I'd made a friend. Mainly because I fed him, I thought with a smile.

The thing about animals is that they don't whine about life, yell at you, complain about what you have or haven't done, and they don't tell you to mind your own business. Animals just plain accept you for what you are. Either they like you, or they don't – nothing in between.

My newfound friend hissed when footsteps crunched over the stone covered driveway. Green eyes narrowed and ragged ears flattened against his head. Hair bristled along Evergreen's back, and he hunched lower before disappearing underneath the deck in a flash. Apparently, I had company.

A stranger walked along the yard and around the garage. He limped to the right as he stepped past the building. His jeans, as work worn as the boots he wore, showed signs of better days. *Ahh, this must be the builder.* No fancy shirt and tie, no architectural renderings. Nope, this guy was a worker. He got his hands dirty and probably enjoyed every moment of it.

He rounded the garage and stopped short when his eyes lit upon me. I remained still while he grinned and approached me. The blue eyes were familiar, and the body husky and rugged. The limp was less pronounced than before, and I wondered what caused it. *There's that curiosity thing again.*

"Hi, you must be the owner of this property?" he said with a twinkle in his gorgeous blues. He removed his boot while he sat on the step and shook a stone out onto the ground. That took care of the limp question, I thought.

Familiarity gave way to recognition. This was the firefighter who'd retrieved my sorry ass from the car accident. Small world, huh? No. Small state.

"Yes, I'm Vinnie Esposito. Aren't you the guy who hauled me from a car accident the other day?"

"That would be me, Jesse Crane." Those rich blue eyes rested on me as he held out a hand to shake mine. "I'm only part-time with the fire company. I build and restore the rest of the time. You left a message about this garage?"

Rising from the lounge, I shook his hand. A pale, thin scar crossed his chin. Funny I hadn't noticed it the other day. Light brown hair topped the high forehead and rounded face. He wasn't too hard on the eyes, I thought.

I stepped toward the damaged building with him in tow. Checking inside and out, he asked questions about the age of the structure and what my insurance would cover. A typical Rhode Islander, he wanted to know what was in it for him, and if he'd get paid. I smirked when he wasn't looking and assured him the insurance would cover the repairs.

A grin covered Jesse's face as he turned toward me. "You do realize the damage is repairable? This shouldn't take but a couple days to put right."

"That would be great. It's an eyesore and I'd like it completed as soon as possible. Could you show me a sample of work you've already done?"

His eyebrows gathered together as surprise filtered across Crane's face. I guess nobody requested that before. I just wanted to make sure he wasn't a hacker, though it was unlikely Aaron would recommend one. I motioned for him to follow me.

We ambled into the house and I pulled the insurance card from my wallet. I handed it to him and said, "Call this number. Mr. Palloni will give you the particulars of my coverage."

"Great. If you want to take a ride, I can show you a job I finished not too long ago," Crane offered.

Now call me stupid, but I took this guy on trust, even if

Evergreen didn't. He'd rescued me from the brink of death, and for that I would be forever grateful. Besides, I knew self-defense techniques. Marcus and Aaron were also perks in my life, and this man was aware of them.

The door locked behind us as we left the house and headed toward the street. A dark green pickup truck loaded with roofing material, tools, and a generator hugged the curb out front. We climbed aboard and headed west. I had no idea where this man was about to take me.

The questions Jesse asked mostly concerned the garage and the house. He got around to Aaron and I wondered if he realized that Aaron was FBI. The answer to my curious mind soon became known.

"Aaron Grant recommended me, huh?" he asked.

"Yes, he said you're reasonably priced and have a good reputation. How do you know Aaron?" I just had to know.

"He was engaged to my friend's distant cousin, Lou Anne, for a short time. They met at the Gaming Commission."

I often wondered if there were other women in Aaron's life. He never brought anyone to the apartment, and it always seemed like he was working. Cops, all types of cops, are driven by their jobs. My curiosity hiked to an all-time new level. "Oh. Still engaged, are they?"

"No, they aren't." He smirked and glanced at me. "He lives upstairs from you, huh?"

"Indeed, he does."

"Hmmph. Well, the engagement was made in hell and Lou Anne...." He hesitated. "Well, never mind about Lou Anne. Just suffice it to say, you won't be bothered by her, in case you're wondering."

"Oh. We're not romantically involved or anything. He's just a tenant and friend. That's all." Why I clarified that I couldn't imagine, but I needed to do so.

We'd nearly passed through the town of Foster by this time. It's a 'country bumpkin' type town with a post office but nothing much to offer, unless peace and quiet were of utmost importance.

Former news anchorman, Tom Brokaw, once called it a bedroom community. I guess he was right.

There were no cinemas, stores, or shopping malls, and the town liked it that way. Every house sat on at least five to six acres of land and the town liked that, too. No neighbors packed on top of one another here. A tree farm every now and then with agriculture at its finest. The town even touted their very own nudist colony along with a country club for golfers. Not necessarily nude golfers though.

The truck turned toward an area I rarely frequented, and thoughts of DeGreico popped up. A silent alarm ran along my nerves as we wheeled down the narrow road. What if I ran into him? He lived down this road somewhere, I was certain of it. Crane hung a right hand turn, and we swung through the gate of The Valley Horse Farm.

Corrals, bordered by high white fencing, lined the dirt driveway as we rolled toward the horse barn. Gorgeous roans, a palomino, and a Canadian Chunk roamed the paddocks. A red barn, doors wide open, squatted toward the left while an oversized, white ranch house sat toward the right.

The truck slowed, and stopped near the barn, and we alighted. Hesitant, I glanced around the grounds, peered at the horses, on the lookout for anyone familiar. I wasn't surprised when DeGreico sauntered forward. Shit, this would be my luck – so much for life turning around.

Tony didn't say anything to me, just wore a snarky grin on his face. Jerk, I thought. He shook hands with Crane, who introduced himself, and asked if we could look at the apartment built onto the barn. I wanted to run away as fast as I could, but I was stuck in a hard spot. Apparently Crane had no idea of the history between Tony and me.

"Sure, go ahead in. I have to round up the horses for feeding. Just take your time and have a look." He was friendly, but I wasn't fooled for a second when those beady eyes scrolled over me.

Once again, I was at a disadvantage. I wouldn't run away nor would I admit that I knew this swine. If Jesse knew it, that was another issue, but I didn't think he did.

"Are you ready?" he asked.

I was so lost in thought, that Jesse was several feet away before he realized I wasn't with him.

"Sure thing," I said and hustled along beside him.

After we entered the neat quarters, he kept up a rolling dialogue about the job and how long it had taken. I glanced around at the, neat-as-a-pin dwelling that put my housekeeping efforts to shame. I figured DeGreico must have a maid.

Glancing inside closets and cupboards, I looked for notepaper. Opening drawers and cabinets as though buying the property – not illegally searching it – I turned to find Jesse staring. I gave him the most beguiling smile I could manage and Jesse responded as most guys do.

Before we finished the tour, I made note of the fact there wasn't any notepaper hanging around. Nothing similar to what I received in the mail anyway. I nodded as Jesse showed me the dovetail work he'd included in the cabinets and molding. I made what I hoped were the right responses.

"The work you put into this place is wonderful. I won't need this detail in the garage, but you definitely have the job. By the way, do you know the guy who lives here?" Even though he introduced himself, I wanted to double check.

"No, this work was completed before anyone moved in. I've never met him before. Why?"

"Just wondering, is all. When can you start the garage?"

"As soon as I speak to your insurance agent, the building inspector, and the fire marshal we'll get started. Does that work for you?"

"Yes, that will be fine," I said.

DeGreico strode through the door as we readied to leave. He glanced at me and smirked again. I gave him a look that said a lot but I never uttered a sound. He shook hands with Jesse before we left.

The trip home was quick, and I couldn't wait to get there. Jesse asked a few more questions about the garage and left me at the doorstep, with a salute. My mind rolled over the information I'd gleaned from him, about Aaron, while I waved goodbye.

The search of DeGreico's residence was a total disappointment, but then I hadn't expected to find anything after I saw how neat the place was. His smirky attitude left me wondering about the letter. Odds were that he'd written it to make me uncomfortable. Well, he'd managed that.

Aaron's black Yukon sat parked next to my Altima in the driveway. Since the yellow Volkswagen was missing, I guessed Lola's cousin reclaimed it. My thoughts turned to Lou Anne and Aaron. What happened to Lou Anne? Was she still around? Why hadn't the engagement worked? Aaron was a secretive man. Questions swirled around my head. I just had to know, but I had no intention of asking.

Didn't someone say that the road to hell was paved with good intentions?

Chapter 16

The day was waning as I backed the car from the driveway and drove toward Cranston. Unwilling to go into the house, on the chance that I'd run into Aaron, I buckled up and hit the road. My mother would have dinner on – probably roast beef or spaghetti. Either way, I was ravenous and would be welcomed for a meal with the family.

I hit speed dial on my cell phone and told my mother that I was coming for dinner. It was always acceptable. I flipped the phone closed and scooted over the back roads. The car handled like a dream. I sped toward my parents' house, elated to have a decent car once again.

At the intersection of my parents' street, my phone jingled its lofty tune. The number displayed belonged to Marcus. I wondered if he were checking on my whereabouts. Unwilling to listen to his nagging, I ignored the call and let it go to voice mail.

The house smelled of roast veggies and beef done to perfection. My father slid the salad bowl onto the table with a glance at me. My mother set the serving platter, loaded with succulent fare, between the four place settings. Not just for the three of us. I should have known better.

A glass of wine in hand, I settled at the table with my parents. Nonni stepped through the living room door and I rose to kiss her cheek in greeting. Her eyes glistened with pleasure; at least I hoped it was pleasure, when I gave her a peck on the cheek. I hadn't expected Nonni to be the fourth diner, but I was happy about it. A break from Marcus and Aaron would be a change.

"Ahh, *bella mia*, how hava you been?" Nonni's heavy Italian accent was ever present. Surprising, since she'd lived in America for a billion years. At least she'd lived here before my mother came into the world. The fact that Italian was the only language spoken in their household when Mom grew up may be the reason for Nonni's accent. Gio and I learned Italian at an early age.

"*Bene, molto bene,* I'm good, Nonni. You look as wonderful as ever. Mom says you've been at the seniors' center, huh? Checking out the guys again?" Laughter followed my question, and Nonni's eyes crinkled with humor. Thank God for small miracles. She'd have smacked me with a wooden spoon if she were offended.

"Not me. I'ma no wanta any old men. I hear you gotta gooda man now, eh?"

Unsure to which man she referred, I just nodded and gulped my wine. My eyes slid to my mother with a silent plea for help.

She rose to the occasion and motioned for us all to hold our plates up while my father served layers of thin-sliced, rare roast beef. I spooned veggies onto my plate. My mother filled hers with salad and waited for my father to serve Nonni and then her.

Mom's eyes moved toward the door and a pleased smile slid over her features. My glance followed hers and widened when Marcus knocked before entering. *Dang, no break for me, I guess.* My mother stood and placed another setting at the table in record time. God forbid anyone should starve. I grinned at Marcus, though I'd hoped to have a private meal with my family.

A slow smile spread across Richmond's face as he glanced around the table. His eyes settled on my grandmother and he removed his campaign hat while I made the introduction.

"Nonni, this is Marcus Richmond. He is a very good friend of mine. Marcus, this is my Grandmother Ciano."

She inclined her head while her dark eyes took him in, all of him at once. "You may calla me Nonni," she said and turned a tiny smile of approval to me.

Dad scowled at me after he greeted Marcus with the usual gruff welcome. An eyebrow arched, but I didn't utter a sound to my father. It would only lead to a head-butting incident. I should have figured I couldn't get away with the silence thing.

"Lavinia, is everything all right?" he asked with dark-eyed suspicion.

"Yes, Dad, everything is great. I picked up my new car today. It's parked in the yard. Why do you ask?"

"You didn't mention Richmond was coming to dinner, is all. Everything good with you, Marcus?" my father asked.

A grin split Marcus's face as he answered the query. He reassured my father that all was well and that he'd been in the neighborhood and saw my car. It seemed like everyone was in my family's neighborhood lately.

My father grunted and resumed his dinner. Nonni mumbled to him in Italian and he mumbled back. It was difficult following everything since they mumbled so. I assumed Nonni gave my father an attitude adjustment because he soon became more cordial.

Awhile later, we all sat back, stuffed to the gills with excellent food, and I waited to hear what Marcus wanted. It didn't take long for him to speak up. My Italian manners must be rubbing off on him.

"I called your cell phone, but you didn't pick up."

"Did you? Well, maybe you left a voice mail?"

He knew I sidestepped, and a thick eyebrow hitched upward as a new gleam entered his eyes.

"Why, yes, I did. You should check it later." The smile was back in place. "Where did you get off to this afternoon?"

Okay, I know I promised Aaron I'd go straight home, and I did. Just because I didn't stay there shouldn't matter. I have a life and won't be managed by anyone, especially two controlling, egotistical men.

"I went to Foster to look at a building," I said.

My mother stared at me for a moment. "Dear, are you planning to buy a building?"

"No, I wanted to see some construction a local contractor had done. The garage needs repair, and I want a reputable builder to do it." I made no mention of the fire and hoped no one

[135]

else would either. *Fat chance of that happening.*

Hazel green eyes gleamed at me, and I knew that Marcus wouldn't let me off that easily for breaking my promise. My mother took the information for what it was. As for my father, well, he's a different story. No matter what – I knew I wouldn't get off the hook.

Dad's dark brown eyes stared at me. "Does anyone know who set fire to your garage? It was on the news. I'm surprised you didn't call and tell us."

Dang, I was in for it now.

"It wasn't bad. The investigating officers have everything under control. It was undoubtedly just an accident. I didn't want to worry you."

"An accident? How could someone 'torching your garage' be an accident, Lavinia? Your life seems more accident prone than usual lately. Have you been sticking your nose where it doesn't belong?" Dad's voice turned loud.

Marcus leaned back in the chair as my mother removed his dinner plate and replaced it with coffee and apple crisp. If I wasn't mistaken, his expression showed he enjoyed my father's interrogation. *What had I done to deserve this?*

Mom doled out dessert and coffee as I stammered, looking for an excuse. Nonni waited in silence, interested to see where the conversation was headed.

"N-no, I'm not sticking my nose in anyone's business, other than my own. I have enough on my plate to keep me busy. Tomorrow I teach at the university and over the weekend, I'm sure to have guests drop by. You do realize the art show is this weekend, and Scituate will be clogged with thousands of people?"

The fork stopped midway to my mother's mouth. She set it onto her dish and stared at me as though I'd developed two heads. What ran through her mind was on its way to her mouth. I could just tell.

"What will you feed these people, Lavinia? Your cupboards are always empty."

Lordy, was food the only thing she worried about? My

garage was torched, my aunt was a mafia moll, and I'd been run off the road. All this in a matter of days, and my mother was concerned over what I'd feed my drop-by guests. It was the last thing on my mind at the moment.

Grinning from ear to ear, Marcus dipped his face toward his plate, concentrating on the dessert. For a lawman who carried a gun – a big gun I might add – he was too much of a chicken shit to get involved with this conversation. *Men, what can ya do about them, huh?* His enjoyment was just a little annoying, though.

"Mom, I'm not worried about what I will feed them. The bakery will have plenty of goodies on trays, all ready to eat. I'm not getting nuts over this."

"If you say so. I just thought you might need something substantial."

"Nothing like that, honest. Just some snacky things. I'll stop by the bakery on my way home tomorrow."

I glanced around the table, took in Nonni's nod of approval, and realized my father still awaited enlightenment on the fire. Marcus was the one with the information. I was about to say so, when he spoke.

"The fire marshal has made his report," Marcus said to my father. He continued with an explanation of how it might have started and the ongoing investigation. That managed to satisfy my father. When he finished, Marcus rose and thanked my mother for the meal. His gorgeous smile lingered on Nonni, and she grinned back with a wink.

Okay, now we know where Muffy gets her wicked ways. My grandmother was about a hundred years old and still raking in the guys. Young guys. Gosh.

In minutes, with a bag of goodies in hand, I left for home. Marcus waited outside for me. I thought he'd gone, but he was lying in wait instead. *I really hate when I'm caught off guard.*

"You want to tell me what really happened this afternoon?" he said in a soft tone as he stepped next to me.

The bag of food landed on the front seat, and I swung around to face him at the window.

"Just what I said. I went with the builder to see his work. End of story." I admit to being defensive, but anger lay just beneath it. My inner struggle with it was a losing battle.

"When you say you'll be home, we expect you to be there. How can we protect you if you're all over the place?"

His arms were crossed again as he leaned against my new car. It meant he was going to be difficult. I recognized the symptoms. What the hell? Might as well get it over with, I thought.

"First off, I don't need a babysitter. Second, nobody was around to protect me, and third, I'm a big girl in case you hadn't noticed," I hissed.

"Oh yeah, I've noticed all right." A hand snuck around my waist and pulled me close. "You just can't stay out of any dilemma you come upon, though, and sometimes being a big girl is no help when that occurs."

My body temp hiked a couple notches at his touch. While a cold wind blew, my clothes clung to the hot skin beneath. Marcus had this effect on me way too often now.

He nuzzled my neck as his warm hands roamed my body. Good Lord, right in front of my mother's house, too. It was a good thing they thought I'd left. *Or had they?*

Edging away from him, I stepped aside and leaned one hand on the car and one on my hip. Staring at him in the dim light, I considered the fact that he wasn't as cool as he'd like me to think either. Unable to take advantage of him at the moment, I changed the subject.

"If I need assistance, I'll call you. You're on speed dial, and so is Aaron for that matter. By the way, I don't know if you're involved with this investigation he has going on, but I caught him questioning my mother. So, I'll tell you what I told him. If you want to know anything, ask me, not her. Okay?"

"Sure, but I'm not involved in his business at the moment." He glanced at his watch and then said, "I'd better get on the road."

"See you tomorrow?"

"You bet. Stay out of trouble and go straight home, please."

His grin belied his persistent, and all too obvious worry over my incapacity to deal with my own life.

Afterwards, I listened to the voice mail Richmond left on my cell phone. It occurred to me that I'd managed to make it through thirty-odd years of life without any state troopers or FBI agents running my affairs. While I was glad to have them around and the two men cared about my welfare, I could manage without their interference. Maybe they needed to realize that, too.

The car eased to a stop in front of the garage and after locking up, I went toward the house. Automatic lights flicked on as I crossed the driveway. My feet crunched over the stones, when the door suddenly swung open. Aaron stood on the bottom step of his staircase. I swallowed the sigh that was about to leave my body.

"I thought that was you. Where have you been?" he asked.

"At my mom's. I have leftovers. Want some?"

"No, I grabbed a bite to eat in the city," he said, trailing into the apartment behind me.

Filling the fridge with the leftovers, I kept thinking about the big girl thing. It was time these two guys were reminded of it. When I turned around, Aaron stood just inside the door where he leaned negligently against the doorframe. I couldn't read his expression and wondered what was coming next.

"Did you hear from Jesse Crane?" he asked.

"I did." The Lou Anne thing popped into my head and nearly out of my mouth. Instead, I swallowed and said, "He took me to see a place he'd worked on. Nice job. I gave him the repairs on the garage."

"You went out with him, alone?"

"Indeed. It turns out he was one of my rescuers from the car accident the other day. I also realized you wouldn't recommend a creep to me."

"Oh," he said.

I left him nowhere to go with the questions about Jesse, and wasn't that a relief?

"Did he tell you anything about his life?"

"No, though he did tell me that he appreciated your referral." I know, it wasn't exactly what Jesse asked about, but it came close enough without me bringing up Lou Anne.

"I figured he could use the work. He's a decent sort."

It was too good to resist, so I had to ask. "How do you know Jesse?"

"We have some of the same acquaintances."

With a nod, I stared at him and watched as he became distant. Yep, he knew that I knew of his relationship with the cousin. Aaron hedged against the doorjamb and glanced around.

"Have you had any other dead-air calls?"

"Not recently. Who do you have in common with Jesse? Work friends, or what?" I asked. Just call me nosy – I can't help it.

"We, um, well, I was kind of involved with his friend's relative."

The advantage was mine and I wanted to press it, but the phone rang and Aaron showed signs of relief. I lifted the phone off the cradle.

"Hello, Vinnie speaking."

Nothing. Absolutely nothing. The line went dead and I set the phone back in its resting place. Caller ID listed the number as unknown. Someone was annoying the shit out of me, and I would find out who it was if it killed me. Honest to God, this pissed me off.

"Who was that?" Aaron asked.

I shrugged. "Nobody, or a wrong number, I guess."

"That seems to happen a lot lately."

"Indeed," I said with another shrug. "It's late and I've got to get up for an early class in the morning. What are you up to tomorrow?"

"Just working, that's all. Look, be careful crossing the bridge tomorrow, will you?" A hint of a smile lay at the corners of his mouth. I nodded with a grin on my face.

"Will do. Thanks for the ride today."

He smiled full on and stepped toward me. Strong hands lightly encased my arms, and he leaned in for a kiss. I responded with the thought that Marcus was a better kisser. With that silent reminder, I stepped back and smiled.

"Good night, Aaron."

"Good night, beautiful. I'll be right upstairs if you need anything." His eyebrows waggled, and I chuckled.

Aaron left the apartment and headed upstairs. I locked up after him and headed to bed with thoughts of Lou Anne, Jesse, and Antonio the businessman rambling around my brain. Was there a connection between any of them?

My head swam. I was too tired to figure it out tonight. I'd run it by Marcus in the morning and see what he thought.

Chapter 17

The wind howled around the corners of the house, waking me with a start. Heavy rain lashed against the windows. Grey light filtered through a crack in the drapes and I realized I'd forgotten to set the alarm. Great, I'd just make it to the university on the other side of the state, providing some moron didn't cause a pile-up on the interstate. I prayed that if there were an accident, that moron wouldn't be me.

Black jeans and a red sweater topped the black high-heeled boots that I yanked on. I hustled out the door with the heavy book bag slung over my shoulder. Foregoing a shower, I'd done the bare essentials. My hair was held off my face by a scrunchy at the nape of my neck. I'd applied little to no make-up to a face that needed globs of it today.

The black denim jacket caught the worst of the rain as I raced from the door. Aaron's truck was already gone, and I made a beeline straight across the driveway to the Altima. Fumbling with the keys, I unlocked the door with the fob and scrambled inside. Rain pelted the windshield while I backed into the street and raced toward Providence.

Traffic was fairly light as I drove past the connector toward the interstate. Interstate 95 proved easier than I imagined, and I managed to cross the three lanes onto the eastbound expressway then headed toward the eastern side of Rhode Island. This was where the fun always began.

Rounding the curve, I settled into a steady flow along with all the other drivers who jockeyed for a spot in the traffic. We all had to be somewhere right away, and this was the fastest lane to get there. I moved into the middle lane and kept an eye in the rear view mirror, tracking anyone who looked as though they'd approach my fender. There would be no careening off the road today, if I could help it.

The slew of cars sped across the George Washington Bridge and roared toward the Massachusetts State Line. I veered off the highway, taking my exit toward the less-traveled road leading to the university.

I work at one of the most beautiful universities in New England. Cars and trucks rolled past as I slowed at the entrance to the campus. Relieved to have made it, I parked in the usual spot, to the left of the building where my class was held.

Rummaging through the book bag, I found the plastic bag stuffed with the note-card. Assured it was safe, I scooted through the raindrops, across the lot, and into the foyer of the building. Students filtered through corridors and conversations hummed like a swarm of honeybees.

The clock on the wall hit the hour, and I realized I had a few minutes to spare. Doing the Indy 500 worked to my advantage. Good thing Marcus wasn't around to clock my speed. I'd have been lugged to jail, no questions asked.

A hand touched my shoulder and I jumped. My fingers curled into a fist before I turned around. Checking myself, I tried to soften what must have been a nasty glare, with a smile.

The dark eyes of Dario Ramirez widened as he stepped back. Obviously unsure of his welcome, he still grinned at me and then walked alongside me as we headed to the classroom.

"Having a bad day, teach?" he uttered with a smirk.

An undercover cop, he always played the part. I figure he didn't know how not to. Some life, I thought.

"Yeah, I'm running a bit late. Looks like you are, too." I took in the coffee colored skin and black hair curling around Dario's collar.

"Nah, I just stepped outside for a smoke. You know how it is – rules and all that." He grinned and nodded toward another student as she passed us in the corridor.

I chuckled and said, "She's too young for you, so knock it off, Ramirez."

"That's the truth. These kids get younger and younger every year. Or maybe I'm getting older and older. What do you think, teach?"

"Either way, she's still too young for you. I'll bet she's just eighteen."

We'd entered the room. I slung the book bag onto the desk and then shook the rain from my jacket as I peeled it off. Damp was the day, and so were my clothes.

Ramirez grinned and took a seat. He slid down and stretched his legs out in an uninterested manner. I knew his routine was part of his act. He glanced around the room and then at me. Four other students entered behind us. I unloaded the sheets of paper for fingerprinting instruction.

Each table held the tools needed for fingerprint identification. The students would 'buddy up' and share their workload and findings. They'd learn how to obtain fingerprints and then identify the matching points using computers geared to their needs.

I'd always taught the class to start from scratch, the old way. But with the computer technology available, we'd stepped into the now instead of the then. Some departments still used the old way of doing things. Crime labs were stepping into the future, and I figured these people deserved to be familiar with the latest equipment available to them.

This particular class was smaller than usual. I'd lost several students who were pulled due to work schedules. The atmosphere remained charged with egos, and every now and then a smart remark would ignite an argument between departments. Whether they were cops, Two-Point-Fives, or wannabes, these people were highly competitive.

Paired up, everyone had a partner except for Porter Anderson. I'd singled him out since he would be the one to work on my note card. If there were any prints, he'd find them. Ramirez watched as I took Anderson aside with a nod of my head. When I glanced at Dario, he grinned and turned back to his partner.

After I explained what they needed to do, I demonstrated the use of the powder and brush to get the print to come forward. Then I lifted it from the surface, using common Magic Tape. Keeping it simple is always best. Everyone started to work on separate sets of prints while I wandered over to Porter, the wrapped note card in my hand.

I leaned toward him and softened my voice. "Porter, I need a favor," I said.

"What is it, Vinnie?" Grey eyes searched mine and then rested on the note card I slid forward.

"Print this card and envelope to see if anything comes up. Then run it through the system. Keep this to yourself, will you?"

"Sure. Don't want Richmond or Grant to know what you're up to?" He grinned.

"Exactly. They just worry for nothing."

"Yeah, right. By the way, I heard you lunched at Da Ravioli with the mob."

"Who told you that?"

"A little bird. Don't go there again, Vin. It isn't a smart idea right now."

"So I'm told," I said. "I'll take your advice into consideration."

Anderson nodded and started to dust the paper. His technique was excellent, and I knew he'd done this before. Why he took the class was a question I couldn't answer.

Wandering around the room, I assisted the students, answered questions, and took some ribbing about my driving skills. News of the car accident made the rounds within the various departments and was stretched to unrecognizable proportions. Around eleven thirty, we broke for lunch and everyone headed to the dining hall for a quick bite to eat.

The jingling of my cell phone caught my attention as the last person left the room. Rummaging in my purse, I pulled out the small unit and flipped it open.

"Lavinia," my mother murmured into the phone. "He's here again today. Antonio, the businessman is at the seniors' center. I don't understand what he's doing here."

I rolled my eyes and gave a mental head slap as I took a deep breath.

"Mom, what do you want me to do about it?" I asked. Hello, I'm only human. No miracles available today, for sure.

"Well, dear, I just thought you should know. It can't be a coincidence that he's at this same center again today. Do you think he's looking for Mafalda?"

"Don't even tell me she's hanging out with him again, Mom. I'll wring her neck after what she put me through with court and all. She's not there, is she?"

"No, when she saw him come in, she hid from sight. You don't think something bad will happen, do you, dear?"

"No, Mom, I don't. Look, I have to go now, but I'll call you later, okay?" *Anything to get her off the phone.* I adore my mother, but sometimes she amazes me. What could I do about Antonio? Nothing. That's what. *Cripes.*

She disconnected the call. I tossed the phone back into my purse in disgust. The apple I crammed into the bag this morning rolled out through the dusting powder and across the table. I grasped the fruit and tossed it into the trash as Marcus stepped through the door.

Dark powder smeared my hands as I slapped them together, hoping to rid them of the mess. Marcus took some towels from the paper holder and handed them to me with a grin.

"Here, try these." He chuckled and shook his head.

"What are you doing here?" I asked.

"Just making sure you made it all right this morning. The governor no longer needs me, so I'm on patrol. It's a good excuse to stop by and see you at work." Marcus prowled the room and glanced at the progress of everyone. When he reached Anderson's table, he looked at me with questioning eyes.

"Why is this person working on a different project when everyone else's work is the same?"

"His is a special project. This guy is way ahead of the others. I think he took the class just to get out of work." I lied. I had to.

A nod of his hat kept me from seeing the expression on his

face. He lifted the pincers and plucked the paper from the table. Turning it over, he read the message inside. His eyes traveled upward and he glared at me.

"You got this note and didn't give it to me? What the hell were you thinking?"

"Now, Marcus, don't get angry. I wanted to spare you the anguish of worrying about me. Besides, I figured that Porter could do this and we'd run it through the system at PPD. The Providence department has great resources and I'd know who sent the miserable thing."

"The state police have great resources, too, Vin. In case you've forgotten that," he said, his voice on the rise.

"I'm not discussing this with you right now. By the way, did you know that Aaron was engaged to someone named Lou Anne?" How's that for a change of subject?

"We'll discuss the fingerprints later. I promise." He glared at me but laid the card back onto the table. "No, I'm unaware of Aaron's romantic status. How did you find out?"

"When I went with the contractor yesterday, he told me."

"How does the guy know about Aaron?"

It was clear that I pressed his patience as he folded his arms across his chest and took his usual stance.

"Well, he's kind of a friend of a relative to the not-bride-to-be," I said.

Skeptical, Marcus slanted a glare at me. At least, it looked like skepticism.

"And this means what?" he asked on a sigh.

Yep, he was skeptical all right. Annoyed too from the looks of it.

I rarely let that get in my way though, so I said, "Umm, when I met some of Aaron's acquaintances once last summer, they said it was good that he decided to move on with his life. He'd laughed and said he was just moving in, into a new place. Later he confided he'd been injured on the job and had told his friends he'd given up working for the FBI. They'd been relieved when he said he'd gone to work for the Gaming Commission.

It's only a cover, though. Jesse said Aaron met Lou Anne at the Gaming Commission and that they were engaged."

"Odd that he's never mentioned it. Are they still involved?"

"Not according to Crane," I said. "He was vague about where she is now, but he said I needn't worry about being bothered by her. 'The engagement was made in hell,' he said."

Interest filtered across Marcus's face. I could tell by the gleam in his eyes that he'd entered the 'dog with a bone' stage. Guys are worse than women when it comes to gossip. I thought my need to know was bad, but most men have it much worse than I do.

"I'll see what I can find out. In the meantime, stay out of this, and when you finish fingerprinting that item," Marcus pointed to the letter, "I want it. Understand?"

"Yes, I understand." After all, he spoke English.

"In the future, it would be helpful if you'd cooperate with me instead of hiding evidence, Vinnie."

"Right." I checked my watch as a couple of cops wandered back into the room.

Curiosity over Richmond's presence was evident, but I refused to indulge the students. He nodded to them and they returned the same as he left the room. It's a cop thing, that's all I know. Respect for the badge and all that stuff.

* * * *

The day grew to a close. So far, nothing was visible on the note card. It was too much to hope for, but I'd hoped anyway. After the tables and the supplies were cleared up, everyone left the classroom. Ramirez stayed behind and walked me to the car.

"Was that the man in your life, Vin?" he asked with a grin.

"Yeah, sometimes he is. Why? What's it to ya, Ramirez?"

"Nothing, I just wondered. Did he pitch a fit when he saw Anderson at work on your special project?"

"How do you know Anderson's got a special project?" I asked, ignoring the rest of the question. Duh? How stupid did I think these people were? Not stupid at all.

"It doesn't take a genius to know that Anderson is way beyond this class. He knows what he's doing and is probably here to keep an eye on you. You do have a lot of mishaps, Vinnie."

"You may be right. I thought he took the class to get out of working. Foolish, huh?"

"No, just naïve, that's all." Dario grinned.

With that, he left me at the car and headed toward a pickup truck parked a few slots away. I watched as he roared past and I contemplated his words. Maybe he was right and Anderson was protecting me. Another man who thought I needed protection. Ugh. I started the car and drove off.

En Croute, the most fantastic bakery in Rhode Island, is located on Federal Hill. The small shop resides next door to a social club rumored to be inhabited by thugs, bone breakers, number runners, and other deadly dudes that supposedly work for the mob. If I were asked to swear to that statement, I'd have to plead out. I have no knowledge of anyone who socializes there and don't want to know either. But the bakery, well it makes the trials of traffic and danger on the Hill so very worthwhile.

The Altima eased into a parking spot, the one and only spot I could find on the street outside the social club. I snuggled the car up to the curb and hoped nobody peeked out the windows. Scooting from the car into the bakery, I stood just inside the door. The sweet smell of whipped cream, sugar, and fresh baked pastries hung in the air. It was heavenly and my waistline grew without so much as a taste of the succulent delights stored in the glass cases.

Marianna Patroni stepped to the counter. With her hand on her ample hip, she said, "What'll it be, Vinnie?"

Now Marianna is a big woman. Not just big, she's huge. Her breasts hang in front of a wide girth, and she needed a B-52 'silver bullet' bra to hold them up. Marianna's demeanor was always harsh, but I suspected a heart beat inside the broad-chested, square-shouldered woman. Gray hair and large hands that were red from too much washing, were the two other things one noticed first about Marianna.

She had a crush on my father when they were young and she still had a soft spot for him. Her musings over the old times filled me with curiosity for a time I'd never know. As well it raised questions about what my father was like in those days – certainly not the same man he was today.

"I'm here for pastry. With guests coming this weekend, I need to feed them something spectacular."

Hearty laughter filled the small bakery, and she slid trays of wrapped Italian cookies, rich pastries, and baklava toward me.

"Your father called today and said you'd need these for the weekend. Wait here, I have more out back for you."

Incredulous, I stood in silence for a moment. The bell jingled over the door as someone stepped inside. Without thinking, I turned to see who waited behind me. Two huge brutes stood in the doorway, hands clasped in front of their expensive-looking overcoats. Man, this was bad, I thought, and gulped. Aside from these two stood another man in a rich tan cashmere overcoat. He stepped forward and whispered in my ear. My gut tightened and I froze in place. Fear riddled my senses as I listened to his words.

"Lavinia, you shouldn't be here. Get your stuff and leave, understand?"

"Yes sir, I-I do, and I w-will," I stammered, sweat breaking out under my armpits.

I couldn't take my eyes off the ham hocks that passed for the hands of the two 'enforcers.' God knows I nearly shit myself from fear right there in the bakery. The two men had shoulders as wide as refrigerators, and from the looks of their faces they'd taken one punch too many. Cold flat eyes stared at me, and my stomach curled into itself. *Oh, yeah, I was leaving, uh huh.* No problem.

"Your father asked that I make sure you were unharmed when you came by. I can only do that once, so make this the only trip here, will you?"

I nodded, dumbfounded that my father not only anticipated my stop, but he'd ordered the pastry and requested protection by the mob – from the mob. *Good grief, what the hell was going on?* And where did Gino Esposito get that power, I might ask? I intended to find out.

From the back room, I heard the clatter of pans and raised voices speaking Italian. Marianna strode through the door laden with a wide box of delicacies – my name was scrawled across the plastic wrap. I paid her an unholy sum of money and proceeded to gather my packages. The two thugs stepped forward, took them from me and handled the box as well. After bidding Marianna farewell, I hustled through the door and to the car as fast as my feet would carry me.

The trunk sprang open, and while I considered what ghastly thing I might find stuffed inside, I found it was devoid of anything. The packages were transferred to the space and the trunk lid closed. The threesome nodded and waited for me to leave. I sped down De Pasquale Avenue, hooked a turn onto the highway, and raced home. My shaking parts quieted a bit more with each passing mile.

With the sweets packed into the fridge, I warmed up leftovers and settled in the living room to eat. I'd scooped the mail from the post office before coming in to roost, and flipped through the envelopes while I ate. There weren't any earth shattering messages, so I pulled the newspaper open and caught up on local happenings. I just finished supper when a rap sounded on the door. Folding the newspaper, I tossed it aside and answered the summons.

Muffy stood in the hallway. I stared at her, my mouth gaping open. What could she want? Why was she here? *I deserved this how?*

"Come in, Auntie," I said. "Can I get you something?"

"Just some coffee, if you will." Plainly, something was on her mind.

While the fresh brew perked I put two cups, milk, and sugar on the counter. Auntie hiked her short stature onto the stool across from me. Her legs dangled from the stool like she lived in the land of the little people. Suddenly she opened her mouth.

[151]

"Your mother and I were at the seniors' center today. Antonio came in while I was there. I hid in the closet of the office since I couldn't get out the door without him seeing me." She stopped, took a deep breath, and then glanced at me.

The coffee was ready and I poured two cups. I slid one toward Muffy and added milk and sugar to mine while I waited for her to continue. Surprise topped my list of reactions. Not only for her showing up on my doorstep, but for the fact that she'd tell me about Antonio.

"Is this a bad time, Lavinia? I can leave if it is."

"No, not at all, Auntie. Just go ahead and tell me what happened." *How did I get stuck with this shit?*

"I wanted to avoid him after he left me at the mercy of the cops and now that he's in so much trouble. Anyway, I hid in the office closet before he entered the room. He sat at the desk and rummaged through the books like he owned the place. I could see him through the crack of the door. It wasn't closed completely." She sipped her black coffee.

"What happened then?" I asked.

The man with him closed the door to the office and then shut the closet door tight. I couldn't see, but I could hear. You know how the Ciano's have excellent hearing."

Yeah, I knew. My mother could hear a fly buzzing at two hundred yards. That hearing got Gio and me in a lot of jams as kids. She would hear us conspiring and nip our plans in the bud. We'd become more adroit in keeping our schemes secret after that.

"Uh huh, then what happened?"

"I heard him tell the man to pick up the bag and take it to the bank for deposit. A woman entered the room and he said the laundry was done for now. I know it was a woman because she answered him with a smart-ass remark and he got mean about her attitude."

"Stay away from the seniors' center. Go somewhere else for your community service. The judge won't mind, and you'll feel better about it."

"Do you think they're laundering money through the center, Lavinia?"

"It sounds that way, but let's not jump to any conclusions. Let me see what I can find out. In the meantime, distance yourself from the center."

Aunt Mafalda nodded and sighed in relief, or maybe despair – hard to say. She scooted off the stool, grabbed her purse, and strutted toward the door. I was right behind her and kissed her cheek before she left.

Once the outer door closed, I leaned against the wall and banged my head against it. *How do I get into these things?*

Chapter 18

Dirty trouble seemed to follow me wherever I went. I collected it like a magnet. No other way to describe my affliction with problems, no sir. In an effort to lighten my mood, I slipped a jacket on and headed out the back door.

The rain had ceased and crisp, cold air swirled through the neighborhood. Soggy leaves littered the yard as I scooped the empty paper plate off the deck and tucked it into the trash bin. Since Evergreen hadn't made another appearance I guessed he found better accommodations. I shrugged and stepped off the deck, heading toward the street.

Silk Lane, a short road that led around the block, lay across the street to the left of the post office. I strode through the quiet neighborhood and headed down the lane. Lights filtered from the windows of homes huddled close to one another. Few overhead lights illuminated the lane, but I could see well enough and had a tiny Maglite stuffed in my jacket pocket. With a few quick strides, I ended up back on my own street.

The red light on the corner changed to green as I approached. I stood on the sidewalk waiting to cross over to Lola's deli. The deli was closed, but I could see the kitchen lights were on and knew she was working. Before I stepped into the crosswalk, a black truck slowed and the window slid down.

"Do you need a lift, Vinnie?" Aaron smiled.

"No thanks, I'm heading to see Lola." I hedged my answer, uncomfortable with the knowledge of him and Lou Anne.

Dark brows hiked up and he nodded. The window closed, and the Yukon rolled away on quiet wheels. I watched the truck pull into the driveway of my house before I crossed over to the deli.

I rapped on the front door and waited for Lola to answer. It took a minute or two for her to unbolt the locks and let me in. Glancing around the street, I quickly stepped through the door.

With nerves wound tight, accompanied by a stomach in knots, I greeted Lola.

"Got any tea? I could use some right about now."

"Yeah, sure, come into the back room. What's going on, Vin?"

"I'm sorry. I should have asked how the meeting with your publisher went. It's just that my life is out of control, again," I said and swiped my hands through my already tousled hair.

Laughter tinkled from across the room as Lola put the kettle on to boil. She grabbed our tea mugs and a tray filled with Danish pastries. She set them in front of me, continuing to grin while she stared at me for a moment.

"The day was great and thanks for asking. So, when isn't your life out of control? I don't remember a time when it wasn't, Vin. Why all the stress about it now?" She smiled.

I filled her in on the events of the day and the note card. I also explained about protection from the mob, by the mob. Her eyes crinkled with humor, and it was apparent that I'd taken this whole situation much too seriously. Either that or Lola had some good drugs in her purse – the result being, everything tickled her funny bone.

"I'm glad you find this so hilarious," I said and picked at the pastry then licked honey from my fingers. "I'm getting absolutely nowhere with finding out who is calling me and hanging up, why someone ran me off the road, how my father has the power to select a judge and command the mob guys, and now I find out that Aaron had been engaged to someone."

"Hey, you left out the Aaron thing. Tell me more." She leaned closer.

The tea was strong and hot, scalding my tongue as I sipped it. I set the cup down.

"There isn't much to tell. He was involved with a woman he

met at the Gaming Commission, got engaged, and it ended. That's all. I know nothing more. He's kind of edgy right now, though. I'm not sure if it's the investigation or if he realizes that I know about Lou Anne."

"Lou Anne who?" Her dark chocolate eyes widened.

"I don't know. Kinda makes you curious, though, huh?" I chuckled at the expression on the freckled face before me.

She nodded and Lola's halo of rich auburn curls settled past her shoulders.

"Uh huh, it does. If I had a last name, my brother could run her through the system and we'd find out more. When Jesse comes to work on your garage, why don't you ask him?"

"If you insist," I said and grinned.

We finished the tea, locked up, and Lola gave me a ride to the house. With a beep of the horn, her MINI Cooper sped away from the sidewalk. I turned away and walked to the house.

The door swung open as I put my hand on the handle. Face to face, Aaron and I stared at one another.

"Can you come upstairs for a minute?" he asked.

"Sure, no problem. Is everything all right, Aaron?" I asked with a sense of impending doom. *Was he going to move out? Would he tell me he had resumed his relationship with Lou Anne and was getting married?* My mind flew over the possibilities. *Did he know my father had mysterious powers over mob guys and judges?*

We entered the brightly lit room, and I took a seat at the counter. His kitchen was similar to mine in many ways, just a bit smaller. Counters gleamed and the appliances sparkled. They should, I thought. The man never ate at home, or cooked either. It was usually a case of his having leftovers in my apartment. I'd have to look into possible tax deductions.

"I guess you know that I was engaged, huh?" he asked bluntly.

"It was mentioned. You know, it's none of my business, Aaron. You don't owe me an explanation." I was dying for one, though.

"I know that. I'm not going to explain my life to you, but I wanted to tell you that it's over. Last summer, when I rented this place from you, I said I was unencumbered. I meant it."

"Oh, well, fine then. I had wondered, but now that you've put me straight, that's fine." What else could I say? *Tell me what her last name is so I can run her through the National Crime Information Center?*

The NCIC would tell me if she had any offenses. But if she was an innocent, then I'd find out nothing. Yeah, right, he was about to tell me nada – nothing at all. *Dang, doesn't that just toast my oats?* Yep, it does.

"Is that all you wanted to say?" I asked, with intentions to escape. He wasn't in his usual friendly mood, and I didn't know what to expect.

"No, it isn't. There's definitely more." The brown eyes glued me to the seat. "You were on the Hill today, were you not?"

"Ah, yes, I was. I went to En Croute for pastry. I know there'll be people dropping by this weekend."

"You couldn't go elsewhere? Lola couldn't supply you with refreshments? Did I not ask you to stay off the Hill?"

He was in a snit and now I knew why – how he found out. Spies are everywhere. His spies. Dammit.

"Lola has her own stuff to do for the weekend crowd. I like En Croute's pastry and I figured I would only be there for a moment, which I was. I apologize for not staying off the Hill," I said with a brave front that was far from what I felt. I'm not ten years old and I refuse to be treated as such, though I realized this man was concerned for my safety so I made allowances.

"Do you know who the men were that escorted you from the premises?"

His eyes were extra dark and I figured he was real upset.

"No, I have no idea. They didn't introduce themselves to me. They just helped put my parcels in the car, is all." No way would I tell Aaron that my father arranged it.

"Just that? Nothing more?" Strong hands spread on the countertop. He glared at me, holding his magnificent body upright as he stared me down.

"No, nothing more," I lied. "They looked like businessmen to me."

"Right. Businessmen." He stifled a gasp of disbelief, but it sat there on his face anyway.

"Is that it? I have to get stuff ready for class tomorrow," I lied again. To hell – that's where my soul was going. Straight to hell. All the novenas in the world wouldn't save my sorry ass.

An eyebrow arched as his face took on an ominous glare. Dang, he knew I lied and if I didn't get away, I'd be put in a chair with a blinding light dangling over my head for interrogation purposes. I could envision it as I slid off the seat.

"That's all for now. Let me say this, if you think about going to the Hill again in the future, don't do it. Things are about to get nasty, and I won't have you interfere with the investigation. You have enough to handle as it is, Vinnie, and I'm concerned for your safety."

"I appreciate your concern, Aaron. Really, I do." My butt flew down the stairs, and I locked myself in my place. Man he was angry – and rightly so. I had made a promise and broken it without a thought. Well, when I made the promise my fingers were crossed, so it didn't count. Right?

After a change of clothes, I wandered into the office. Sweatpants and a sweatshirt were the attire for the night. I sat scrunched down in the leather chair and rummaged through class assignments. My glance caught the blinking light of the answering machine and I hit the message button.

"Lavinia, this is Antonio. I was wondering if we could talk?" The mobster's message went on to give the phone number he wanted me to call. I stared at the machine, wondering if I should call or not. It would only be a call, and I had to know what he wanted. It might be something important. It would be rude to not call. I justified my curiosity.

I lifted the phone from its charger and dialed the number for Antonio, the businessman. It rang three times before someone answered.

"Hello, Antonio speaking."

"Hi, this is Lavinia Esposito. You called me?" I held my breath.

"Lavinia, my dear. I wanted to ask you about Mafalda. How is she doing? She won't take my calls and I'm very concerned."

He wasn't too concerned when he left her to rot in a cell at the PPD, though. There was more to this, and I wanted to know what it was.

"She's fine, just a bit shaky after her stay with the Providence Police."

"Mmm, that was most unfortunate. She is such a wonderful woman. Quite a temper, too, eh?"

"Well, yeah." I'd have been angry, too, if I was left in jail.

"I'm told she's doing some work at the seniors' center. How is that going?"

"I don't know…fine, I guess. Why do you ask?" *Ah, hah.* That's what this was all about. Interesting, very interesting.

"An associate of mine said he saw her there and before he could speak to her, she disappeared. I wondered about that."

"I have no idea. Maybe she didn't recognize your associate. What can I say, Antonio? She's probably still angry with you. Give her some time to cool down. I'm sure you'll hear from her."

"If you think that's best. She hasn't said anything to you, though, huh?"

Yikes, did he have spies in the village? Was he aware she came to visit me? Good God. Would I ever have a mundane life? Unlikely.

"No, she hasn't uttered a word about anything, Antonio."

"Well, thank you for calling back, and I'm sure I'll see you soon," he said, and disconnected the call.

Did he mean his goons would haul me in? Was he threatening me or was that just a common saying? My hand shook as I placed the phone back in its holder. I rubbed my hands over my face and smoothed my hair back.

The clock on the desk shone bright as it neared ten o'clock.

Where had the time gone? I could hear muffled footsteps cross the upstairs floor and knew Aaron was still up. Not too late to give up some of my information, and maybe get some in return.

Gathering courage, I slipped thick socks on and hustled up the stairs. A quick rap on the door brought a summons to come in. It was now or never, I thought, and I swallowed hard as I entered the apartment.

"Aaron?" I called.

"I'm in the front room. Come on in, Vin."

I strode through the rooms I'd painted over the summer and ended up in the warm-hued room that my friend Larry had faux finished. Dark brown leather furniture set off the amber walls to perfection.

I hadn't seen this area since the furniture was moved in and was intrigued. Ornate lamps rested on oak tables and a huge bold pastel chalk drawing centered the wall over the burning fireplace. I recognized it as the one I gave Aaron in August. The carved frame he'd chosen suited the accessories in the room.

A large deep burgundy rug, edged with cream, covered the center of the hardwood floor. Dark gold silk drapes sloped from the corners of the window casings, adding warmth to the furnishings. The room's overall effect was astonishing.

My eyes traveled the room before they landed on the man in front of the fireplace. Both Aaron's fireplace and mine were gas and were fired by the thermostat. He used the remote and it came on. He stared at me and his glance took in my attire.

"Ready for bed, are you?" He smirked.

I pushed my sweatshirt sleeves up and wandered further into the room. Photos – probably of his family – littered a table and bookcase nearby. I glanced at them but saw no woman, other than an older woman who resembled Aaron in coloring and smile. *Must be his mother.*

"You've never been any further than the kitchen, have you?" he asked.

Aaron's mood seemed to have lightened, but his face still had a tightness to it. I wondered what lay behind those usually warm chocolate eyes. *There's that curiosity and the cat thing again.* My nine lives were tallying up fast lately and I was in no position to refuse help from anyone. The saying 'Keep your friends close and enemies closer' is oh, so true for me.

"No, I haven't. Can we talk? I think there are some things you should know."

He hand beckoned me to sit down. I took the leather chair nearest the fireplace while Aaron lounged on the sofa. I was cold and wondered if that was due to a culmination of fear from all the recent events.

"I was rather short with you earlier, and I apologize for that Vinnie," he said with sincerity.

If he was working me, I didn't care at this juncture. There were things that needed to be said, and I planned to unburden myself.

"No apology needed. I know I drive you and Marcus nuts. It's just the way I am. Sorry. I need to tell you something important though. You may already know, but whether you do or don't, I must tell you." With that, I took a deep breath and shared Antonio the businessman's dealings at the seniors' center. I also told him of Aunt Muffy's visit to me earlier, and about the phone message from Antonio and our conversation when I returned his call.

While I spoke, his face tightened, loosened, and tightened once again. At one point, a nerve pulsed in his cheek. I thought that only happened in novels or the movies, but honest to God, it happened right there before me. Dark eyes gleamed and then he smiled. *Whoa, now what?*

"I'm glad you decided to share all of this with me. I did know some, but not all of it. We wondered where he was laundering the money. It seemed farfetched that he used the seniors' center to do so. Does he think Mafalda has become aware of his business dealings? Is that why you're so worried?"

"I'm not sure that he knows, but it's a possibility. He's never called before. I can't imagine why he would have called me otherwise. His call seemed of the fishing-for-information variety. Although Muffy isn't taking his calls, I'm certain he could just march up to her front doorstep and invite himself in. Why not? Why would he call me?"

My feet tucked under me, I twirled a lock of hair around my finger as I thought. When I looked at Aaron, he was smiling.

"Any other thoughts roaming around in that inquisitive mind of yours?" he asked with a chuckle.

"Um, not that I can think of. I do wonder, though, if he knew Auntie hid in the closet of that office. Maybe he wants to know if she heard what he said. She's a shrewd woman, and he's aware of it. She'd figure out what he was about, and then she'd be in danger."

"True enough, but I think your imagination is on the fly here. Don't let it take control of you. Think in conservative terms and you'll be fine." Aaron smiled again.

I realized he was making an effort to defuse my overactive imagination. *Lots of luck there.*

Rising from the warm chair, I wandered toward the kitchen. Behind, I heard his soft tread and knew Aaron was on my heels.

"Thanks for listening," I said.

"Thanks for sharing. It will help us out with the investigation. Funny how you become embroiled in every case I have." A small grin played around his mouth.

"Right. Good night."

Chapter 19

Students waited in the classroom for the last lecture on fingerprinting. Before noon they finished their projects and Anderson managed to lift a half print from my card. He told me that if the front hadn't been glossy paper, he wouldn't have been able to retrieve any print from it.

After the lecture, a question and answer session on fingerprint assessment started. The remaining hours flew. With little time to spare, the students used the computer program and started the chore of matching the prints they acquired. While they worked, I stepped over to Porter Anderson and mumbled to him under my breath.

"Is it possible to attain the identity of the person for me through the PPD?"

"I'll see what I can do. There may not be enough of a print, but I'll give it a try. By the way, I saw your name in the newspaper yesterday."

"My name? What was I in the newspaper for?"

"You were listed in the 'Obituaries', Vin. Was it a joke by someone?" The steady grey eyes watched my features.

"Not that I know of." Startled, I tensed. "If it was a joke it's in bad taste, don't you think?"

"Yeah, I do. I'll run this print, and call you later."

"Great. You have my cell phone number, so just call anytime. I appreciate your help. I owe you, Porter."

"How about dinner, then?" His grin widened.

"Thanks for asking, but I don't date my students."

"I'd heard that from some of the others you turned down.

Just thought I'd ask." He continued to smile, gave me a wink, and left after packing up his equipment.

Ramirez sidled over with a smirk. "Did he ask you out?"

"Why do you ask?"

"I told him you wouldn't date students, but he didn't believe me. Even made a wager."

I'm sure my eyes opened wide. "A wager? How large a wager?"

"He bet me twenty bucks you'd agree to dinner."

"You're in the money then, aren't ya?" I laughed. These egomaniacs were too much for me. Their antics never failed to amuse.

As I crossed the parking area, Marcus waited for me. His cruiser was parked so close to my car, it nearly kissed my bumper. He unfolded his arms and wandered toward me.

With a light kiss to my forehead, he stood with hands on my arms. "Hey, lady, how about dinner?"

I started to laugh and he stepped back in surprise. Within a space of a few minutes, I was asked to dinner twice by law enforcement. I wondered if there was a bet between Marcus and Ramirez.

"What's so funny?"

"You don't have a bet riding on the invitation, do you?"

"No, why?"

"Well, every semester, I get someone who thinks I should date them, and I was just asked to dinner by one of the students. He bet Ramirez that I'd go out with him for dinner. Ramirez made an easy twenty bucks." I chuckled.

"Who asked you out last semester?"

"Patty DiFrizio. I definitely refused that invite." Patty was a great person and good cop, but sexually she swung in both directions and I avoid that issue at all costs. 'Each to his or her own' is my motto. That lifestyle just wasn't for me.

Laughter echoed across the parking lot. Marcus's chest heaved and then he settled down. I ran my hands over his arms and watched him sober. Yep, that was the effect I waited for, uh huh.

"What are you doing after going to dinner with me, ma'am?" he asked.

"Why do you ask, Trooper Richmond?" I said as I stepped closer to his body.

One hand reached around my waist and dragged me into his tight grasp. I could feel Mr. Winky stand to attention and knew I'd won the day. Control was exulting, even if it was only over Mr. Winky.

"Maybe you'd like a snuggle later?" he asked.

"Is that what we're calling it now? A snuggle?" I laughed so hard he released me.

"Let's get some dinner. You're spoiling the moment, lady." He hustled me into my car, and I followed him from the parking lot.

At the Crimson Dragon, Marcus slowed and we parked side by side. *Oooh, Chinese food, yum.* I eat Chinese fare whenever I get the chance, but it doesn't happen often. Mostly 'cause I dine with my parents and that's usually Italian cuisine – and free. My mouth watered as I left the car and joined Marcus at the door.

In a corner booth at the back of the restaurant, Marcus ordered our favorites. Sharing the food was something we did every time we ate out. I handed hot tea to Marcus, in a little bowl, and saluted him with mine.

He chuckled and casually sipped the tea until someone moving past jarred my elbow and I spilled mine. I didn't notice who it was, but jumped up as it burned through my slacks. Marcus gave me his napkin and poured me another cup. He never even blinked at the fact that I may have third degree burns. *Crap. No sympathy there.*

"Are you finished messing around now?" His voice was calm.

"Yeah, I guess so. I could have serious burns, you know." I whined and I knew it.

"You'll be fine. It wasn't that hot." He shook his head and then looked at me with that wolfish grin. "If you like, I'll check it out later."

"Great. I look forward to medical attention."

He smiled broadly. I adore that smile, by the way. My grin

[165]

matched his until I turned my head. At the table across the room, I caught the stare of Tony DeGreico. The smile froze on my face and Marcus caught the look.

"Who's that?" His eyes raked DeGreico.

"Tony DeGreico, the guy who stalked me," I muttered, suddenly uneasy. *Had he bumped me?*

A cold hazel green stare turned to Tony and then to me. I reached across the table to take Marcus' hand. A tightened jaw and frigid attitude settled over Richmond's features and that increased my uneasiness. The cop demeanor fell into place as he stared at me and sipped tea. What was he thinking?

"I was just clumsy. Let it go."

A cool customer, Marcus wouldn't step across the room and pop DeGreico in the face, though it was probably on his mind. Instead, he focused on our dinner and me. With an effort, I relaxed enough to enjoy the meal and company. By the time we finished, DeGreico was gone and I didn't even see the dirtball leave.

"Now, was that so difficult?" Marcus wondered aloud, once we were outside and his arm hung around my shoulder.

"Was what difficult?" Thought fled when his hand slid down my back and his warm lips covered my cheek with tiny kisses. My heart pounded and my blood pressure soared.

"Nothing." He grinned. "Are you ready for first aid and dessert?"

"You have something good to offer?"

"No, I have something fantastic to offer."

I laughed. I couldn't help it. The ego thing was there in front of me. I glanced down and said, "Yes, you do."

We agreed to meet at the house and I drove away, my spirits heightened with anticipation.

The car slowed and turned into the driveway. I eased next to the Yukon and parked. The door locks clicked when I closed the car door. As I wandered toward the house, I wondered how long it would be before Marcus arrived.

A step behind me crunched on the uneven stones of the driveway. It happened so fast that I didn't have much time to react. Hands roughly grasped my shoulders and shoved me to the ground. I pitched forward and lost my balance.

Sharp edges of crushed stone cut into the soft skin of my palms that dug into the driveway. A heavier shove between my shoulder blades and I landed on all fours. Pointed tips pierced my knees as I turned my face away from the jagged surface. My hair flung forward, blocking my vision. For an instant, I just kneeled there, and then, when I realized I could, I scrambled to gain my footing. With fisted hands I took a few steps toward the house before whipping around.

The yard lay empty. No sound of footsteps could be heard. Exterior lights blazed as I whirled in a circle, taking in the entire yard all at once. The driveway was completely deserted.

The contents of my purse were splayed across the ground. Bent in half, I picked up everything and stuffed it all back into the bag. The whole time, I listened for any noise that would alert me to a possible repeat performance. With my purse full, I limped into the house and slammed it on the counter.

A half hour later, Marcus pulled into the yard in his truck. He'd gone home to change and get his own vehicle. While I waited, I picked stone bits from my palms and cleaned bleeding knees where the rocks jabbed through the material of my slacks. Band-Aids covered the small wounds now.

Relieved, I swept the door open and launched myself at the man. Though I had Band-Aids on my hands, I clung to Marcus like a life raft. So much for bravery.

"That glad to see me, huh?" he asked with a chuckle.

When I stepped back, he stared at my face. Then his eyes moved to my hands. One swooping glance took in my whole being. His face tightened as he waited for my story.

"What the hell happened between the time I left you at the restaurant, and now?" he demanded.

"I got home and there was a surprise visitor waiting in the shadows for me. I never saw who, but someone shoved me to the ground before I could defend myself."

A strong hand came up to my hair and smoothed it before his

palm cupped my face. He leaned in and kissed me with emotion. I moved closer and wrapped my arms around his neck. It was quite a while later before we had a moment to talk. By then, I was happy, Marcus appeared happy, and Mr. Winky was completely relaxed and asleep.

Nestling into Richmond's shoulder as we lay in bed, I could hear the thump of his heart under my head. I smoothed a hand across his chest and the heat from his body warmed me. This was nice, real nice. I liked these diversionary tactics.

"Who do you think attacked you outside?"

"I haven't a clue. There were no footsteps that I could hear. No sounds to even indicate a car drove away from anywhere in the neighborhood. You know how quiet the town becomes in the evening."

"That's true. Maybe we need to look closer at who might have set the fire. Might be the same person has now attacked you? It could be you pose a threat to someone. They might have been coming back for a look at the garage, you know."

"Do you think so?" My heart clenched in my chest and my breathing seemed sporadic.

"It occurred to me that the fire might not have been set, but was an accident instead. No signs of a cigarette were found, only burned matches, but that doesn't mean anything. If someone were smoking, and the flame caught the tree, and then the garage, there'd be panic and the person would flee. What do you think of that theory, Vin?"

"It makes more sense than someone purposely setting fire to the garage. I never did like that thought, Marcus." I snuggled closer while he stroked my hair.

"How are your hands and knees feeling?" he asked.

"What hands and knees?" I asked with a chuckle.

"Then my tactics worked?"

"Indeed they did."

"You got any coffee made? I could use a cup right about now." He swept the covers back and a cool draft sent goosebumps across my body. *Dang, I was so comfortable, too.*

"Coffee it is," I said and slipped a robe on before heading into the kitchen.

From the bathroom Marcus hummed some country tune, totally off key. I smiled and wondered if he planned to stay the night. Gosh, what was I thinking? It bordered on a commitment kinda thing. Lordy, Lordy – somebody help me keep those thoughts at bay.

While coffee brewed I slipped on a football jersey, followed by a pair of sweatpants – and left the robe behind. Fluffy socks covered my feet and I pulled my hair back into a clip. When I returned to the kitchen, I poured coffee into mugs, slopping milk into both, and all over the counter.

A grin covered Marcus's face while he watched. He shook his head and tore paper towels off the roll. With a quick swipe, the milk disappeared and he tossed the sodden paper towels into the trash bin.

"You never cease to amaze me, never ever." He grinned.

"I know I'm an amazing person. By the way, did you find out anything about Lou Anne yet?"

"Yeah, she's a guest of the Rhode Island Women's Detention Center. Her name is Lou Anne Begoni. She has relatives on the Hill and they're a dysfunctional family. Rumor has it that Aaron started romancing her to get the goods on the family. When the facts came out, she was into every deal up to her brown eyeballs. A twisted woman, too, I hear. No wonder Jesse told you it was an engagement made in hell."

"Aaron didn't talk about it much. He wouldn't explain, and I didn't ask him to."

"That must have been a difficult task for you. Knowing your penchant for the 'need to know,' it must have eaten you alive."

"Hey, I'm insulted by that." I pouted, imitating hurt feelings.

"Right, but you don't deny it." His laughter ignited mine.

"True enough. I also shared some information with him about Antonio, the businessman. He seemed pleased that I came clean, since he realized I had information of sorts."

"We figured you'd spill your guts sooner or later."

"Who's *we*?" I asked, but I knew the answer.

"Aaron called me when you showed up on the Hill for pastry. I explained what you were doing and that you'd be staying for a brief moment or two."

"How did you know?" I gasped.

"I just figured it out," he said with an air of mystery.

"Great, I have no privacy at all with you two around. Who would ever have thought an undercover FBI agent would be such a blabbermouth?"

"You're lucky, and you know it, Vin. He and I have to keep tabs on you for your own sake," he said, while studying his fingernails. When he glanced up at me, I caught the teasing glimmer in his eyes.

I swatted him as my cell phone jingled its tune from deep inside the handbag. I hauled it out, flipped the cover open, and answered the call.

"Vinny, this is Porter. I have news for you."

My glance strayed to Marcus who yawned wide, and stretched. I knew he listened. No sense in pretending the caller was someone else.

"What did you find out, Porter?" I asked, my eyes on Marcus.

Hazel eyes rested on me while I listened to the fingerprint results. I thanked the man and ended the call.

"Porter Anderson got a partial print off the card in class. He found a match for the owner of it."

"Are you planning to tell me or not?" At attention, Marcus leaned his elbows on the counter and waited for me to answer the question.

"Antonio, the businessman."

Silent, he leaned back and shook his head. It wasn't the response I expected, but then I seldom knew what to expect from this enigmatic man.

"Well, well. Antonio, huh? I can't believe it. We found a connection to the damage on your Taurus that led us to his associates. It figures he'd be in this up to his neck. I thought

DeGreico was the perp, to be frank."

"That was my assessment as well. I figured he thumped my bumper and sent me flying. Then someone put my name in the newspaper 'Obituaries'. Porter told me he saw it listed yesterday. When we saw DeGreico at the restaurant tonight, the coincidence was a bit much for me. However, if Porter says it's Antonio, then it must be true."

"Get the note card and envelope to me tomorrow, and we'll double check to make sure. In the meantime, stay off the Hill and out of trouble – if that's possible."

"If you insist," I said, rubbing the palms of my sore hands.

With his fingers wrapped around mine, Marcus kissed each palm. Instant relief flowed through my veins, or were those my hormones raging? I couldn't figure it out and so just let what would be, happen.

Marcus slid an arm around my shoulders and pulled me to him. Mr. Winky was awake again.

Chapter 20

Throughout the village, and up and down my street, vans and moving trucks lined the curb. It was early in the morning, but the artisans had already arrived to set up for a weekend of art sales. The cold weather was sunny, so at least that was in their favor. I didn't envy them three days of chilly winds, but that was their choice. Not a job I'd stand in line for, but they probably wouldn't take mine either. No accounting for tastes.

Blockades would be erected at the intersection by evening, and the weekend would officially begin. Thousands of people with dogs, and kids in strollers would tramp through the village. They'd check out the yard sales and food offered at the church and the deli on the corner. I'd also have more company than I could imagine. If that didn't pan out, I'd have to eat all that pastry by myself.

I grinned, waved at the fire chief erecting barriers, and headed east, driving toward the campus. The car hustled along next to tractor-trailers, mail trucks, cement mixers, and a slew of cars headed toward Massachusetts. We rounded the curve on the interstate highway, and I made it across the Washington Bridge safely, for the third day in a row. *Yes, there is a God.*

When I cruised into the grounds of the university, I noticed Ramirez hanging around outside. He stared while I locked my car, and walked alongside me as I approached the foyer of the building.

"So Teach, did you find out who was behind the fingerprint you had Porter run?" he asked.

Alert, I wondered at his interest. I said, "Why do you want to know?"

"Just wondering. There's talk on the Hill that there's some

heavy shit going down, and I wondered if the print was connected to those people."

"Oh, well, Porter couldn't get a good match. Not enough points to fit it with anyone." I didn't know why I lied. Perhaps it was a case of paranoia.

"Any idea who it could belong to then?" he asked with a sly grin.

What was this about and where was he headed with it? I stared at him.

"No clue. Do you have any?" I wanted to know. "It's alarming to have threats, even subtle ones, made against me."

He shook his head and said, "I'm sure it is. If you hear anything, let me know. I'd be happy to put those scumbags in lockup. Or to stand guard at your place." I shook my head.

"Thanks, I'll keep that in mind," I said.

We entered the room to find the class milling around. As a group they shuffled toward their seats and waited for me to take attendance. The only person missing was Porter Anderson.

About an hour into the class, the door opened and Porter sauntered into the room. He glanced at me with a slight smile and a wink as he took his seat. I continued on until the lecture was finished and then dismissed everyone for a break. It would be an early day. Fridays usually were. I kept everyone for a full day most seminar days, but Fridays were different.

The room emptied, except for Porter. He hung around until I glanced at him. The bag with the note card in it was suspended between two fingers. He slid his chair back and strode forward.

"Vin, I ran another test last night and found a print on the glue inside the envelope."

"I assume you know something of use or you wouldn't be so smug." I grinned at his excited expression.

"Yeah, but you won't believe it when I tell you."

"Don't keep me in suspense Porter, spill it," I snapped. Edgy over the upcoming answer, I waited.

His grey eyes widened as he grinned. "Teach got a bit of stress goin' on? Okay, okay. I'll tell you. I ran the print and came up with the name Marianna Patroni."

Dumbstruck, I leaned back against the counter. Bile rose in my throat as darkness zeroed in. *It couldn't be.* Never in a million years would I have come to that conclusion. I could have guessed for a lifetime, but she was the last person I'd have named.

"Vin? Vin, are you all right?" Hands shook me.

I returned to the present and stared at Porter.

"You're shitting me, right?" I asked. "This is no joke, Porter."

"It's the truth, Vin. I'm sorry, but the other print belongs to her. I take it you know this person?"

"Yeah, for years. She and my father go back a long time. What else did you find out about her?"

"Nothing much. She was hauled in about ten years ago for assaulting her other half, and she got printed. That's why she was in the system."

"Cripes, my father's gonna have kittens. Damn." I could see it playing out in my mind's eye. Gino ranting like a maniac over the news. I'd have to placate him somehow. Then he'd get into the married-with-children dialogue that is never ending and I'd have to listen to that lecture as well.

A chuckle brought me back to earth and I glanced at his face. Yeah, easy for Porter to laugh. He didn't have my father as a parent. A father who, when he was young, had a fling with a woman who scared the crap out of me. I didn't know what to think and couldn't make up my mind whether to tell him or not.

My little inner voice, you know the one that lectures me on the rationale of dating cops, started to nag me. *Your father will be angry as hell over this. You better keep it to yourself.* Hah, I thought. Why would I listen to it now? I never did.

Maybe I'd rethink it, though.

The class filtered in, we covered the remaining material, and I dismissed everyone early. My afternoon agenda included talking to my father, and I wasn't about to delay the visit.

Wind, clouds, and sun fought for equal time as I left the building. Within seconds, Anderson and Ramirez joined me. They walked on either side of me and checked my car before I got inside. Dramatic as it appeared, I was glad they made the effort. It also occurred to me that there could have been something left out of Porter's report.

My car rolled from the campus onto the highway. I got off the interstate and drove toward my mother's part of town. When I passed the seniors' center, I noticed her car and U-turned into the lot. I came to a screeching halt and left the vehicle at a trot.

Old folks wandered around holding bingo paraphernalia while others played pool in the billiard room. I could hear music and went in search of the sound. There would be refreshments to accompany the music. I had no doubt that's where my mother would be located, too.

The room was decorated with flowers, and tables had linen covers. Teapots and cups ranged across the surfaces. Lots of tiny little cakes adorned plates in the center of each table. Women and men alike, from their late sixties and beyond, listened as a soprano screeched an operatic melody. *God help me. When I reach this point, just shoot me, somebody, please.* If I start drooling at that age, then it's a definite request.

The music continued as I sidled along the back wall in an effort to reach my mother. She stood behind the counter of the serving station with two other women. Muffy was absent, so she must have listened to my well-meant advice.

"Mom," I whispered in her ear. "Where is Dad today?"

"He's at the Knights of Columbus Hall with his card-playing buddies. Why, dear?"

"I need to talk to him about something. I'll call you later." I kissed her cheek and walked away from the blaring screech of the off-key soprano. These folks must have been deaf, especially since the singer couldn't carry a tune. She also slaughtered the Italian language with her voice.

I scooted through the back streets to the K of C Hall. Dad's car was parked among several others, and I pulled alongside. My heart sank at the thought of the upcoming confrontation. A sense of dread enveloped me. Maybe Porter was mistaken. What then?

I could always wait until Marcus ran his own tests and see where that led. What if it ended with the same conclusion? I'd still have to face my father. No easy task, that.

With a hearty breath, and all the courage I could muster, I left the car and headed inside the hall. Laughter filtered down the hallway. I knew the guys would be in the same room as the last time I was here. That time, I had told my father someone had threatened my mother's life. That went over real well, as you can imagine. I shook my head at the memory.

I'd been lucky my dad hadn't broken my neck when I uttered the words. Instead, he'd ranted and raved about the fact that I was still single, needed to find a man and settle down. 'Have a family,' he'd said. 'Be a soccer mom. Make spaghetti.' Yeah, that's a job I'd stand in line for. Besides, there wasn't anyone to take me off my hands. *Thank you, God.*

Hovering outside the door, I peered around the frame and watched the dealer prepare the cards. My father glanced up and stopped, mid-sentence. He grimaced and then muttered some words to the man next to him. The whole table of men turned in their seats to stare at me – the card game interloper. The interruption of their game was a serious offense. I waved, one waved back, and then they all grinned and said hello. I waggled my fingertips at them again as my father reached me.

He was tense, clearly wondering why I'd come. Probably remembering the last time. We strode into the same ballroom as before, and a sense of *Deja vu* struck me. *Was I in for the same lecture? God, please spare me the same old ranting.*

"There've been some issues lately. I have to tell you something, Dad."

Braced as I was for the onslaught of my father's grim outlook on my lifestyle, I was unprepared for what came next.

"Are you pregnant, Lavinia?" he asked.

Geez, was that his question for all the issues in my life? Did he think all I did was drop my drawers? Couldn't there be anything else going on other than sex and trouble? Anger simmered just under my breath, but I swallowed hard and hoped it would stay down.

"No, I'm not pregnant. It's the last thing on my agenda, Dad," I stated, with animosity in every syllable.

After I told him about the note and having it fingerprinted, he stared at me a moment.

"Someone's threatening you? You're in danger? What does this have to do with me?"

"There were two prints on the card, Dad. One print belonged to Antonio, the businessman. The other belonged to Marianna Patroni."

His expression was a prelude to bad things to come. I could feel it in my bones. The signs and symptoms were evident, and I didn't know where to take the conversation.

"You're sure, Lavinia? The prints, they are beyond doubt, eh?"

"Yeah, they are. I'm sorry Dad, I know you and Marianna go back a long way."

"Who told you that?" he asked, his voice gruff.

"She did. She explained how you two had been an item when you were kids and she never forgot it. She was disappointed when you married Mom, but said she understood."

"I never had a relationship with her. We grew up in the same neighborhood, but her old man was bad. I wouldn't have anything to do with her. You must have got it wrong, Lavinia."

How did this end up my mistake? I didn't misunderstand the woman. She had been in love with my father. They were an item until he met my mother.

"Dad, I'm telling you. She said you'd gone out together, that Mom stole your heart – that kind of thing. She even regaled me with stories of your youth." I stared at him. "I couldn't imagine you involved in some of the stuff but I didn't question it either."

"What kind of stuff?" he asked with narrowed eyes.

"Just stuff." I shrugged. "I also want to know how you got the judge to come into court on his day off and how you managed to have thugs on the Hill protect me from others like themselves." I was on a roll and paced back and forth, my agitation out of control.

"The judge is an old flame of your aunt's. I called and asked for the favor or she'd be in jail as we speak. He was happy to do it. As for the guys on the Hill, I went to school with them and I'm the godfather to one of their children. There isn't anything underhanded goin' on here, Lavinia. So don't get huffy."

"Huffy? You call it huffy? Dad, I nearly dropped dead from

fright when those three thugs entered the bakery. I almost shit my drawers, for cripes' sake."

A glint of rare humor entered the dark eyes. My father even smiled a bit at the outburst. *He thought this was funny? God help me.*

"You were actually afraid of these guys? They weren't there to harm you, Lavinia."

"When I turned around and saw these guys with ham hocks for hands and shoulders like pro ball players, I nearly fainted. Honestly, you could have warned me. Who was the guy dressed in camel-colored cashmere?"

"It doesn't matter who he is. He did as I asked and got you safely out of the bakery." A flat look entered my father's eyes as he stared at me.

"The bakery? You were worried about me being in the bakery, not because I was near the social club? Did you know about Marianna?" *Why hadn't he warned me?* This man, my father, the chef of all chefs, knew about Marianna?

"I know a lot of things that you don't need to know, but I'm sure you'll try to find out. Richmond was positive you'd head to the Hill, as was I, when you mentioned a bakery. Lavinia, you can't stay out of anything, can you? You need a change in your life." He sighed.

Agreed. It wasn't my fault that I was plagued by unfortunate mishaps. They just happened. You'd have thought my father would know that by now. Geesh.

"Don't start the 'marriage, kids, and spaghetti argument', Dad. I'm really not in the mood for it. There's been enough crap in my life lately without you spouting off about the need for grandkids. If you want grandchildren, talk to your son about it, but give me a break." *Wow, had I really said that to my father?* I stopped talking when he became quite still.

He nodded at me and simply said, "Watch your step, Lavinia. There are dangerous people around who would like to change your life. Just be careful what, and who you take on." With that statement, he turned away and walked back into the card room.

I stared after him and wondered what the hell he meant by that ambiguous statement. Now I was really nervous.

Chapter 21

Popcorn kernels, an empty wine glass, and a half-filled wine bottle littered the coffee table. I sprawled across the sofa and watched dumb television ads. I flicked through the channels with the remote and finally settled on a movie. *The Godfather* played for the umpteen millionth time – Al Pacino's dark good looks covered the plasma screen.

When another commercial came on, I turned the television off and lolled on the sofa, staring at the ceiling. What was I supposed to do next? I couldn't get a grip on all that had happened lately.

My feet hit the floor with a thud as I stood up. This was no time to lollygag around and indulge in a pity party. So many unanswered questions. *Who torched my garage? Who shoved me down in the yard? Why would someone want to force me off the highway?* I was determined to find the answers as I paced the room. *But how?*

After wracking my brain for several minutes, I decided to hike upstairs and grill Aaron for some answers. Answers, I was positive, he wouldn't want to give me. The man was secretive on a good day, unless he decided to spill the beans about me, that is. *What had he found out from my mom?*

That was it. I would work him like he'd worked my mother.

With my apartment door to the front entry wide open, I climbed to the first landing of the staircase and listened. Muted sounds of Mozart caressed the walls. Footsteps crossed the room as I wandered up the final five steps to the door of Aaron's apartment.

Dirty Trouble

After a light knock, the door opened and Aaron ushered me into the living room. The fireplace was already lit and cast a soft glow throughout the room. Shadows danced on the walls, and firelight reflected off the wood floor surrounding the area rug. *Ah, ambiance.*

Dressed in my usual sweatpants and jersey attire, I slouched into the chair nearest the fireplace and folded my legs beneath me. Aaron stared for a brief moment and then settled on the adjacent sofa. He offered me a drink, but I shook my head. Clear thinking was the key to good interrogation tactics.

"Are you sure you don't want some coffee, at least?" Aaron asked.

"No, thanks. I've got some questions for you, though." My courage started to evaporate, but I conjured up more and took a deep breath. "What's the connection between Marianna Patroni and my father? You must know, since you know everything else."

"They lived in the same neighborhood. Other than that, there was nothing between them. Marianna's father was connected to organized crime, and she picked up a lot of his bad habits. What's this about, Vin?" His warm chocolate eyes glowed in the soft firelight as he studied me. His handsome features lay half in light and half in shadow. A handsome devil, for sure.

My inner voice started its ever present nagging. *Stay on the subject. Don't get involved with another lawman.* Okay, okay, I'll listen this time.

"My father and I had a discussion today, and he said about the same thing. However, I know she has a connection to my family somehow. I'm sure you could tell me if you were inclined to do so."

His face turned thoughtful as he stared at me. "If I provide the answer to your question, what will you do with it? I can't afford to have you interfere with the ongoing investigation, especially at this stage."

To avoid his question, since I didn't know what to answer, I asked another.

"How far into the investigation are you? Also, do you have

any idea who put my obit into the newspaper?"

Eyebrows arched and a smirk covered his face. "Someone actually did that?"

"Indeed, one of my students saw the article. Should that intimidate me? Is someone looking to make my demise an actuality?" My hand cupped my chin as I leaned on the arm of the chair. I felt his eyes on me as my long, wavy hair fell forward.

"As far as the investigation goes, you know I'm unable to share. This newspaper imprint could be a joke – a poor one – but a joke all the same. No one has mentioned it to me. I'd be on guard if I were you. It doesn't hurt to stay aware of your surroundings, right?"

"Uh huh. So you're not worried by this?"

"I didn't say that, but let's not over-react or let this grow out of proportion." Aaron smiled. "Like I said, stay on guard, Vinnie."

Relief fluttered across my nerves. No serious threat – then I'd be fine. Maybe he was only trying to reassure me. His words had done so, that was for sure.

"Have you had any encounters with Tony DeGreico?"

I nodded. "I ran into him on a few occasions, but he's kept his distance. I think he enjoys making me uncomfortable. I've had about enough of it, too. I say that with certainty."

"Oh? Does that mean he had better watch out, or what, beautiful?" A smile sneaked across his firm, full lips.

"I'm not sure what it means, but it just annoys me to have him ogle my chest and smirk as though he has a secret that I could never guess. To hell with him."

"I can't blame him for ogling your chest, Vin. But the smirk thing would get on anyone's nerves. Try to ignore him. It's the best defense, and you know it." The square white teeth gleamed when he smiled. A seductive smile, one I thought was meant to mesmerize.

Foolishness, pure unmitigated foolishness, that's what it was. I'd stepped into the lair of a gorgeous man who thought I was beautiful. He'd only answer my questions with questions of his own and I'd go away empty-handed, again. *If he made a pass at me, how would I react?* Marcus sprang to mind and I hefted my weight out of the chair.

"I'd better leave. This conversation isn't helpful and I'm sure you won't give me any worthwhile answers anyway," I said with a grin. In bare feet, I padded across the rug to escape the temptation of him. I had too much wine, that's all it was.

"What's the hurry, beautiful? You've only asked me a couple of questions that I have no real answers to. Ask away and if I can help out, I will. After all, you shared your knowledge of Antonio, the businessman and his association with the seniors' center."

"Okay, I'll have some coffee then." *Was I about to tempt fate or what?*

"Sure, coffee it is. Wait here, I'll be right back." A wide grin covered his face as he left the room.

Toes toasting in front of the fire, I leaned back in the chair and relaxed. I also considered what else I could inquire about that might end with some answers. My father's latest actions couldn't be revealed at any cost, that was for sure.

A tray balanced on one hand, Aaron entered the room and set it on top of the coffee table. I watched while he poured two cups and handed me one. His cup lifted in salute and I raised mine as well.

The brew was strong and scalding, but that was how I liked it. After a few sips, I set the cup on a nearby table.

Aaron watched in silence. I couldn't read him to save my soul.

"What are your plans for the weekend?"

"Tomorrow afternoon when the tourists have cleared out of town, I'm headed to the cemetery to visit Aunt Livvy's grave. I haven't brought any fresh flowers lately, or chatted with her, and I should, you know?"

"That's a good idea. Where's the grave located?"

"At the corner on Silk Lane, I go straight past the house under the pine trees. The road leads right into the cemetery. Her grave is just down the hill, on the left, overlooking the reservoir."

"So what else is going on this weekend? You're expecting guests?" He smiled, knowing I'd bought an embarrassing amount of pastry that needed to be eaten.

"Usually a bunch of people I know wander around the art show and then stop in. When I first moved in they started coming by, and now it's like an open door invitation."

"What, no yard sale?" He chuckled. Everyone along the street had signs up and junk piled high on tables made from sheets of plywood resting atop sawhorses.

His manner was friendly and warm, but I figured he was trying to work me or make me relax. Either way, I was here for the duration…wouldn't leave without some information. I arrived here with a mission, and I'd be darned if I'd give up without a good try.

I chuckled. "No, no yard sale. I'll leave that for the neighbors. I think it's just their way of unloading all the junk they've managed to collect. By the way, I think Lanky Larry will be here."

Larry, the gay little meatball that he is, is a great friend who supported me through the death of my Aunt Livvy. My nasty cousin used him the summer before to find out about smuggled gems. Larry had also worked on this apartment with me to ready it before Aaron moved in.

The two men took a liking to one another. Larry thought Aaron had biceps worth swinging from, while Aaron considered Larry a fantastic artist.

Different to a fault, Aaron stood well over six feet, had a tan women would kill for, was way too handsome, and was built like a wrestler. Larry, on the other hand, stood a bit over five feet tall, was round as a soup bowl, and bald as a melon. Generous and extremely talented, Larry showed great artistic talent. We'd met in college and had been fast friends ever since.

"He will? That's great. I haven't seen him around since we arrested your cousins."

"He's been busy with his faux finishing business, but he shows up here every season without fail."

"So what else is on your mind besides this art festival?" Broad shoulders leaned against the leather sofa and firelight flickered across his strong features.

"I was shoved to the ground outside the apartment last night and I wondered if you heard or saw anyone when you arrived home earlier in the evening?" My eyes never left his face as I waited to see if he knew anything at all. He never gave an indication of what he thought, just shook his head.

He poured another cup of coffee and sat back. If I hadn't known better, I'd have thought he might want to see how I worked a person. He should know by now that I'm a tenacious sort.

"Did you see who it was?" he asked, after a long pause.

"No, I didn't. I'm curious, though, since the person came out of nowhere. Kind of odd, to say the least," I said. "So tell me more about Marianna Patroni."

The coffee cup tilted, and Aaron caught it before the beverage could spill onto his slacks. As he glanced up, I realized he hadn't expected to return to that topic. How interesting, how very interesting. *Why didn't he want to speak to me about Marianna? Was she involved in his FBI probe? Hmm.*

"I think you're fishing, but I don't know what you're fishing for. I'm not at liberty to tell you anything, Vinnie."

"Then tell me about Lou Anne," I said, just a bit annoyed at his put-off attitude.

"Jesse told you about Lou Anne, huh?" His lips tightened, and his eyes darkened.

"You knew that but didn't want to share. I figure this whole investigation is connected to my family somehow and I have a right to know. Now, what does Lou Anne have to do with my family?"

"She is Marianna Patroni's daughter. She has nothing to do with your family. Satisfied?"

"Why did you get engaged to her if you knew she was related to the mob? I wouldn't think it would be a wise move." There had to have been more to it than a need for information. *Like love, for instance?*

[184]

"Man, you are a news bag." Aaron shook his head and set the cup aside. He leaned forward, elbows resting on his knees, and stared at me.

"Yeah, I know. Now tell me."

"We, the FBI, found out there was illegal betting taking place. Around that time, I'd been injured on the job and in recovery mode. My doctor released me to return to work, but nothing physically demanding. So, I took the assignment and went to work at the Gaming Commission."

His strong hands ran through his dark hair as he leaned back. Silent for a few moments, I couldn't tell if he was thinking about the whole scene, or what he was willing to share. I sensed he'd talk about Lou Anne if I just kept my mouth shut. As unlikely as it seemed, I did just that.

With a sigh, Aaron said, "I met her after my first week of work. She was good-looking and a bit crazy, but I was there for a purpose and that was that. After a few weeks, she hung around and made it obvious that she was interested in me. I took advantage of it and started to date her. One thing led to another, I was introduced to the family, and then everything came to a screeching halt.

"Not one single clue could I get about the how, where, and why of illegal betting. I was stumped, until I realized they were suspicious of me. It was then I took it upon myself to woo Lou Anne with a whirlwind courtship. All the while, my boss was climbing all over me."

"So you used her for information on the family?" I asked in a soft voice. Was he using me to get information on my family? Did he think all Italians were mob related?

"Yes, I did. She's a woman who probably suffers from an untreated bipolar disorder, I think. She would fly into a rage one minute and be fine the next. Man, it was a challenge at times. I never knew what to expect or when to expect it. I'm not proud of what happened."

"You think all Italian families are related to the mob?" Now I leaned forward, my elbows resting on my knees. I needed to know if this man suspected my father of being a racketeer.

"Don't be ridiculous, Vin. Of course I don't think that. Why would you ask such a question?"

"Because you worked my mother for information. That's why."

"Did it ever occur to you that I worked your mother over for you? That maybe I would like to be more than your neighbor?"

Stunned, I sat back. Was this a lie? Had he tried to find out how best to approach my father?

"Surprised? I thought for sure you realized it." The handsome devil sat back, his eyes agleam in the softly lit room.

"Indeed. I mean, well, we have gone out a few times, but I, well, um." I stopped, took the foot out of my mouth before I choked on it, and sat back. *Cripes, what was I supposed to say? Dammit, how did I end up in these situations?*

"Cat got your tongue?" He laughed. "That would be a first."

I chuckled and nodded, too embarrassed to think of a quick response. He had asked me out several times during the summer, but I figured he knew I was involved with Marcus. Dang, didn't this put a damper on my question and answer period? Uncomfortable and confused, I rose from the chair, and headed for the door.

"I won't take up anymore of your time. Should you find out anything concerning my safety, I hope you'll tell me first, not Marcus." My hand on the doorknob, I turned back, smiled a goodnight, and nearly ran down the stairs.

The lock clicked as I scampered toward my apartment. I realized that Aaron had gotten rid of me with one sentence. *Wow, the man was good.* I hadn't even seen it coming either.

Once the other doors were closed and bolted I slid the French door open a crack. I slopped some leftovers onto the paper plate on the deck for Evergreen and locked up for the night.

Chapter 22

Sunbeams crept through the crack in the bedroom drapes. The smell of coffee brewing in the kitchen caused me to thank myself for setting it on automatic before I went to bed. Catlike, I stretched under the covers then rose to have an eye-opening cup of java.

The rear hallway door opened, and knuckles rapped on the apartment door as I left the bathroom. The kitchen door swung open and I stepped aside to greet Marcus. His knock had become familiar. That was way too weird. Not only could I identify the sound of his cruiser and his truck, now I knew his knock as well.

The smell of coffee permeated the kitchen, and he sniffed with appreciation. Since he was in uniform, I realized he had to work and just stopped by to pick up the envelope and note card for further fingerprint tests. It deflated my ego to know this visit was strictly business.

"Good morning, Vin. Just get up?" He chuckled.

Did I look that bad? Nah, I'd just combed my hair, washed my face, and brushed my teeth.

"As a matter of fact, I did. What do you want, Marcus?" I asked with my most sarcastic Italian attitude.

He grinned. "Sweet as ever, huh? I just stopped by for the note, some coffee, and anything else that's available." His eyebrows waggled.

"Here's the note and the coffee," I said with a smirk, pushing both in his direction.

"Nothing else, huh?"

"Nope, not today. When do you think the print results will be ready?"

"Later this afternoon. One of the guys is coming in special to run this test. I'll let you know what I find out."

He eyeballed the tray of Italian cookies on the counter. I tore open the cellophane and slid the delicacies toward him. His eyes lit up when he withdrew a sfogiatelle to go with his coffee. The clamshell shaped pastry crunched as he bit into sweet thin-layered strips, dusted with powdered sugar. The inside was filled with sweet-flavored, thick ricotta cheese.

"Mmm, this is heavenly. Did this come from En Croute?"

"Uh huh. I have more if you want to take some with you?"

"No, I can't really. I have to get going. Stay out of trouble today, huh?"

"Will do," I said, as he strode through the hallway.

At the door, Marcus turned, leaned into me and kissed my lips. A brief kiss, it warmed me to the core. This man affected me like no other ever had.

Smiling, I wiped away his powdered sugar grin and ushered him from the building. I watched Marcus' car leave the driveway and roll onto the street. From the corner of my eye I caught a swift movement near the evergreen trees edging the property next door.

The movement caught my attention, and I peered at the line of greenery. Nothing moved, no branch swayed, and everything remained calm. Everything, except me.

Determined not to overreact, I hurried into the kitchen, grabbed a pair of sneakers, and slid them onto my feet. I hustled toward the driveway and the tree line. Motivated by anger, I yanked back the branches and stared toward the Masonic Hall.

Not a single movement other than leaves rustling in the wind. Barging through the line of evergreens, I strode the length of driveway and rounded the garage. Again, nobody appeared to be around.

It wasn't my imagination. I knew someone had been there.

I took an exasperated huff of air and returned to the house. Before I could enter, a yowl of pain echoed from the side of the garage. I rushed toward the sound. Footsteps pounded across the

Masonic Hall's parking lot and I turned in that direction.

A tall, baseball-capped form ran full tilt. In attack mode, the huge cat snarled and growled as he leapt from the ground. Claws extended, the beast sank them into the neck of my peeper. He tried to fling Evergreen – the miniature mountain lion – off his back while on the run.

Screams of anguish and pain continued as the fellow careened toward the corner of the building. He jumped up and down flailing his arms while twisting disjointedly in an effort to disengage the beast. The sounds faded along with the footsteps. I stopped the foot chase and walked idly past the Masonic Hall, only to come up empty again.

Proud of himself, Evergreen pranced into view. The scar-ridden beast rubbed against my pant leg, his purr like a jet engine ready for take off. I glanced down at his scraggy appearance and smoothed the fur on his wide head. His body wound through my legs before he sat in front of me, staring upward.

"You think you're quite ferocious, don't you?"

His head tipped to the side. I admired the ever-present smile on the face of the beautiful, albeit ragged features. I stared at this furry phenomenon that had entered my life and now considered himself my protector. All Evergreen needed was a cape. And leotards. He was a regular bad boy, and we know women like bad boys.

If he answered my question, I'd have been hauled to the looney bin. I scratched his ears and together we set off for the house. Whoever peered at me through the trees would think twice about doing it again. All the same, it would be prudent to watch for anyone with major damage to their person, possibly from my guard-cat's rapier claws.

On the deck of the house, I set out more snacks than usual for my newfound protector. Evergreen snagged the food from the dish with talon-like hooks that emerged from his soft paws. He woofed it all down in a flash. His manners left something to be desired but maybe he didn't have a mother like mine. I went indoors and left him attending to his daily ablution after his tasty fare was gone.

Dirty Trouble

* * * *

The town was about to fill up fast with leaf peepers, art hunters, and treasure seekers. It wouldn't be long before the streets were jammed with cars parked bumper to bumper. The first day of the festival was crazy. I hustled to straighten up the house and start the fireplace. While the sun rose above the trees to warm the town, people bundled in heavy sweaters, sweatshirts, and jackets, bustled past on the sidewalks. Yep, the art festival weekend had officially started.

By late morning, a knock sounded at the door. I opened it to find Frankie DeMagistras and his latest 'arm candy' on the doorstep. I gave the Providence cop a hug, gave her a smile, and invited them inside. The front gate creaked open as I turned away and I glanced back. Detective Michael Bellini, also from the PPD, strolled up the walk and grinned unabashedly. Wow, I thought. Bellini came to visit me? How had I managed to get this lucky?

The smile broadened, and I grinned. What the hell, it could be worse. It could've been the mob who tramped into my yard. I waved him inside. A cool wind whipped along behind him. He hustled indoors while I closed the heavy outer door behind him and left the apartment door open.

Coffee, Amaretto liqueur, and pastry were laid out on the dining room table. I had decided it would be an easier task to serve from there rather than the kitchen, and I was right. Frankie helped himself to a dish filled with small cakes and Italian cookies. He poured black coffee into his cup and added a splash of Amaretto to it.

His arm candy, Shirley something or other, was tall, leggy, overly made up, and underdressed. Yeah, she'd freeze her ass off today, I thought, with a cordial smile. I offered her refreshments and turned toward Bellini.

In front of the fireplace in the living room Bellini gawked at the artwork on the walls. He turned, admiring the lion sculpture on its pedestal.

"I didn't know you were an artist, Vinnie. You're full of surprises, aren't you?" Bellini asked. He couldn't resist the lion, and caressed the smooth surface.

This creature had played an important part in the gem smuggling adventure last summer. It stood upright, a couple feet in height with front legs splayed as though expecting an assault.

"Most of the artwork here was done by my aunt. There are only a few pieces that are my work. Livvy sculpted the lion, and it's my favorite piece. Can I get you something to eat or drink, Michael?" I asked. My mother would have been proud of my good manners. Bellini usually brought out the worst in me.

"Coffee would be great. My wife is across the street at the yard sale, and I couldn't resist the opportunity to see your house," he said following me from the room. He greeted Frankie with a nod, and gave Shirley a wide, lascivious grin.

What is it about sets of legs and bodacious breasts that bring out the worst in men? Maybe the fact that her clothes were too tight and skimpy had something to do with it. Leave it to Frankie to hang out with a chick like this, I thought with a mental eye roll.

Handing Bellini a cup of coffee, I motioned to the food, and left to answer the door. To my surprise, Trooper Jonah Franklin stood on the doorstep. In jeans and a sweatshirt, he appeared less formal. He greeted me with a wide grin, and I ushered him into the house. Just as I started to close the door Lola hustled up the walkway.

"Glad to see ya, Lola. What are you doing here? Thought you had to work?" I asked.

"The help is running the place for now. I needed a break and figured your house would be the place to take it." She chuckled and left me on the doorstep.

At the sound of her voice, Jonah turned and stared at the auburn-haired beauty. As his eyes widened I knew she'd given him the Julia Roberts smile. It never failed to have the same effect on every man. Introductions made the rounds while more food was consumed and the coffee pot worked overtime.

Bellini's wife, an attractive blond with a great sense of humor, joined the crowd. I wondered what she saw in this overbearing man, who tested my patience. Though I think we were even on that score.

When I returned to the dining room to refill the coffee carafe, I noticed the crowd had grown even more. Aaron had made his appearance, and a few other friends had dropped in to visit.

Lola and Jonah stood near the fireplace, deep in conversation. When Lola glanced my way, I smiled and winked. She had struck a home run with Jonah. He seemed totally mesmerized by Little Miss Dynamite. I wondered if his interest would have any effect on Aaron. Probably not, after his revelations concerning me, I thought.

People stopped in, chatted, and toured the apartment until late afternoon. The last of the crowd left around four, and I cleaned up snack debris for the last time. Most friends came by on Saturday and Sunday. Monday was my day to take in the artwork and consume clam cakes and chowder at The Lions' Food Wagon. Those guys served the best clam chowder this side of the Rocky Mountains. *Do they serve clam chowder in the Rockies?* Pondering that question, I got ready to leave for Livvy's gravesite.

Chapter 23

Once the dishwasher was loaded I stepped out on the deck to get the potted plant I bought for Livvy's gravesite. Evergreen was nowhere to be seen. I glanced around twice to make sure nobody lurked in the bushes. Paranoia seemed better than fear to me at this point.

The sliding door lock clicked in place. I checked all the other entrances as I passed back through the house. I slipped on and secured my heavy, hand-knit autumn colored boucle sweater. Blue jeans and running shoes completed the outfit as I headed down Silk Lane toward the cemetery.

At the sharp curve in the lane, I walked straight through the right of way and wandered down the hill past aged grave markers and statues. I never slowed my pace until I reached Livvy's grave. I brushed aside the crisp leaves that littered the surface. I removed the remnants of flowers from my last visit and settled the new pot of rich burgundy mums in their place.

"There, that's better, Auntie. They're your favorite color, too," I murmured. "Lots of people came by and admired the house today. You'd have liked that, I'm sure."

The sentence caught in my throat, and I swallowed hard. Livvy, a staple in my life, always backed me up when I was hard pressed to win a battle with my father or Giovanni, my twin brother. She had been my cheering squad and number one fan all rolled into one aunt. *She was now dead.* God, I missed her. I stared down at the headstone and wished with all my heart this wonderful woman were still alive.

"I truly miss you, Auntie," I whispered, running my hand

over the stone.

"What are ya doin'? Talkin' to yourself?" I heard the smirk in the voice rather than saw it on DeGreico's face. Bracing myself, I turned to face him. There'd be no backing down this time.

"That's none of your business," I said.

"Maybe you should spend some time at the funny farm and get a taste of what it's like. That's where people who talk to themselves end up, you know." He smirked again. The nasty expression on Tony's face accompanied his forceful stride forward.

I stood my ground, angered by the fact that he'd listened to the private conversation. Tony's knack of showing up where he was least wanted, or expected, irritated me beyond reason. It got on my nerves. Today it would be my turn to take the upper hand.

Pissed off and put out, I watched the jerk move up the knoll toward my aunt's grave. Toward me. I stepped aside onto even ground, unwilling to allow him near her. It was probably irrational to feel so, but some things are private and this happened to be one of them.

"Get away from me. Now," I said, as he came within range of me.

His hand shot forward as I took a defensive stance. My strongest leg braced my body, and I fisted my hands at my sides. I blocked the blow with my arm before it reached my face. By lifting my foot, I ran the ridge of my running shoe down his shin. The look of painful surprise on Tony's face was gratifying.

His snarl accompanied curses hurled in my direction. Before he could react, I raised my left leg and stamped down hard on his foot and then punched him in the face. His open palm missed its target when he swung at me.

I learned these and other defensive tactics after Tony stalked me two years ago. During the past summer my house was broken into and I had scuffled with the perpetrator. These same techniques had proven handy, not to mention the kickboxing lessons I'd recently taken up.

Tony lost his balance and grabbed my sweater as he fell

backward. I tumbled to his side. He grabbed a handful of my unbound hair. With a yank he brought my face toward his. My knee leaned into his chest as water streamed from my eyes at the pain of having my hair ripped out.

His fingers wound so tightly into the long tresses I could have cried. Maybe I did. I'm not sure, but before he could inflict any more damage, my knee sank harder into his chest to quell his breathing. I slugged him in the face as hard as I could, over and over. Pain spread across my hand into my wrist, but no crunching sound of broken bones accompanied it.

Shoving me backward he rolled away and yelled, "You rotten bitch!"

I tumbled over clumps of dead grass and landed away from him on my face. In a matter of seconds, Tony regained his balance and started toward me again, swearing all the while. In an effort to distance myself from him, I scrambled onto my backside and scooted sideways on all fours, like a crab.

A triumphant look replaced the painful one he'd worn seconds ago. Blood seeped from his nose, smearing across his face as he wiped it away. I was less sure that I could win this fight. I breathed heavily as I watched him advance toward me. With my feet flat underneath me I stood and regained the defensive stance. This time, I had my hands up like a boxer and balanced on the balls of my feet.

He stopped about four feet away and stared a moment.

In silence, I stared back.

"I said, get away from me now. And stay away from me," I yelled awaiting his response.

"Like hell I will. It's your fault I lost two damned years of my life, and you're gonna pay for it." He moved so fast he caught me with a one-two-punch before I could effectively block it.

Flung backward, I grunted as I hit the ground hard. Tony rushed at me as my leg and foot came up in defense. Scared, I kicked outward, caught him in the gut, and rolled sideways. Away from him – back onto my feet. Now, I know I was supposed to run rather than stay and fight, but fear and anger made a lethal combination.

The jerk had yanked out my hair, shoved me in the dirt, and hurt me. Yeah, I was on overdrive now. No way would I retreat from this creep. Well, maybe if I were losing the battle or got tired, I'd reconsider.

He landed backward and stayed on the ground for a second or two. I wasn't fooled with the ploy. If I ventured near, I'd be in a precarious situation. Not me, nuh uh.

When Tony crawled to his feet I saw his bloody and bruised face was twisted in rage. Again, I stood my ground, not realizing a third party had entered the scene. Tony didn't know it either as he charged me head on. I was just too pigheaded to run, so I danced in place.

I was backing up as fast as I could but realized it was too late. There was no time to strike a worthy blow before he brought me down again, flat on my back. His tackle left me breathless enough to give him the advantage. Tony raised his fist to hit me. In one brief second things changed. He straddled my thrashing body ready to do me grave harm and suddenly he was yanked up in the air like a marionette on strings.

It was more than I could comprehend. *What the hell just happened?* I lay still for a moment and listened, gulping in deep breaths of air. A heavy thud sounded as he hit the ground with a bellow of pain, followed by a string of curses.

I lifted my head, Tony lay flat on his stomach while Aaron twisted his arm backwards, toward his neck. With brute strength Aaron hauled him off the ground, pushing him toward the lane. Jonah stood at the end of Livvy's gravesite. He grasped Tony by the arm when Aaron handed him over. Tony ceased to struggle once the two men entered the scene. I guessed he knew when to quit. With a backward glance, Jonah saluted me before he dragged Tony off to who knows where.

Dirt and dried grass covered my clothing. My sweater was all stretched out of shape. I must be a sight, I thought, as I brushed the worst of the debris off my clothes. I promised Marcus I'd stay out of trouble, too. Now I'd be in for it. I sighed and ran my hands through my hair, pulling it back into some sort of order – hoping it wasn't too bad.

Mumbling about the inconsiderate actions of some people, I whispered an apology to Aunt Livvy. Aaron approached me, his face an unreadable mask. Hastily I glanced away and continued dusting off my clothes.

"You just can't stay out of trouble, can you? Are you hurt, Vinnie?" He glanced at my bedraggled clothes. He tilted my chin and looked at my face.

"No, I'm not," I lied. "As for the scuffle, Tony fared poorly, didn't he?" I spoke with a smirk while tears threatened to overflow. I blinked hard to push them back before they could trail down my undoubtedly filthy face.

This stoic attitude of mine must have been too much for Aaron to handle, and he grinned and nodded.

"Yeah, you were great, Vinnie. Have you thought of taking up boxing?" He chuckled and shook his head. "There was some street fighting in there, though." A muscular arm slung around my shoulder as he drew me to him. He smelled good, like the outdoors and aftershave. I leaned into him for strength. We headed toward the lane, his arm still holding me close.

"How did you know where to find me?" I asked.

"Jonah and I were at the deli. Lola said she'd heard Tony mention that he'd kept an eye on your place all day. He and his cronies were having coffee while Tony bragged about how he'd get even with you. I called the house and got no answer, then remembered you were planning a trip to Livvy's grave."

"You arrived just in time. I had the upper hand for a brief period, but it didn't last long. Thanks for the rescue."

Instantly, I became folded into a strong pair of arms and hugged so tight I thought I'd break. Enjoying the moment, I still stepped back before it could get serious. A smile tugged at his lips, and I responded to it with one of my own. I couldn't lead this man on. It just wasn't right.

"Lola was the real help. If she hadn't been such a fountain of information, we might not have gotten to you."

"What else has Lola been informative about?" I asked. *Did he know my dad called in mob-related favors? Was he aware that the guys on the Hill outside En Croute were friends of my father? Was I just jumping to conclusions again?* Yeah, undoubtedly.

"She mentioned that your father would never have anything to do with the mob. She insists that he was strict with you and Giovanni. You and your twin must have been hell on wheels, huh? I need to meet this twin," he said with a chuckle.

"My father was tough on us and stricter than most parents, even in our extended family. He was determined we'd never have anything to do with guys named 'Joey Bag O' Donuts' or people like that. We gave Dad a run for his money and had some scrapes with the men in blue. Nothing serious, mind you, but we're law-abiding citizens now."

"I'm glad to hear it. I believed Lola when she said those things. She's an ardent defender of you, and your family, Vin. Quite a good friend you have there."

Determined to move the subject off my family and the mob, I tossed my thanks out again. "I know, she's the best. Thanks again for the help."

"You did well to hold Tony at bay. When I took off at a run, Jonah wasn't far behind. We weren't sure what we'd find, if anything. I figured you wouldn't take any crap from Tony this time." He glanced down at me. "I'm glad you're all right. Sometimes you scare me, you know?"

"That's what Marcus says, too. I figure I'm damned lucky to have the two of you on my side."

Lola was probably a wreck by now. We passed the library heading for The Salt & Pepper Deli nestled on the corner. My adrenalin had crashed, leaving my energy level nil. If I stopped walking and sat down, I knew I'd be finished. Sustenance, that's what I needed. A sandwich maybe, one of the Lola-type sandwiches she offered. Ah food, the cure for everything.

The traffic light at the corner changed as we approached, and vehicles moved on. Only a short time before, the streets were packed with cars, trucks, motorcycles, and various other conveyances. The curbs were visible now, the street nearly deserted. The light changed to red but before we could step across the street, a grey SUV blocked our path.

The light bar straddling the roof flipped on and strobe lights flashed with intensity. The window descended as Marcus leaned toward us.

"You okay?"

I nodded.

"Go into the deli and I'll meet you there." He frowned at my disarray before he closed the window. The SUV rolled around the corner, and the light bar went off.

We hustled across the street and entered the deli by means of the front door. Marcus entered through the opposite side of the building. Hands on his hips, he stared at me in silence for a moment while shaking his head. Unable to tear my eyes away from his stare, I stood transfixed.

"I heard you had a tussle. You don't look too much the worse for wear." Marcus grinned.

Nodding, I smiled back. He reached me in one quick stride and asked, "Are you sure you're all right?" Warm knuckles ran along my cheek before he held my arms in a loose grasp. I nodded in assent.

Just then, Lola hustled in from the back room. Auburn hair sprung in wild profusion around her face instead of being tied back in the usual knot she styled when she cooked.

I whispered, "Yeah, I'm fine." Gosh, no ranting or raving. *How did that happen?*

Marcus chuckled when Lola stepped between us, brushed him aside, and gave me a hug. Lola was much shorter than me and over her head I caught the gleam of humor in Marcus's eyes. He turned his attention to Aaron.

The two men walked away, mumbling to one another. I couldn't make out what they said, but I didn't care. Lola stepped away then requested coffee, tea, and sandwiches from the two wide-eyed teens behind the counter. She pointed me toward the sofa. I glanced around the empty deli.

Dirty Trouble

Lola marched forward, ordering the two men who towered over her, to take seats as she hauled the overstuffed armchairs closer to the coffee table in front of the sofa. She set the tableau up for customers who simply wanted to relax, read the paper, and lounge around, like at home.

Everyone's seating was arranged and the teens followed Lola's orders. I escaped to the rest room to take stock of the damage to my person. The large carved mirror, suspended on the wall over the sink, showed the damage was minimal. A couple scratches to my dirt-smeared face and a bruise along the brow. Nothing major, thank God. I washed my face, ran fingers through my hair to organize my wild tresses, and then scoped out the knuckles on my right hand.

Across the top of my hand some skin had been scraped off. It stung when I held it under the running water. No other damage appeared on the surface. I couldn't feel any broken bones as I flexed my fingers and fisted the hand. Nope, I was lucky and God watched over me. Why? I couldn't say.

Back in the dining area, I burrowed into the soft cushions of the armchair to relax. The two men sipped steaming beverages and sucked down hefty sandwiches. Lola handed me a mug of Earl Grey tea. The aroma wafted from the cup into my nostrils. Immediately, calm descended. Nothing could relieve stress like a cup of tea. No wonder the British drank so much of it.

"You'll press charges against Tony, I imagine?" Marcus asked with a raised brow. "You know you must take his threats seriously now, don't you?"

I should have known that while there'd been no barking about the altercation, he would harangue me about the issue somehow. At some point.

"I took them seriously from the beginning. I just didn't make a big deal out of it. Everyone else did that, remember?" I said with attitude. "It would have been counterproductive for all of us to act paranoid at the same time. So, I let you guys have a go at it first." I raised my hands in a stop motion and smiled. "I know it's unusual for me to behave that way, but I'm able to show some common sense now and again."

Laughter met the statement, since we all knew that I tend to go off on a tangent at any given moment for no good reason. If I feel there's been an injustice done to someone over something, then I have to know the whys and wherefores of it and make it right.

"Answer the question, Vinnie."

Squinting, I stared at him. "I thought I did. I took it seriously. Do I need a lawyer to answer that question?" I smirked.

"No. Now answer the other question." The soft voice belied the demand. "Will you press charges against him?"

"Indeed I will, Trooper Richmond. He will go straight to jail. He will not pass go, and he will not collect his two hundred Monopoly dollars, because he has violated his probation. It's that plain and simple. I'm surprised you didn't know that," I answered with a short-lived, smug, superior attitude.

"I was aware of it. I wondered if you knew. You've tap danced around this guy since he first approached you outside the barbershop. I've known everything about his incarceration since Jonah called me that day. This guy took on a losing situation from the outset." He grinned. "I also realized that you'd take as much of his crap as you could before he'd be on the receiving end of your temper."

The three of us listened in silence as he rambled on. Then I grinned at him with a nod. "You're right, of course." I turned to Lola. "It's late. Do you need help clearing up for tomorrow?" Anything to change the subject. I had all I could stand of Tony DeGreico.

She glanced at the wall clock. "I sure do. If you'd be good enough to straighten this room and wash the tables, then I'll finish up in the kitchen."

The teens left after serving us, and it was the least I could do to give this good friend a hand. She'd been part of my rescue today, and I would never forget it. I cleaned the tables with Aaron's help after Marcus left for the barracks. The place shone as Lola emerged from the kitchen.

Lola set the alarm, locked the doors, and headed home.

Dirty Trouble

Aaron and I strode up the lamplit street toward the Colonial. The brisk evening air sent shivers along my body while long strips of my dark hair tickled my face. I caught it in a twist and tucked it under the neck of my sweater.

The town lay quiet as we made our way into the yard. It was good to be going home.

The house was shrouded in silent darkness beyond the reach of the streetlamp. After Aaron unlocked the outer door, he headed upstairs and I entered my own apartment. He reached the first landing and stopped. I waited in silence.

"Would you care for a glass of wine?"

"Sure, give me a chance to change my clothes. Then I'll be up, okay?"

"Great, we need to talk," he said and continued on his way.

Terrific, we needed to talk. Just what did we need to talk about? I wondered. If this were going to be a lecture, I wouldn't stay long. If it were about him and me, then I definitely wouldn't stay long. If this was just me jumping to conclusions again, well, I gave myself a mental head slap and changed my clothes.

Chapter 24

On the way home, I was cold from the wind whipping through my clothes and I was quick to change into something warm and comfortable once inside. Within minutes a lightweight sweatshirt smothered my body with such snuggly warmth that it curled my toes. Thick, hand-knit fuzzy socks covered my feet as I shuffled up the stairs to Aaron's apartment. Flames fluttered in the fireplace, and the door stood open in welcome.

On the last step, before entering the apartment, I heard Grant's deep, rich voice. He spoke to someone on the phone while he paced the kitchen. Being a curious creature, I sidled into the living room and listened while I leaned flat against the wall.

"Yes, I understand. 'Take down' at ten on Monday. I'll be there." He paused and then said, "No, she doesn't know. I haven't said a word." Another pause and the floor creaked. The footsteps moved closer. *Was he coming toward me?*

I hustled out the door to the first landing on silent feet. Cheerful-voiced, I called Aaron's name and scrambled into the living room. Aaron's long stride brought him into the room, the phone in his hand. His eyes narrowed as he stared at me with suspicion and then quickly turned away.

"I'll see you then. Thanks for calling." He disconnected the call, cradled the phone in a huge paw, and turned toward the kitchen. A moment later, he carried in a tray holding wine, cheese, and two goblets. Aaron's smile welcomed me. His suspicions tucked away as he slid the tray across the coffee table.

Stuffed into the armchair by the fireplace, I toasted my toes near the flames. I knew this 'Calgon, take-me-away' moment couldn't possibly last. With a nod of acceptance, I clasped the goblet of ruby red wine and nibbled sharp, tangy cheese.

"Anyone important on the phone?" I asked.

"Just a friend checking in. Why?" His eyebrow rose as he stared at me.

"You sounded business like, and I wondered, is all."

"There's something you should know, Vinnie," he said and took a seat across from me. "I hope you'll understand when I tell you. Try not to get angry."

Oh, my God. My father's imminent arrest is what he planned to tell me. I just knew it. Or maybe the arrest of Aunt Muffy, and my father's arrest would happen on Monday. What about my mother? What would she do? How would she handle that? These thoughts scrambled through my befuddled brain.

With a deep breath, I nodded and gulped the wine – not tasting it.

"Monday, there'll be some arrests made."

Oh, God, I knew it. Here it comes.

"Okay," I said.

"You should stay in town. Go to the festival – enjoy your houseguests, or whatever it is you do during this weekend. Just don't leave the village. Do you understand?" His serious face, his dark eyes held me pinned to the chair. I couldn't move, though catapulting from the room entered my mind.

"Okay," I mumbled again. My brain sped away – a freight train out of control. Off I went on a tangent.

Who did the feds plan to arrest? I didn't just need to know. I had to know. I *really* had to know. *Did my father ask another favor of some kind that implicated him in something illicit? What the hell was going on?*

"The Hill is in celebration, as usual, for the Columbus Day holiday. On Monday, an FBI team, along with the PPD and state police, plan to arrest certain members of the social club next to En Croute." Aaron sipped his wine and paused. "Marianna will also be taken into custody for her part in the crimes. It's imperative that you stay here in the village. I can't worry about you being caught up in the situation, especially if something goes awry."

"Exactly who will be hauled in?" I asked, my voice just above a whisper. *God, please don't let it be my dad.*

"I can't tell you that. Just promise you'll stay out of it."

"I promise," I lied. My fingers, tucked into the fold of my sweatshirt, were crossed and double-crossed. *Would my father be arrested for a crime he hadn't committed?* If so, then damn straight I'd be involved up to my very dark eyeballs. *What could this lunatic be thinking?* Well, I couldn't blame Aaron. He wasn't Italian and didn't understand the pull of family responsibility.

"Convince me that you'll stay here in Scituate and not interfere, Vinnie." Furrowed eyebrows creased the tanned forehead of the handsome brute before me.

"How would you like me to do that, exactly?" I queried him with a twitch of a smile on my lips. Why I smiled I'll never know, but the tension in Aaron's face eased.

"That, my dear, is a leading question. However, if you show me your hands and swear that you won't show up on Federal Hill on Monday, then I'll take your word for it. You see, I know that when you cross your fingers, your promise doesn't count." The smile broadened into laughter, and white teeth gleamed in the firelight.

How did he know that I crossed my fingers? Why would that matter to him? Caught out in the act of fibbing, I raised my hands, wiggled my fingers, and issued a few words to the effect that I wouldn't interfere.

Placated, Aaron chuckled and said, "That didn't really hurt, did it? You planned to show up when you heard me on the phone. Why, I wonder?"

Indignant, I blustered over the fact that he'd known I'd sneaked into the apartment while he was on the line, but I failed to mention why the arrests interested me so much.

"You only had to ask," I said. "I'm happy to agree to this request. Honest."

"So, why would you consider showing up? Afraid someone important to you would be arrested?"

"No," I lied. "It's just that I figured you'd tell me more than what you've shared so far." I plucked the edge of my sweatshirt ribbing and refused to look at him, afraid he could read my mind.

"It's impossible for me to say anything else. I could get into serious trouble for divulging this much." He leaned back against the soft leather sofa, hands behind his head, staring at me.

"It's all right, I can respect that. Besides, I'm certain the take down will go without a hitch. With so many professionals in one place, it has to, doesn't it?" Yeah, right, with a slew of professionals and all that testosterone topping off egos, a screw-up somewhere along the line couldn't help but happen. It's just the way it goes.

The phone rang downstairs, and I hitched off the chair to scoot down into my apartment. My stocking feet slid across the hardwood floor, and I raised the receiver to my ear.

A tad breathless, I answered the call. "Hello."

"Is this Lavinia?" the male voice asked.

"Yes, it is. Who's calling?"

"This is Peter Bedeek, the gentleman who assisted you outside of En Croute. Remember me?"

"Uh huh, I do. What can I do for you?"

"I wanted to warn you that things on the Hill will get sticky Monday. You need to keep your parents away from the area. Understand what I'm tellin' you?"

"Got it, no problem. I'll make sure they won't show up. Thank you for calling. I appreciate it." *Appreciate it? Am I nuts?* Slipping the phone into the charger, I leaned against the desk, drumming the enamel on my teeth with the tips of my fingernails.

Some thug calls me on the phone and instructs me to keep my parents off the Hill and I'm supposed to be happy about that? Not only did the FBI want me out of the way, but now thugs issued orders to me. Do I look like a mob moll? Someone who follows orders from a pack of witless wonders? Nah, not me.

Slowly I returned to the hallway and yelled up the stairs that I'd be turning in for the night. Aaron yelled down that he'd see me in the morning, and closed the door. I swung my door shut and twisted the lock in place.

I'd been toasty warm in front of the fire, and relaxed from the wine until the phone had rung. I ambled into the bedroom, pulled the thick down comforter away from the pillows, and snuggled underneath. It didn't take long for body heat to radiate throughout the bed.

My eyes drooped lower and lower as sleep descended. I had no clue how this evening managed to get beyond my grasp. Not that I'm a control freak or anything, but I do like order – even though it doesn't seem that way.

* * * *

I awoke to another day of company. The guests rolled in and out while my pastry supply dwindled. Nothing out of the ordinary took place. At the end of the day I heaved a relieved sigh.

Around seven o'clock that evening, I turned on the fireplace, set out wine glasses, and waited for Marcus to tumble in. Aaron had been gone since five. I wondered if he was prepping for the arrests the next day.

The phone rang as I settled on the sofa. The voice I'd come to know so well brought a smile to my face.

"Where are you, Marcus? I'm waiting here by the fire for you," I said.

"Sorry, Vin, I can't make it. I've been held over and am pulling another shift."

"Cripes, now I'll have to drink all this wine by myself." I laughed as his chuckle crossed the distance.

"Did you get the results of the fingerprints?"

"Yeah," he said. "They were the same as what Anderson found."

"I figured as much, but it was worth a try. Right?"

"Indeed. I've got to go. Stay warm and I'll see you tomorrow sometime, all right?"

I rang off and settled in for a movie and a glass of wine.

Chapter 25

Sunshine cascaded through the French doors in the kitchen while I prepared a pot of coffee. My glance strayed to Evergreen, parading back and forth on the deck outside. Every now and then, his keen eyes glared through the glass while he waited. He wanted a snack, so I rifled the fridge to comply with the silent demand.

Chilly, brisk-moving air filled my lungs and tickled my nose as I stepped outside to deposit the plate on the deck. I murmured soft words of welcome to the beast and watched him wolf down the food. In no time flat the dish was empty, licked clean and shiny by his sandpaper tongue.

The rangy animal licked his lethal paws before he washed his fluffy face. I watched in awe as he cleaned toes that concealed spring-loaded claws. Every now and then, Evergreen chewed one claw while all the others sprang forward. I turned and left him to finish his bath and went inside to take one of my own.

When the phone rang, I hustled to answer it. My mother's voice echoed in my ear.

"Lavinia, your father is heading up to the Hill today. He's going to march in the procession to the church. He'd like us to meet him there for dinner at the Piazza Di Aglio. Do you have any guests coming by today?"

"No guests today, Mom, but I hoped you and Dad would come here and take in the festival." No such idea had entered my mind, but I needed to come up with an excuse so my parents would stay away from the action on the Hill.

"Oh dear, I hadn't even thought of that. Well, can't we just go up to watch your father march and then have dinner at your house?"

My mother, the compromiser. If she could make things work out for everyone, she would, but not today. A sense of panic took hold of me, I wondered how I could keep my father from making the trip to the Hill. *Dang.*

"Does he have to participate in that affair? I really looked forward to having you both here for the day." If nothing else, I could always use emotional blackmail. It might work on Mom, but Dad was another matter altogether.

"I'm sorry, dear, but he's left the house and I won't see him until we meet later." Her voice sounded tense. Maybe it was guilt. I wasn't sure.

"Fine, then, I'll come by and pick you up. We'll head to the Hill together." Shit, now I would be in trouble with Aaron. If Marcus found out, I'd be in double trouble.

Family first, then whatever comes next. That's my motto.

Dressed in jeans, three-inch heeled boots and a heavy burgundy sweater over my turtleneck jersey, I drove toward Cranston. Inching into the driveway, I noticed Aunt Muffy's car parked behind Mom's. Great, I'd have to deal with Mob Moll Muffy as well as my parents. The day had taken a nosedive, and a sense of weighted doom settled over me like a cloak of chain mail.

A pathetic sigh left my lips as I stepped up the stairs and into the house. Muffy sat at the table, dressed to the nines, handbag at the ready. My mother strode through the kitchen door, her scarlet jacket draped over her arm.

"We're ready to go. You look a bit stressed, dear. Is everything all right? You haven't had a disagreement with Marcus or Aaron, have you?" Her face and voice were filled with concern, and I knew I couldn't utter a sound about my real issues.

With a shake of my head, I said, "No, I wanted to tell you that Tony DeGreico has been arrested. He's violated probation and will be sent to jail." I left out the why and how of it all.

"I'm so relieved. He deserves to be in jail, especially after what he did to you, Lavinia. How did you find out?"

"Marcus told me last night that he'd be headed back to a

cell." *How's that for lying by omission?*

The three of us left the house, heading for the car, as the grey SUV blocked the end of the driveway. My mother smiled and waved to Marcus. Aunt Muffy just stared at him, and then her black eyes slanted toward me. After she gave him a nod, the two women entered my car to wait. Marcus strode up the driveway and grasped my arm, hustling me toward the street.

"We need to talk, now."

"Fine, but take your hand off me before you alarm my mother." Alarm me, is what I meant.

His hand dropped from my arm as he turned to face me. Marcus's face wore a grim expression which meant that his news wouldn't make my day any better. *Crap, I hate when that happens.*

"What is so important that you came by my mother's house?"

"I called your cell phone, but you didn't answer. After I found you weren't home I swung by here. Tony was bailed out of jail this morning. A big-time attorney coughed up the bail money and made some kind of deal with the DA and the judge. I want you to be extremely careful today. Tony will be nastier than ever if he finds you."

Quaking inside, I nodded in agreement. Marcus leaned in and kissed my lips ever so tenderly. For a moment, my breath caught in my throat.

"You be careful today, too. Why don't you stop by later tonight for pizza?" I asked.

"Sure. And dessert, too?" His brows waggled, and a wicked grin crossed his features.

Laughter bubbled up from somewhere deep inside, and I nodded. How I could find humor at this point in time was anybody's guess. I watched Marcus drive away and I strode back to the car. My mother and Aunt Muffy had mile-wide, all-knowing grins on their faces as I slid behind the wheel. A chuckle from me brought soft laughter from them as we left for the Hill.

"You serious about this cop?" Aunt Muffy asked.

"Yeah, I'm afraid so." I chuckled at her shaking head.

"He'll break your heart, ya know."

"So could anyone else. Life is a chance I have to take." My little voice felt compelled to agree with Auntie at this juncture, but I switched it off and drove toward Federal Hill.

Throngs of viewers milled around the Hill, peering into quaint shops as they slurped down pepper and meatball sandwiches, munched on doughboys, and sipped espresso. My mouth watered over the doughboys. When fried in unhealthy fat, rich bread dough puffed up and was then mounded with granulated sugar. *Ah, don't you love unhealthy stuff?*

I scanned the crowd for a glimpse of my father, but he was nowhere to be seen. Lined with parade enthusiasts, Atwells Avenue, the thoroughfare that ran the length of the Hill, began to quiet down as the procession for Saint Christopher started.

Poking my elbows out, I edged closer to the street and caught sight of my dad. He marched proudly with a few other men, holding the flag of the Knights of Columbus before him. On either side of my father, Grand Poobah Gino Esposito, walked the two thugs who accompanied me from within En Croute not so long ago. My heart flip-flopped in my chest and then sank to the bottom of my high-heeled shoes.

Cheers followed the procession as they made their way to the church three-quarters of the way down Federal Hill. Politicians smiled, shook hands, and passed propaganda sheets to anyone who'd take them. I recognized the Chief of Police and a few of his cronies. Some cops from the PPD straggled along the rope cordoning off the parade route.

A hand reached out and touched my shoulder. Startled, I nearly fainted and then turned on the person with a fierce attitude. My mother stood before me with a worried look on her face, and I bent my head toward her. The noise of the crowd drowned her words as I hustled her toward the back of the crowd.

"What is it, Mom?" I asked, my mind flying in all directions at once.

"I've lost Mafalda. She took off when my back was turned. I

can't find her anywhere. You don't think something has happened, do you?" A worried frown covered my mother's attractive features. I put my arm around her shoulders, affectionately giving her a hug.

"Maybe she needed to find a rest room or went to buy a snack, Mom. Stay with the parade, I'll go find her for you. We'll meet you at the church, okay? Make sure Dad remains there with you so we don't get separated and lost completely." If they were together at the church ceremony, then I could at least account for their whereabouts. Verifying Aunt Muffy's whereabouts was a different matter.

Mom nodded and followed the crowd toward the western end of Atwells Avenue. I turned toward the piazza where most of the restaurants were situated, Da Ravioli was among them. Quiet surrounded the piazza now that the parade had passed.

With a deep breath, I headed toward Da Ravioli. My gaze sped over the patrons who awaited a table and it landed on Andre Messino, the undercover cop-turned-waiter. I leaned forward to glance into the dining room. *No Muffy*. Dang. Now what would I do?

"May I help you, ma'am?" Messino asked as he approached me. His bland facial expression belied the look in his eyes. He didn't appear happy to see me. Why, I wondered?

"Yes, you can. Has my aunt been in yet today?" Nervous, I danced from one foot to the other, my composure wracked.

"You mean Mafalda? Yes, she just went to the Ladies' Room and will be out momentarily. Follow me, will you?" He turned on his well-polished shoes and strode away.

I followed him down the corridor, past the palm fronded plants, and out of sight of the patrons. Once around the corner, I noticed he waited with dark eyes that glittered in the light. Oh, yeah. He was pissed about something.

Up close and in my face, he whispered, "What the hell are you doing here? It's a bad place for you today. You promised you wouldn't come back after the last time."

Surprised, I cocked an eyebrow at him and slid my hand to my hip. "This is a free country, at least the last time I checked anyway. Why shouldn't I come to this restaurant?" Then it hit me like a Mack truck. This place would likely be the take down spot. After all, hadn't I waved to the FBI guys the last time I was present? Shit.

The cop waiter nodded as he watched realization dawn on my face. "Exactly, Vinnie. Get your aunt and your asses out of here now. Hear me? Right now." He emphasized each word as he whispered it, making sure I got the point.

The rest room door opened and Muffy emerged just as the Men's Room door swung wide and Antonio stepped out. Dang, this would happen now, I thought. They stared at each other as Muffy smiled a nasty smile, one that boded ill. I wouldn't want that look pointed in my direction for anything.

"Well, well, if it isn't the asshole of the year." She reached into her bag and hauled out a small canister of spray.

I stared, immobile, watching the scene. In one swift movement, she lifted a petite container and sprayed Antonio directly in the face. The smell drifted toward me and Andre dragged me down the corridor away from them. My aunt had just doused Antonio with pepper spray, inside the restaurant no less.

"What the hell is she doing?" he demanded.

"Getting even, I think." I smirked and gave the sixty-something woman silent applause for having the nerve to do it.

"She has to leave now, and so do you," he murmured to me. I nodded. Andre headed toward the corridor once more and came back seconds later saying that Muffy had disappeared. Antonio lingered in the bathroom, rinsing his eyes.

Panic welled up within me and I strode down the corridor to fling the Ladies' Room door open. No Muffy. *Crap. Where had she gone?* I couldn't imagine she'd hang about after she took her revenge. Nuh uh. Muffy was too smart for that.

My mind raced over the possibilities. Where could I find the short, round troublemaker? Andre and I headed into the kitchen where the chefs were deep in preparation of culinary delights. I stopped to smell the aroma of Italian cooking, but Messino prodded me toward the rear door of the restaurant.

Once outside, we split up and raced off in different directions. As I turned the corner of the restaurant, I glimpsed a crew of armed and dangerous men wearing SWAT gear, headed for the front door. A swift change of direction took me back the way I came, only to see another crew advance toward the rear of the building.

In an effort to escape the danger, I hauled ass down the alley and into the nearest tenement house. To my surprise and delight, I found Mafalda sitting on the step inside the door, catching her breath.

"What the hell are you doing here?" I asked. Maybe I yelled, I'm not sure. Relief flooded my being as I slumped against the wall.

"I had to escape that man. He swore at me after I sprayed him and then pledged to kill me. The idiot meant it, too. Imagine that?" Muffy's incredulous face caused me to roll my eyes.

What the hell did she think would happen? Could she have assumed Antonio would thank her for pepper spraying the shit out of him? I couldn't believe it, but what concerned me now was finding a safe way out of here.

I cracked the door open and peered outside. The cops were nowhere to be seen and the alley stood empty. My hand enclosed Muffy's, and we slid outside. With a furtive glance up and down the filthy lane, we scrambled along the wall of the three-story apartment building. Approaching the street, I straightened my clothes and whispered to Muffy, "Act natural and don't look around. If we appear guilty of any crime, it will draw attention. Understand?"

"Okay, Lavinia. I'm sorry that you're involved in my actions."

"It's okay, Auntie. Just keep moving." I led her down the street.

The woman had no idea what I'd seen or that the cops were inside the restaurant arresting everyone and anyone on their list of suspects. Muffy thought life was all about her…but then we all feel that way sometimes.

At the corner of the street, I caught sight of my parents in front of the church. My father paced back and forth as my mother wrung her hands. When we arrived, Mom lectured Aunt

Muffy in Italian. My father stared at them and then turned to me.

"What happened while we waited for you? I started to worry."

"Auntie got carried away with her act of revenge and scared herself silly. Nothing to worry about, Dad." *So I lied. What else could I do?* God had my number. When he got tired of forgiving me for lying, then I'd be punished. That's it. End of story.

"You're sure that's all there is to it, eh? Nothing more you want to tell me?"

"There's nothing else to say, Dad. Let's get out of here and go have something to eat at my house for a change." The invitation came as a surprise to my father. I guess my mother hadn't told him.

Anxious to leave the Hill, we found our cars parked where we left them at the bottom of the lot on a back street near a school. I drove off alone while my family followed at a sedate pace. My father drove, and I'm sure my mother harassed him over his low speed.

The radio newsman announced the arrest of several high-ranking mob officers in a raid on Federal Hill. He listed those arrested, which included Antonio the businessman, and Marianna. The charges brought against the detainees included racketeering and interstate smuggling of contraband. No big surprise there. Just before the announcer finished his newscast, he mentioned Tony DeGreico was the son of Marianna and was an accomplice to the smuggling ring. *Can you beat that? All these years and I never had a clue.*

At the red light outside of Scituate Village, I leaned back and rested my head on the headrest of the car seat. If I could get through the day without any further mishaps I'd consider myself lucky.

The light changed and my car crept forward through the crowded village toward the house. Pedestrians stepped into the streets without looking and glared when I honked the horn. Ah, festival weekend, a great time for those who live dangerously.

My parents arrived within a short time and sat in the living room, sipping wine in front of the fireplace. The day lengthened and a chill permeated the air. I bustled around the kitchen and tossed ingredients together for a frittata. Potatoes and eggs melded in the fry pan and smelled heavenly. I added Italian seasoning, salt, and pepper to it before I flipped it over onto the platter set out next to the stove.

A knock on the door preceded Richmond, who strode in like he owned the place. I smiled as he glanced around.

"Where's the pizza?"

"We're having a frittata instead. No dessert until later though." I grinned.

"Your parents are here, huh?" He chuckled. "I saw their car in the post office parking lot. Where's Romeo today?"

"You mean you don't know?" I whispered.

"Don't know what?" Marcus murmured.

"His team arrested a bunch of hoods on the Hill today while the parade took place. Tony was one of them. Isn't that great?"

"What did you have to do with it, Vin? I can tell you were involved up to your gorgeous eyeballs."

With a brief explanation of what happened at Da Ravioli, I watched Marcus try to hide the humor he saw in Muffy's actions. He suddenly laughed aloud as his body shook with mirth.

"She does get her stockings in a twist, doesn't she? You saved the day again and didn't need any help, I assume?" Eyebrows hiked as he spoke.

A smile hovered around my lips. I refused to admit that if it hadn't been for Andre Messino, the undercover cop-turned-waiter, I'd have been out of luck.

Marcus wandered around the counter and sniffed the steaming omelet while his arms encircled my waist. He nuzzled my neck and my knees went all rubbery. It didn't matter that my family sat in the front room waiting to eat. I could only think about Marcus as a delicious snack. No calories, just tasty. I leaned back and smiled at the man who raised my body temp with a look and a touch.

Chapter 26

The art festival ended for another year, and within a day or two the village returned to normal. Classes at the university resumed with my Two-Point-Fives, flashlight cops, and real Five-Os studying for mid-term exams. Life was good. I couldn't imagine it any other way.

The day started out on a late note. I arose to an alarming racket outside the back door. Evergreen meowed. Well, not meowed exactly, maybe more like he yowled. He yowled until I opened the French door and asked what his problem consisted of so early in the day. I knew it had to be a food issue, since he only came by to beg a free meal, kind of like my trooper and FBI agent friends.

Green eyes narrowed with disdain as if I'd insulted the freeloader. Good gosh, I'd have to claim him on my income taxes next. I fished around in the fridge for some leftovers and tossed a couple chunks of cheese onto the deck to placate him until I could find a more appropriate meal. While he wolfed the cheese down, I filled a dish with remains of the food left from the festival.

Unable to tell if Evergreen had a taste for pastry, I scraped the chocolate off the éclair into the trash and split the pastry apart on the plate. Yellow cream filling oozed out to cover everything else. I slid the door back and extended the loaded plate to the monstrous beast. He gulped it down in record time and then started his bath routine.

With a glance at the clock, I realized I would be late for the daily race across the bridge so I hustled into the bedroom for a set of clean clothes. With my hands full of clothing and underwear, I streaked into the bathroom to shower. The blow dryer took most of the moisture from my hair then I scooped it into a loose ponytail.

Some screeches and wild yowls came from the back yard. Curious to see what happened, I slipped my shoes on and hurried out the door. More noise and a bunch of swearing caught my attention as I followed the sounds.

"Get off me you hairy monster," a tall, lanky kid yelled, as he tried to disengage Evergreen from the back of his heavy shirt.

With folded arms I watched the kid struggle against the ferocious cat. Long claws embedded in the young man's wool jacket as Evergreen tried to maul him. I noticed crusted-over scratches on his neck and realized this must be the person who committed arson and peeped at me through the bushes.

"What the heck are you doing out here?" I asked using a Marcus stance.

His thin body hunched as he attempted to shake off the creature. Fair-haired and light skinned, he wasn't familiar.

He stopped his struggle and stared at me for a moment. The cat hung suspended off his coat. The yowling stopped at the sound of my voice.

"Just lookin' around, that's all," he mumbled.

"For what?"

"Just lookin', I said." He spoke with more belligerence this time.

"Did you start the fire here in my garage, young man?"

Wide eyes turned toward me. "It was an accident, ma'am. Honest, I was too scared to confess. I'm sorry about it. I was here the other day lookin' to see how bad the damage was when the cat tore into me."

"Is that why you shoved me to the ground?"

"I didn't and wouldn't do that. This other guy who drives a beat up old pickup truck did it. Sorry I couldn't help, but things worked out okay."

Ah, Tony. I should've known.

"All right then. Why don't you come closer and let me get Evergreen off your jacket? Then we can talk about restitution."

The gangly kid drew near, and I lifted the cat from his coat, taking great care to release the claws.

On the ground, Evergreen strutted away as though his job were finished. I smirked at the independent creature and turned back to the kid standing nervously before me. He was sweating profusely and looked ready to run. He also was dressed too lightly for the weather. He shivered....

"Come inside. It's cold out here, and I have to get ready for work. I can only spare a few minutes, but we need to discuss your actions." I grasped his arm and led him into the kitchen, and made a quick call to Margy Gluck, the Secretary of All and Everything, to have someone fill in until I could get to class.

His blue eyes roamed the room as he smoothed down his wind-tossed locks of hair. The kid appeared awestruck and I wondered why. The house and furnishings weren't exactly from a designer magazine.

"Nice place you got," he said.

"Do you want something to eat or drink?" There's that Italian hospitality thing again. I would be late for class at this rate.

"If it isn't too much to ask, yeah."

I poured him some juice and whipped up some toast. I was handing him the butter and jelly when the sound of footsteps on the stairs caught my attention. I figured Aaron had seen the whole incident from his deck and couldn't contain his curiosity.

"What's your name?"

"Eric Strom."

"Well, Eric Strom, eat up and tell me how you think we can work out a deal to fix the garage."

Round blue eyes widened. I figured the kid's age to be around fifteen or sixteen years old and it was obvious to me that he had no money. His clothes weren't quality, and his jacket had frayed edges which meant he probably wore hand-me-downs, or the clothes were just plain old.

"Ma'am, I don't have any money to repay you for the damage."

[219]

A knock sounded at the door. I strode forward and opened it. Aaron stood outside, concern evident on his features.

"Not now," I said. "Come back later, okay?"

"Sure." Aaron nodded.

The door slid shut and I heard the feet move back in the direction from which they came. A smile twitched across my lips at the thought of his protectiveness.

"Eric, it occurred to me just now that maybe the builder, who will start work on the garage within the next few days, could use a hand with the job. If you're willing to help him out, then we can call it even. What do you say?"

"You mean you won't call the cops?" Eric's eyes rounded again.

Being the softhearted dummy I am, this kid got to me. I nodded and he actually smiled.

"Sure, I can do that. As long as you don't call the cops."

"Great, then we have a deal. I'll give you the phone number and you call him. Explain that I want you to help him out and he can call me to confirm it. All right?"

"Sure, ma'am. I'll call him right away."

"Call me Vinnie, please. Also, tell me how the fire started."

"I was smoking out back. The wind blew the ash and it caught the evergreen tree. From there it burst into flames. The trees are pretty dry and dead back there and should be cut down. I could do that for ya."

"Sure thing. Let's get the garage done first, though. If you want to earn some extra money, I can keep you busy with a few odds and ends around here."

"Great, ma'am. I mean, Vinnie."

"We'll keep the garage incident between us. There's no need for anyone else to know about it. You can work with the builder after school. Is that fair enough?"

His smile lit up the thin face, and I realized the kid probably hadn't had much of a break in his life. Some of us only think we have it tough, I thought, as my father's lectures came to mind.

Eric Strom left the house with a smile on his face and maybe a sense of relief as well. My book bag lay on the counter, the contents strewn about when the door opened and Aaron strode inside. He leaned against the door casing and stared at me.

"That kid set fire to the garage, huh?"

"Yeah, but it was an accident. He seems a good kid and has agreed to assist the builder."

"You're sure this is how you want to handle the situation?"

"Well, he showed remorse and has an aversion to the police. So, yes, I do want to handle it this way."

A wide grin crossed his handsome face as the huge man stepped forward. He kissed my cheek and said, "Good, I'm glad you're willing to give him a break."

"I didn't tell him you're an FBI agent either."

"By the way, were you on Federal Hill the other day? Some of my guys thought they saw you enter Da Ravioli. You did promise to stay away, didn't you?"

"It must have been someone else." I lied with my fingers and toes crossed.

"Mmm, I'm sure." He smiled good-naturedly.

Nah, he didn't believe me, and who could blame him? I chuckled at the handsome brute, gave him a peck on his cheek, and dragged my bag off the counter. Then I headed out to teach cops how to be cops.

Author's Biography

J.M. Griffin has been writing humorous cozy mysteries and artful non-fiction for many years. She lives in rural Rhode Island, a state she considers colorful and interesting.